A FEARFUL SYMMETRY

"He's dead," he said. "He's dead."

He said it over and over, rocking the body more and turning the head toward me. Blood was congealed around the ears and eyes from a massive wound to the temple, where the skull had caved in. But the face was recognizable.

It was Carlos Smith, lying where Worthing had lain before. One eye was crushed and bloodied by the blow that had killed him. The other stayed painfully open. The skin had turned to a bluish pallor. But it was Smith.

The wind gusted painfully in my face as I stood and gaped. Some hideous cosmic prank. Or a plan so grisly and complex as to overwhelm belief.

"He's dead," the man repeated.

"ENGAGING." *—San Diego Union*

"FAST-PACED!"
—Los Angeles Herald Examiner

CHIAROSCURO

PETER CLOTHIER

A SIGNET BOOK

NEW AMERICAN LIBRARY

In fond memory
of
MICHAEL BLANKFORT,
friend,
Saba to our Sarah,
writer and art-eater
extraordinaire

With special thanks to R. B. Kitaj, who made the drawing which was one of the seeds for this story; to artists Gary Lloyd, Gene Sturman, and Maura Sheehan, from whom I borrowed images or ideas; and to Carlos Almaraz, who cheerfully lent a first name along with the images of his Echo Park drawings. He is not Carlos Smith. By the same token, none of the artists or other characters in this book bear any relation to any real person, living or dead. Any resemblance is purely coincidental.

ONE

◇

The thin gray light of a New York winter's morning spread evenly across the richly textured marks of charcoal on heavy rag paper.

It was going to work. Tomorrow, maybe, I would be able to push through the last few details that had been holding me back: There was something there I had still not fully understood. I looked from the drawing to Laura. She sat cross-legged, her thighs spread easily, and gazed across my shoulder through the studio window.

"How's it going, love?" I asked. My voice broke quietly through two hours of silence. I knew how long it had been by the way my fingers had set around the blunted end of charcoal until they were cold and stiff.

"Okay."

As usual, she seemed to wake from a trance. She was the best model I had ever had. Patient, composed, intelligent, she understood instinctively what I was looking for. And after work, we could relax together, making love with genuine affection.

She rarely stayed over, living a life outside the studio about which I knew only snippets gleaned from casual talk.

For my part, I pursued the life I had dedicated wholly to myself and to my art. A selfish life, perhaps, but that's what I had settled for. The hell with the art world.

She was too young for what I offered, and needed more than I could give. Laura had come to New York from a Philadelphia ghetto a couple of years ago, wanting to be a fashion model. She had never made it for the simple reason that she wasn't fashionable. First, she had too much body. Then, she was black—too black, and she lacked the supercilious sophistication of the competition. She exuded a warmth and compassion alien to the cover of a glossy magazine.

It was the special quality of her warmth that I was trying to reach in all the drawings that surrounded us, pinned up in various stages of completion on the studio wall. I used other models. But it was Laura I was trying to reach—right down to her great, generous soul.

"Are you getting somewhere, Jake?" She brought coffee on a tray and fit herself in around me on the sofa.

"Somewhere," I said. "Soon. Good God, if I could do you right."

She smiled. She put her coffee mug on the floor and snuggled up close. I set down my mug on the side table. Then I slipped both arms around her. I closed my eyes and put my head back on her arm. I sensed that she was about to kiss me when the telephone rang.

The telephone in my studio sits on a table out in the hall, by the front door. It rings rarely and when it does, it's normally answered by the tape deck. That morning I had forgotten to reset the tape.

"Goddammit."

Laura laughed and shifted her weight while I got up to answer the thing, more to be rid of its shrill insistence than to talk.

"Yes."

"Jacob Molnar, please."

"This is he." My tone was meant to be discouraging. I picked up the phone and paced across to the studio door, leaning against the post to watch Laura.

"This is Carlos Smith."

I knew the name and the reputation through the glossy art journals, which were my only regular contact with the art world. I used them to justify my isolation.

Carlos Smith. Neo-expressionist, so-called. Raw anger on raw canvas. What Tom Wolfe had once called "radical chic" dragged back in new clothes. I could have hung up, but didn't.

"I'd like to meet you," Smith said.

"Meet me?" Unconsciously, I allowed the accent to fall on the second word. I looked at Laura and found her laughing at me.

"Listen, Molnar, I take it you don't like my work, if you know it. I understand that. I play the game, you don't. That's why I need to meet you. I need your help. Your advice."

"Go talk to your dealer, Smith," I told him.

"Nice," said Laura, interrupting. "Very nice." She arranged herself on the sofa and patted the cushion beside her. Giggling, she allowed the silk of the robe to fall away from her breast.

"Well," Smith said, "they said you'd be like this."

"Like what?" I asked.

"Holier than thou, I guess."

"With the thous in this business, what did you expect?"

Laura shook her head at me and wagged a finger.

"One more time, Molnar. I want your help. Remember Patty Drayton? Remember her?"

Drayton. A suicide, perhaps two years ago. Punk artist, spiked orange hair, a skinny girl-child, permanent scowl. She did performances, too, and tapes. I called to mind the image of her coarse male figures fashioned out of wire and debris. Switchblades for cocks. Aggressive, hideous females, bristling razor pussies.

I looked back at Laura and chuckled silently at the comparison.

"One of the first in your Samantha Dmitri's stable, if I remember right," I said. "But dead."

"Dead," agreed Smith flatly. "Murdered. Like your friend. Like Worthing Nelson."

The words were added so quietly that for a moment I thought I had misheard. I shook my head and turned away from Laura to the blank white wall behind the telephone. The memory of Worthing's loss returned with a shock of pain, converting instantly to anger.

"You use Worthing Nelson to get through to me . . ." I started.

"I can show you how. I can show you why."

The white wall seemed to pulse and I set a hand against it to steady myself.

"Sotheby's," Smith insisted. "This afternoon at two. You'll come. They're selling *Sam's Song.*"

TWO

◇

Goddammit, I hadn't expected this. A Jacob Molnar at Sotheby's. Bona fide American master. The catalog cover said so.

People were streaming back in and finding seats. Dealers and buyers, consultants and investors, the press. The whole ego-crazy caravan of the art world.

Up there on the dais, the picture I had painted years ago seemed alien, the stepchild of a generation, not the creation of an individual imagination. There were a hundred others like it, signed on the back "J.M." and dated with the month and year. It seemed like a century ago.

So now a single phone call from a virtual stranger, a man I should have expected to despise, had brought me back. Murder, he'd said. Try as I might, I hadn't been able to brush it off as fantasy or lie.

I searched the rows to see if I could spot him. I would know his face from pictures in the glossies.

"Jacob Molnar," the auctioneer announced. He adjusted the microphone and coughed, consulting his notes. "American, born 1934."

The sound system let out an electronic howl.

"Untitled, 1967, eighty-four inches by sixty inches, oil on canvas."

I cringed. I had known "untitled" was a lame excuse. Still, everyone did it then.

"An exceptionally fine example of this distinguished artist's work," said the auctioneer. He squinted through half-moons at the filing card in his hand and read off some details of the provenance. The picture had been sold out of Marlborough to a single owner—a name I didn't recognize. It was part of the man's estate. There was some reference to the piece in Goldman's *Postwar Art in America.*

"Who'll start the bidding? Am I bid fifteen thousand? Fifteen thousand bid, thank you, sir, fifteen thousand, the gentleman on the left."

Someone moved into the row beside me and I glanced toward him as he shuffled down between the seats. Elmer. Elmer Rothstein. Writer, a sometime poet, and art critic for the *Village Voice.* A shortish, plump man of about my age, clean-shaven around heavy jowls, and earnest. Balding in front and long-haired at the perimeters. His jaw literally dropped when he saw me.

"Hi, Elmer." I grinned at him and nodded.

"Jake Molnar?" he said. "Red-beard himself? Jesus, it's been a while! We've missed you, Jake."

He took my hand almost reverentially. I had to laugh.

"You're back with us?" he asked.

I shook my head and put a finger to my lips.

"They're selling my masterpiece." I winked. "Up there."

"Twenty-two thousand, am I bid twenty-two thousand? Twenty-three?"

"Holy cow!" said Elmer. "That's pathetic."

It was going more slowly than I had imagined a work of mine would sell at auction. An emptiness bit at my gut. Not pain. The old ego, the arrogant artist? I thought not: Countless days with soft rag paper, charcoal or pastel, and the breathing of the model had cured me of the need for dollar success. The battle was now between mind and material, image and eye. Not artist and society. Not value and money. I was through with that.

But the emptiness persisted, as though there were something here that I'd missed without realizing—something that had once been part of the texture of my life.

Thirty, thirty-one thousand. There were a couple of bidders left. A tall, ungainly young man was propped against the wall to the left with the look of an injured bird. He was sweating it out, mopping beads from a sparsely covered crown.

"Museum director. Midwest, somewhere," Elmer whispered.

A woman down front had joined in late. Hidden from sight by the crush of intervening bodies, she put a forefinger in the air to raise the bid. The single finger was almost enough. It had to be Cynthia. Cool, well tailored, implacable. Bidding, I would bet, for a client.

The artist's former wife makes bids on the artist's former work.

It left me regretting more intensely that I had come at all.

"Thirty-two, thirty-three thousand, thank you, madam, thirty-three. Am I bid thirty-four? It's against you, sir, am I bid thirty-four?"

The young man nodded anxiously.

"Well, sure, it's a half-way decent job," said Elmer. He leaned over and jerked me out of maudlin memories with a chuckle. "Remember what Goldman had to say. 'First-rate example of its generation.' Something like that. Such a bullshitter! 'Notice,' " he mimicked, " 'how the surface image is built on formidable structural underpinnings, compounding the emotional impact of abstraction with the shock of image.' "

Goldman had really written some such stuff.

"Thirty-four thousand, I'm bid thirty-four. Fair warning. Fair warning, now."

Fair warning. The amplified words came down like some message from the gods. I looked around again for Smith, shrugging down feelings of disgust.

"Thirty-four thousand, bid against you, madam, thirty-four. Am I bid thirty-five? Last call, sold at thirty-four thousand to the gentleman on the left. Thank you, sir."

Snatched from the grasp of lovely Cynthia Molnar by the sweating youth from Missouri. He would go home worrying that he had paid too much.

There was an indifferent smattering of applause as Elmer tugged at my sleeve and made a face. "Goes to show, Jake," he said. "Never quit while you're ahead. You think Andy's work goes for peanuts, or Roy's? Rauschenberg? Johns? Jesus, man, that crap goes for hundreds of thousands. And what did they do? They stayed out there, is all. Look what you could have done."

I said nothing.

"They loved you, Jake. They all loved you. They wanted you to stick around. Well," he shrugged. "We may be a bunch of phonies, but the art world's still the only game that never ceases to amaze and fascinate. Me, at least. But I guess you always were a prickly cuss. Never could make a compromise." He paused and looked at me curiously. "They tell me you've been holing up in your garret, making masterpieces that you'll never show."

"Says who?" I asked.

He shrugged again. "Oh, these things get around," he said. "Even when you don't. When do I get the exclusive?"

I laughed, and watched them haul my painting down from the block. I was still debating going down front to offer condolences to Cynthia when another phantom from the past was resurrected.

"Jake Molnar! I don't believe it!"

People seemed to have difficulty with that. Maybe they'd thought I was dead. The man approached me from behind, a catalog dangling easily at his side.

Dan Traceman. Patron of the arts. Short. Wiry. Very good looking, according to Cynthia. A shrimp, I thought. The only man to whom I had ever refused point blank to sell a picture. In public. And caused a scandal that I'd relished savagely.

"Hello, Dan." I found it hard to repress an old itch of disdain, a bristling irritation for the self-esteem that he wore like a cologne.

"What brings you groveling in the dirt with the rest of us mortals, Jake? Your stash running out?"

I chose to take it as friendly banter. As a name artist, I had been savvy enough on the stock exchange to keep me comfortable well into old age.

"Just curious," I muttered. "Just curious."

"Killed the cat, didn't it? Curiosity?"

Traceman had barely broken step. He breezed past with a smile and a brief wave of his catalog. He left that not-too-delicate perfume of power to fill the air in his wake. Down front he stopped to hold court and Cynthia was with the little crowd that gathered round him. He kissed her on both cheeks and spoke a few words in her ear. She looked back, puzzled. Sweeping back stray wisps of hair, she held a catalog to shade her eyes as she searched the rows to find me. I could have waved.

"You saw the catalog cover?" Elmer seemed barely to have noticed Traceman's passage. "I had to see that thing again."

I turned to study the cover reproduction. *Sam's Song.* 1963. Worthing Nelson soaring, unsurpassed. Even in the tiny scale of a catalog reproduction, the emotional depth of the work was unmistakable.

I had a personal stake in that picture. One of the great memories of my life was that moment of epiphany in Worthing's studio, when I had dropped by to visit after what must have been perhaps the most intense day's work in that intense man's life. I felt his total physical and intellectual exhaustion along with the beginnings of that elation one experiences at the breaking of some immense barrier. We went over the painting inch by inch together and then Worthing had said simply, "I think I can do it."

The work lived on, the man was dead. Murdered? I looked around again, annoyed at the state of my nerves. No sign of Smith.

Another contemporary master reached the block, and the audience buzzed. Stella. I stared at the early shaped canvas, its familiar pastel bands paralleling one another through geometric curves. All right, Frank, or all wrong. A smart artist, smart work. But all wrong. The image of my own most recent drawing replaced the Stella in my mind. Laura. A figure, human, vulnerable, nude. Back to Degas.

There was an eddy of excitement swirling in the

rows ahead: a dark river of hair, the tilt of a turned nose, a flashed smile.

"Samantha Dmitri," Elmer told me, before I asked. "New Wave dealer riding herd on a stable of galloping superstars."

Of course. The stable included Patty Drayton—and Carlos Smith. Both artists she'd created out of nothing but a genius for hype. I turned around and searched the hall for Smith again. Maybe he wouldn't show.

"Am I bid twenty thousand for a prime Frank Stella?" asked the auctioneer. "Am I bid twenty, thank you."

I turned and touched Elmer's arm. "Keep my seat," I said. "I need a breath of air."

THREE

◇

I made a ten-minute tour of the lobby and the exhibition space, looking more at the people than the art, and unsure why I should be so nervous that the man had missed me. The overflow crowd made busy conversation, smoked, and stamped out cigarette ends on the floor.

There was still no sign of him. I looked in the catalog and decided that I would wait for *Sam's Song* and no longer. Enough was enough.

Back in the hall, I found my row and squeezed past Elmer in time to catch the tail end of a burst of applause.

"What happened?"

Elmer shrugged. "Another hit for Samantha," he said. "You wouldn't believe the price for a Patty Drayton. Fifty thousand. Just a little drawing, is all."

The Dmitri woman seemed to be making the most of the occasion. The explosion of strobes from news cameras froze her face in a series of frigid stills as she kissed Dan Traceman on the lips. Fragile, she seemed, in those ephemeral flashes—though her reputation was for toughness. A squadron of gray-suited escorts, young-faced and corporate, surrounded her. Another glimpse, and she was swallowed back into the crowd.

I looked back at the catalog cover and flipped through to the page that referred to *Sam's Song*.

Worthing Nelson. The most honest man who ever lived. The most generous artist. In the catalog, his life was reduced to half a page of facts. In my mind I saw the white head of short, curled hair, the broad face, boldly lined, its permanent smile creases belying the pain of the man's life. Hands like animals, hairy, clumsy, leading their almost independent life, colliding with human things in perpetual surprised innocence. Hands capable of almost laughable gentleness.

Once my mentor, always my friend. Frozen one winter morning on a deserted street, his grand heart slammed to a halt. Wham! Worthing Nelson dead. And, as far as I was concerned, abstract expressionism dead.

With remarkable timing, a Carlos Smith was hauled up on the auction block. Elmer laid his finger on the catalog title and poked it at me, raising a hairy eyebrow.

" 'American Masters,' they call this?" he said. "The guy's barely twenty-five years old."

I shrugged.

"Back to the figure?" said Elmer. "Meets with your approval, huh?"

"God, no!" What I had been after was the human figure in its humanity, not as another easy image in an abstract painting. Smith's crude outlines were a parody.

We watched with fascination as the old game played itself out. The price leapt up to thirty thousand in the first ninety seconds, with bids coming in at the telephone desk. Then up to fifty, with Dan Traceman in there, leading two other bidders. The one on the telephone would be some kind of a partner, I would lay odds.

At fifty thousand, Traceman dropped out.

Sixty. Sixty-five.

Way beyond any value intrinsic to the work—and way beyond anything paid for a Carlos Smith before.

Seventy. The woman relaying bids from the telephone hung up with a smile and the hammer fell to a stunned silence from the crowd, then a wave of spontaneous applause. A flurry of reporters headed for the doors.

Elmer threw up his hands and let his catalog fly. Down there in the front where I couldn't see, the flashbulbs blew and some neophyte collector quivered with the double privilege of owning a Carlos Smith and paying a record price for it. Some folks get their kicks from such distinction. And a pair of speculators, who likely had bought a dozen Carlos Smiths at a couple of thousand each a few months earlier, had increased the value of their stake by quantum leaps. Thus it goes.

I hoped it wasn't Cynthia's client. As I looked around to see if she had left without stopping to say hello, the auctioneer moved easily from the ridiculous to the sublime.

"Sam's Song."

Elmer actually gasped. Beyond all reports of the death of masterpieces, I knew this painting was one of the great works of the twentieth century.

Even like this, manhandled unceremoniously and propped unevenly on the tabletop, the white-cotton-gloved hands of the Sotheby's assistants grasping at its edges—even like this, the painting lived up to its title, singing across the squawk of human presence in the room. It simply sang. It sang in a welter of color and texture, an incredible precision of line and feel for space. With absolute economy: no more, no less. The heart of the painting lay in its gesture, strong and precise—the heavy, self-assured brush marks competing for predominance with delicate detail of scratch and splash. It was a field in which the eye could never rest, nor could one evade the conflict of emotions it evoked.

"The man could paint." I turned to find Carlos Smith had taken the seat behind me and was leaning forward to speak into my ear.

I froze. The casual intimacy revolted me. It insinuated equal standing among Nelson, myself, and Smith. *Sam's Song* alone denounced the notion as preposterous. By Worthing's standards Smith was still in the cradle.

I got up to leave before the bidding started on the Worthing Nelson. I could live without that.

Bewildered, Elmer looked in amazement from me to Smith and back again. Of all people, he'd be the one to understand the irony.

"Jake . . . ?" he said. "Stay in touch, will you?"

"Yeah. Good to see you, Elmer."

Smith followed me out. He shouldered a brilliant yellow thermal jacket with the single word PAIN embroidered in small elegant letters on the shoulder.

"Congratulations!" It sounded like the insult I intended it to be. "Fancy prices!"

"For what?" he retorted. "Fat lot of good it does me. Samantha sold that piece two years ago for a couple of grand. She works at sixty-forty. Sixty for her."

The cold air hit my face as we left the lobby. "Sixty-forty!" Ten years ago, we had gasped at fifty-fifty.

"She sold it to Leo Wolff."

"Wolff?" I asked.

"I'd lay my sixty to your forty that he was the bidder on the phone just now. So far as I knew, he owned the bloody thing. Or maybe he'd given it away so he could buy it back."

Smith laughed bitterly.

"So where do we talk?" I asked.

It was snowing lightly. I stopped and turned now to look at Smith more closely, watching with amusement as he reacted to the Molnar chill. Seen face to face, Smith was more than the shallow kid I had expected. Once his momentary bitterness had cleared, I found myself attracted to an easy grin, the lightly bearded Hispanic features, and above all to the eyes, which glowed with the kind of intensity I associate with sharp intelligence.

"Your place," said Smith. The man had a habit of hitting hard, unexpectedly.

My place. A sanctuary I had taken years to build. No artist or dealer, no critic or collector had once disturbed its silence. There was my library, its single leather chair and standing lamp, the books. The studio itself, all but empty, where the easel stood and where I passed the hours with Laura. I wished myself back there, with her.

"Impossible," I said. "Tell me what you have to tell me here."

I wondered for a moment if he had heard me. His

eyes lost focus, wandering in the stream of people who had followed us out. "Listen," I said. "For Christ's sake, man. You've wasted enough of my time. You have something to tell me, shoot!"

When I tried to grab my arm away from him, the grip tightened. His eyes met mine again, then jumped away, focusing somewhere behind me. A small group jostled out of Sotheby's onto York, turning coat collars up to break the gathering wind. Splashes of bright winter jacket against translucent winter gray.

Some of the party recognized Smith and waved. There were a few words shouted, isolated, brittle against the cold. I read the curious glances directed toward me. Who was Smith talking to? I would have been familiar to this crowd, perhaps, as the image from a decade-old *Artforum* or *Time* magazine.

The group turned south on York, busy with news and shared opinions. But one of them broke off and turned back as if on impulse.

"Well, well, Charlie boy. Surprise, surprise!" The accent was British and the speaker laid a familiar arm around Carlos's shoulder. Smith reacted with a short smile behind which I read something different altogether.

The image was Eighties New Wave: short back and sides, hair greased back, with a small tail at the nape. A strangely naked face with prominent eyes and cheekbones. One ear pierced in several places, earrings spaced at intervals around the lobe.

"Who's your china?"

China plate. Mate. A ragged memory of Cockney rhyming slang flashed back to me.

The curve of his lip was disfigured by what looked like a blood blister or a recent bruise. I looked into the moist blue eyes and met insolence. Contempt for my evident middle age? For the straight-arrow image?

"One second, Brian. Hold on. It's business. I'll catch up," said Smith.

He grabbed me by the arm painfully, pulling me a few steps further up on York. He spoke quietly but with emphasis, still barely audible above the traffic, checking back nervously as if to measure sound and distance factors.

"Look," he said. "I can't hang around here. And I can't have them see me talking to you any longer. Believe me, there's nowhere else. Just tell me where you live and I'll meet you there. Soon. Half an hour. And for Christ's sake don't let them see this. Please."

Standing close by, he took a small package from underneath his jacket and slipped it under mine, pulling the zip front up in a single, urgent gesture.

"Eighteen East Eleventh. Apartment four," I heard myself respond. I wouldn't have believed it.

"Soon. Half an hour," Smith promised. He turned back south, running the few steps to catch up with his friend.

From where he left me standing, I watched as the intensity and fear he'd shown to me were swallowed back into the skin of a public persona, the image of Smith the artist, confident and swaggering. He clapped an arm around the shoulder of the man called Brian and both soon vanished in the surge of workers heading home.

FOUR

◇

Fair warning. The auctioneer's phrase came back like a refrain.

With Carlos and his friends out of sight, I pulled the package from under my coat and looked at it. A stuffed brown mailing envelope, bandaged and sealed with heavy masking tape.

Half an hour, he'd said. I looked at my watch: It was shortly before five—a crazy time to try for a cab. Damned if I'd take the subway.

Scouting the sea of surging yellow traffic for the unlikely vacant cab, I turned east on Seventy-second A lucky break produced a cab just as its previous occupants climbed out. Back in the warm, I laid the envelope on my lap and cursed myself for a fool for ever having left my studio.

Who's your china?

I thought again of Worthing Nelson, dead these past ten years. We saw less of each other in those last strange and secluded years of Worthing's life. Sometimes you need to see a friend, and sometimes not. Not that the friendship had cooled or mutual trust was lost. Regret came later, after his death, when he was no longer there to see at all.

Locked in traffic, the driver lowered his window and hurled a lungful of imprecations at the gathering snow, the cab ahead, a knot of reckless pedestrians. He spat, closed up, and settled down, apparently satisfied.

Sam's Song. I counted back on my fingers, amazed. 'Sixty-three. At that time I had been twenty-nine years old and Worthing thirty-nine. I had married Cynthia in 'sixty-nine. Those were the years—the years of my marriage—when Worthing and I had gone separate ways, acknowledging, always, the strength of the bond between us.

There was one other factor. Worthing was gay. We'd never much discussed it. Never needed to. It was more as a matter of public knowledge than through our communication that I had followed his breakup with Sam—an event that, in its prolonged agony, had become popular sport for the art community. Strange how Worthing, that private artist, could parade his personal affairs in an endless carnival before the watching world. He seemed to enjoy it.

But despite their quarrels, Sam had kept him working. Not so with Sam's successor, Nicholas. A manipulator. Sponge. A drain on Worthing's weakening resources through the early Seventies until his death. There had been illness, too.

It was Nicholas who had occasioned my one half-hearted intrusion into Worthing's personal life. Worthing and I met for lunch one day at the SoHo Charcuterie. Before, we used to meet in his studio, but toward the end he always found some excuse. There's no new work, he'd say. There's no new work.

The cab jolted forward three yards at a time. Outside, the snow fell heavier than before and the traffic seemed stalled beyond hope of movement. I checked the time. It would take me more than thirty minutes at this rate. If Smith arrived before me, he'd have to wait. Well, let him, I thought.

No new work.

At the restaurant Worthing and I had seemed more like strangers than friends for the first time. He looked strained and older than his years. Some of that special liveliness around the eyes had gone. It might have been better if we'd said nothing—just sat and stared at each other. As it was, the conversation had idled over my own recent work, events on the art scene, Nixon, and the war. But without the usual bite or satisfaction. I finally broke the rule we'd developed more in practice than in principle.

"What's with Nicholas? I just don't understand what he has for you. Why?"

Worthing had returned my gaze, acknowledging the empty, idle hours, the loss of drive and vision, the spiritual and aesthetic vacuum of a once rich life. Or so it seemed. Then he'd said simply: "I know. I love the little shit. That's all."

We'd both laughed. Neither had wanted to say more.

It was after five-thirty when the cab finally made it to the corner of Fifth and Eleventh, pulling up at the curb with a shudder. I fished the wallet from the breast pocket of my jacket and paid the fare.

Feeling faintly ridiculous, I concealed Smith's envelope under my coat and pulled in my scarf against the snow. Turning down Eleventh, I looked ahead toward the steps of the house I had taken for a studio. I was too far off to see with any clarity through the falling snow, but I had the urgent sense that something was wrong.

Up ahead, two figures were locked in an embrace so close that I had walked some paces before it occurred to me that they were fighting. I paused, unsure which way to run—to help or get help.

The man who was hidden from me by the second flailed arms around the other's back and was swung suddenly, smashing against the railings under the porch light. The impact brought out a sound that was half-gasp, half-scream.

Carlos! The thermal jacket was a distinctive, almost luminescent yellow. I started to run toward them.

Smith jerked himself loose and lurched down off the top step, steadying himself against the rail and spinning to the sidewalk. He was facing me as he struggled to get back to his feet, but it was a moment before he recognized me.

"Molnar!" he yelled. "Christ's sake . . ."

But his attacker was on him again, hooded, anonymous, violent, and Smith was forced out, winded, into the street.

Why didn't he run toward me? Instead, he dodged a car and took advantage of the second man's delay, heading east on Eleventh. His pursuer slammed into the side panel of the braking car, and then was gone, racing ahead of me.

"Smith!" I yelled stupidly. "Hey, Smith!"

I started off after them but got caught in the second of two equally confounding events: Skidding on a layer of soft, fresh snow, the car with which the pursuer had collided slid noiselessly across the street until its fender and headlights ripped into a parked car at the side. The door burst open and the driver came at me.

"Fuckin' maniac!" he yelled. "Fuckin' maniac . . ."

I would have had his two gloved fists in my face if I hadn't backed off and held up my own hands for protection.

"Hey, wait!" I yelled back. "Wait! Man! I don't know what the fuck is going on, okay?"

He stopped and stared into my face, his rage barely receding. Then gave me the finger, turned, and stamped off down the street.

FIVE

◇

The door opened while I was still looking for my keys. No one should have been there. But the door opened and light flooded out.

Laura. I could have wept with relief to find her there.

"Jake?" she said. She looked out over my shoulder into the street. "Jesus, what's happening out here? Are you okay?"

I closed the door and put my arms around her. "How come you're here?" I asked. "Here when I need you? God bless you, kid."

"I was worried about you, Jake, after this morning. I couldn't reach you on the phone, so I thought I would stop by."

"Something told you, huh?"

She nodded. "It was that damn phone call, wasn't it?"

A siren screeched outside, behind the door, but I left it closed.

"What is it, Jake?" asked Laura. She nodded toward the sound. "What's happening? First thing I hear this ruckus on the steps, and then the crash. By the time I got to the window, this guy was coming for you. I was scared silly."

"Not half as scared as I was, love. Come on, I'll tell you. You can help me sort it out."

I wasn't hungry. Laura had been preparing food but we left it on the stove. She brought me a tall green can of Rainier's ale to the library, where I had set out Carlos's stuffed envelope and a paper knife on the reading table. I sank back into the leather of the easy chair, feeling bruised.

The familiar hiss of the can's seal and the cool malt taste brought me back to the edge of reality. I closed my eyes and went back over the day for Laura. A few hours earlier, I hadn't wanted to explain the call from Carlos: It had seemed too complicated, too unreal. Now, if only to try to explain it to myself, I went back through the whole thing in detail, from the call to the fight on the doorstep.

A blue light splashed its reflection on the ceiling.

"You shouldn't be out there? You shouldn't tell the cops?" she asked when I had finished.

I shrugged. "I don't think I've one damn thing to tell them. God knows where Carlos disappeared to."

"You think he's safe?"

"I've been worrying about that. But I don't see there's anything I could do to make him safer."

She thought about that. She must have agreed. At least she didn't push it any further. "Sounds weird."

"Weird?"

"The whole thing. Come on now, Jake, you know how you are. You don't even like to step outside the door if you can help it."

"What's weirder still," I told her, "is that I kind of enjoyed it. I never realized quite how much I'd shut myself in here." She laughed. "Sure," I said, "even Jake Molnar needs contact with the outside world. Maybe I've just forgotten how to take a risk. It was like a cold shower after a sauna. Shock treatment, but it woke me up."

She stood behind me and her thumbs were slowly loosening knots between my neck and spine.

"And now," I said, "the envelope, please."

It was a plain manila envelope, used and reused to the point where its folds had worn away. Crisscross layers of masking tape held it together, revealing only small squares of the original material. In one square, the grid showed snatches of a typewritten address: "OS SMI," it read. "W. BLE." And on the last line,

"Y.C., N." In another, part of a blue-gray stamp. Like details in a collage.

The knife sliced easily through one long edge of the envelope and I slid the contents onto the reading table. A few eight-by-ten glossies in a protective paper cover. A black-bound artist's notebook, small format. A bundle of newspaper clippings, held together with a red plastic paper clip. A clear plastic slide organizer, folded in half and tied with a rubber band.

"Smith's how and why?" asked Laura.

"I guess." The glossies were on top of the deck. "Let's start with them."

I slid them from the protective folder. There were just four pictures.

"Who's that?" said Laura. "Or should I say, what's that?"

"Patty Drayton. The one Carlos told me was murdered. It's a promotion shot, I guess."

"Promoting what?"

I saw Laura's point. There was something inhuman about the picture. It was a head shot: The stark bone structure was caught from an unnatural angle, slightly below and to the side, to accentuate strangeness. Spiked hair set off in contrast to the white space behind it. Cheeks sallow to the point of emaciation. Heavy mascara round the eyes and lashes. Mouth slightly open, grinning crookedly, revealing a set of teeth that might have been touched with makeup to exaggerate the space between them. The whole image conveyed a deliberate cruelty.

Turning the picture over, I pointed to the Samantha Dmitri gallery label with typed information: "Patty Drayton, 1981. Photo credit: Fergus St. Orman."

The second picture must have been a snapshot blown up to an eight-by-ten. A jolly girl. Full head of hair, reaching down over the shoulders. A natural plumpness straining at the belt that coupled jeans and T-shirt at the midriff. Big, ingenuous smile, lopsided. A second figure would have been standing to her right in a tartan shirt, an arm about her shoulder, but this one had been cropped, leaving the picture unbalanced, incomplete. I passed it on to Laura.

"Same girl," she said at a glance.

I wouldn't have known. But when I flipped the picture I found a handwritten note with the name and date: "Patty Drayton, 1977?" The date had a heavy question mark. I placed the two pictures side by side and took another swallow from the can.

"I don't get it," Laura said.

"Simple," I said. "Friend Carlos has discovered hype, that's all. Take a look at the next two glossies. First the artist, then her work." Laying them on the table, I paired them like the first two. Before and after.

"Look. 'Patty Drayton, ink on paper, 1976.' " I showed her the label and turned the picture over. "Figure drawing, see? Not bad. It's tough to tell from a photo, but maybe the woman had talent I hadn't suspected."

Laura studied the picture under the reading light. "It's not a Jake Molnar," she said.

"It sure isn't that," I laughed. "Okay, now look at this one. 'Patty Drayton, 1981.' Same Samantha Dmitri label. Mixed media, dimensions, etcetera. This is the kind of work she got famous for before she died." A male figure, crouched and ready to spring. The trademark switchblade cock erect and glinting through layers of wire armature and street debris.

"Okay, now look at the price." It was penciled beside the label at seven thousand dollars. "That was two years ago. So the woman dies and makes the press. Gets to be something of a folk hero and martyr, right? And before you know it, the value of her work shoots up. This piece is worth ten times as much today. Easy."

"Seventy thousand?"

"More, much more. A little drawing went for fifty just a few hours back. It's just like any other business. You promote an image and a product, create the demand and manipulate the supply. In this case, Patty's suicide made someone a pile of money. Limited supply and incredible demand."

"But Smith said murder, right?"

"He hasn't proved that to me yet," I said.

The black book was filled with neat lines of memos, sketches, ideas, quotations. There were found objects pasted in, and clippings. An artist's notebook. Inscribed on the cover page: "If found, please return to Patty Drayton, 214 W. Broadway, Studio C." Funny, a youthful touch. Not just the phrase but the handwriting, especially neat and careful, expressed a girlish faith. The notion that it could be lost and returned suggested an innocence one wouldn't have associated with this artist. My journals never left the studio.

I flipped through the pages, debating whether to do a quick overview and then come back, or plod methodically through the entire package. I stopped here and there at a page to read a bit out loud, allowing at least the sketch of a self-portrait to emerge. Brief phrases, visual ideas, the simple arrangement of words on paper.

"Sounds different, doesn't she?" said Laura.

"Different?"

"From the way you'd thought about her. Jake, you're a knee-jerk chauvinist. She's sure a lot different from the cheap hustler you made her out to be."

"I guess you're right," I said. The journal allowed the glimpse of a richness in Patty I hadn't allowed myself to grant her. A complexity of thought. In her sketches, she had the ability to focus and distill the image, capture the mood of an instant. She had a special understanding of the body's language in its poses.

The telephone rang in the hall. I had remembered the tape deck this time, but I set down the ale can anyway. By the time I reached it, the tape was activated and I stood listening to the last words of my own recorded voice announcing frostily that anyone wishing to leave a message could do so after the beep. I waited to see who'd called before deciding whether to pick up.

When the beeper sounded, the hang-up wasn't immediate. An electronic silence, an expectation, as though the unidentified caller were aware of my listening presence there. There were seconds of static silence that seemed heavy with indecipherable meaning. I lifted the receiver.

"Smith?" I asked. "Smith?"

Whoever it was hung up.

"Jake," called Laura from the study. "Jake, who was that?"

"No idea," I called back. "He didn't say."

I paused at the studio door as I went back to the study and grinned at the sudden, unlikely vision of Laura as a Patty Drayton construction. Her picture glowed on the easel in near darkness, and a lucky glance showed me what it was that I had missed before. It was turning out to be one of the best things I had ever done—a work that was beginning to give me that deep satisfaction that comes with finally getting something right. Laura seated, naked, on the floor, her legs half bent and spreading, revealing a mat of shaggy down.

No razors there.

SIX

◇

Laura had the newspaper clippings spread out when I got back to the study. Mostly they were small headlines and short paragraphs, roughly outlined with felt tip markers: "CONTEMPORARY FETCHES $73,000," "AUCTION NETS $40,000 FOR YOUNG ARTIST," "RECORD SET FOR WORTHING NELSON: ZURICH SALE." And so on. Each clipping had been carefully identified and dated in what I took to be Smith's handwriting.

It took us a while to get it in chronological order, and even when it was done, it proved to be disappointing stuff.

What else is new, I thought? Young artist discovers what the market is about. Nor could I get excited over Patty Drayton having been exploited. It had happened to better artists. Worthing had been exploited in his day. I had been exploited too. And let's not forget, I told myself, that we'd done our share of exploiting. No artist is exempt from human maladies like greed. It was only later that I had chosen the other course and refused. No great distinction, really. Many others had done the same back in the late Sixties and the early Seventies. Some—the concept artists—had refused to produce a salable commodity. For myself, I had simply withheld the product from the market. Holed up in my garret, as Elmer Rothstein said.

"More of the same?" asked Laura, catching the drift.

"I don't see much to tell us any different," I said. "The only surprise is that Smith sees anything of note in all this stuff. I wouldn't have thought him so naive."

Rolling the rubber band from the last of the four

items, I found a pink receipt for slide reproduction costs in the fold of a single sheet of transparencies from Photocolor on Sunset Boulevard in Los Angeles. Twenty-five dollars and fourteen cents. I held the sheet of slides up to the light and squinted through them, starting from the top and left.

"It's a Worthing Nelson," I told Laura. One I couldn't remember having seen before. My eye followed the top row, reading from left to right. All Worthing Nelsons. None I had seen before.

"Jesus!" I said.

"What is it, Jake?" said Laura.

I didn't answer for a moment. The next row was the same. And so on, down the sleeve.

"They're Worthing Nelsons. All of them."

"So?" she said.

"I never saw them before. I didn't know they existed."

None of the transparencies were identified. No dimensions. No date or title. No provenance.

"I don't see what's so strange," said Laura. "You'd have to know everything this guy did?"

"Yes," I said simply. "I thought I did."

"Maybe they're fakes," said Laura.

Could be. They'd be hard to fake, but if Smith had stumbled on to a good forger making Worthing Nelsons, it would have been big news.

Squinting up again, I picked a transparency and popped it from the file sleeve, then pulled out the carousel projector from its place on the bottom shelf and loaded the slide into an empty cartridge. I switched on the beam and we watched the picture materialize on the white surface of the library wall.

I would have to see the real thing to be sure. The projected reproduction two-dimensionalized the textured surface of the painting. But the signature seemed clear. The energetic structure, the absolute authority, the color palette. It was different, too. A tone I had never seen in his work before: The fluid expression had taken on an edge of tension. Gestures had become shorter, more abrupt. In fact it was probably the change that made it more convincing: No artist of Worthing's stature could repeat himself forever.

"Well?" asked Laura.

"Sure looks like Worthing," I said. "But it's not quite the Worthing I knew. There's something here I never knew about him. Something that's hard to read."

"So what's the big deal?" she asked.

The image held steady on the wall, stunning in color and complexity.

"Listen," I said. "If a Worthing Nelson I'd never known about shows up, it's no big deal. So he didn't show me a painting. Or two or three. But here's a guy who, for all the art world knew, had given up painting for the last ten years of his life—what the critics called 'the silent Seventies.' One of the most important artists of the century."

"Isn't it possible they were painted earlier?"

"Possible. Lots of artists hold work back when they don't need to sell it. But this has all the ease and authority of his later work. I've never seen anything like it."

I held the rest of the file up to the light. There seemed to be a consistency, too, among the twenty slides, suggesting a full period of growth and change.

Another question. If there were twenty of them, why shouldn't there be more? If the file had been half empty, even less than full, I might have settled for the notion that after all there were a few Worthing Nelsons that I didn't know about. Yet a filled sheet somehow suggested the possibility of more.

"Time, Jake," said Laura. "I'm going to be leaving." She'd already picked up her coat and bag from the hall.

"They said there'd be a lot of snow," I told her. "It was starting when I got home. You could stay." I surprised myself, wishing she would.

"If I know you, you're lost for the rest of the night," she said. "And I've got my exercise class at eight. See you around nine, okay? And stop looking so worried."

I laughed. "Come here and give me a kiss, goddammit."

She let herself out. When she had gone, I loaded the other nineteen slides in the carousel. With growing amazement, I feasted for what must have been hours on the legacy of Worthing Nelson. With a mixture of joy and sadness, I concluded that my friend had deceived me in those last years of his life. No new work, the man had said. Yet here was the evidence. Or part of it. Where was the rest?

It was in the small hours that I awoke to find myself still in the study chair. The projection of a slide glowed on the wall and the projector's fan was clattering to dispel accumulated heat.

And then again before dawn I awoke in bed with a chill fear and a massive hunger for sex—I suppose for a human body to clasp my arms about—to pour it all out of me, into Laura who could bear it better.

I dozed again fitfully, slipping in and out of dreams.

SEVEN

◇

Shaking myself free from the bedcovers, I hobbled naked to the bathroom and surveyed, in the mirror, the last vestiges of a morning erection. The complexity of veins and textures. Drawing again. I was doing it even without charcoal in my hand.

Standing there in the bathroom, I caught the irony of my own narcissism. In the context of the past twenty-four hours, the values on which I'd prided myself before seemed disproportionate and out of place.

I saw myself as Cynthia might have seen me all those years ago. Jake the egotist. All prick, no tenderness.

I continued my examination.

Forty-nine. Thick dark hair and reddish beard. Not tall, powerfully built. To keep in shape, I do daily push-ups and stomach crunches. And three good walks a day. I need the walks as much as I need food. Each time it's a journey into the myriad faces of people. I walk through the streets and watch and devour whole human beings as I go.

The fresh mark of a bruise on the outside of my upper arm surprised me. I remembered the painful pressure of Smith's fingers and wondered what to do. Find him? Would he find me? The contents of his package lay spread out on my study table.

It was close to seven-thirty, later than usual for a morning walk, but I went out anyway. The storm had produced no more than a light covering and the sidewalks were clear enough. I paused on the top step to survey what seemed like a whole new world and headed west, doubling back over the course of last night's chase.

I guess we all have rituals. No matter what route I took, I would always make a point on my morning walk to pass the spot where they'd found Worthing. Just something I did. A salute, perhaps, or payment of a debt.

That morning, I turned south on Fifth and walked through Washington Square, veering east toward the Bowery. There, as always, the wind seemed to blow a little colder and more bleak. Abandoned building sites gaped like absent teeth, and discarded newspaper blew across the street. Even the rusting dumpster at the corner of East Fourth looked the same as the day they had found him.

From a distance, too, the cast of characters looked the same. A couple of figures, one prostrate, the second bending over him. One drunk, the other checking him out for hidden stocks of liquor. Or money. Or usable warm clothing. The scavenger's head was covered with an oily woolen ski hat, from which gray ends of hair stuck out and flapped a little in the wind. He wore an army greatcoat, tattered and stuffed with newspaper. I paused to watch, perhaps to scare him off—though there wasn't much, I thought, I could have done.

He poked at the body with strange little whimpers, as though by shaking it he could bring it back to life.

"He's dead," he said. "He's dead."

He said it over and over, rocking the body more and turning the head toward me. Blood was congealed around the ears and eyes from a massive wound to the temple, where the skull had caved in. But the face was recognizable.

It was Carlos Smith, lying where Worthing had lain five years before. The yellow jacket was gone, but there was no mistaking the face. One eye was crushed and bloodied by the blow that had killed him. The other stayed painfully open. The skin had turned to a bluish pallor. But it was Smith.

The wind gusted painfully in my face as I stood and gaped. Some hideous cosmic prank. Or a plan so grisly and complex as to overwhelm belief.

"He's dead," the man repeated.

EIGHT

◇

    All I had been able to do was call the cops and tell them where to find him. Without leaving my name. I couldn't bring myself to that point.

    Yet the more I thought about the thing, the more I knew it had to have been set up for me. There had to be someone who knew about Worthing and knew that Smith had found the slides. They had to have known he'd contacted me. Worse, it had to be someone who knew my habits. Who'd been watching me. I needed to talk.

    The trouble was, iconoclasts have no one to talk to.

    I dialed Cynthia's number.

    "Cyn?"

    "Jake? Is that you?"

    "Yeah, babe, it's me." I said it out of habit, and wished at once I hadn't. She couldn't stand for anyone to call her babe. There was a pause. She could never make it easy.

    "Saw you at Sotheby's yesterday," I said.

    "I was amazed," she said. "I was bidding on your painting. What brought you there?"

    "Business," I said. "Do you know Carlos Smith?"

    "Of course. His work. I've met him once or twice."

    "He's dead. I found him this morning, where they found Worthing. The precise same spot. He'd been killed. Murdered."

    There was a silence.

    "Cyn?"

    "I'm just trying to get this through my head. I mean, my God! Murdered? Carlos Smith? It's unbelievable! Did you tell the police?"

"I told them where to find him. Cynthia, Smith was the reason I came to Sotheby's. He called me yesterday and told me Worthing had been killed." I gave her the short version.

"I tell you, Cynthia, I'm spooked. It feels like someone has it in for me. But why me? I just don't get it."

There was another pause as she thought that one through.

"You want help?" she asked.

"I could use some," I admitted. "Just to talk. You have time?"

"Listen, today I don't. Not a minute anywhere. And nothing I can break. Lunch tomorrow?"

It seemed like a week away.

"Okay," I said. "I'll pick you up."

The question continued to nag as I tried to get back to the business of the day: Should I call the police again? I padded down the hall and paused, leaning on the studio doorjamb to glance at the work in progress in the morning light. It was a habit that sometimes showed me the way for a whole day's work. I found nothing. Saw nothing but the image of two dead artists.

The front door opened and brought welcome release from thought in the sounds of Laura's presence. I heard her go through to the bathroom to undress and slip on the dark silk paisley robe. By this time I would usually be at the easel, studying the previous day's work, correcting or making notations of detail that needed attention. I hurried to clear the breakfast things and rinse them in the sink.

"Hey, Jake," she said. "You're late. How long were you up last night? You solve your mystery yet?"

My hunger from the early hours returned. I took her face between my hands, grasping the dark hair at her neck and bringing her mouth forward to my own.

"Hey now, Jake, love, what happened to you overnight?"

She smiled and cocked her head to one side, puzzled. On a normal day, it was business before pleasure. Today, I felt an almost desperate urge to bury myself. To go back, back where it was familiar and warm.

"Easy, baby."

I reached out and slipped the silk robe from her shoulders, bringing her body close to me, allowing my head to fall between her breasts. The soft warmth of her flesh responded, shivering at the contact of my prickly stubble. I marveled again at this young woman, barely half my age, who could make me feel like man and child together.

I led her to the studio couch and stood watching her settle into natural rest. The tough grace of her thighs, almost beyond belief; the belly that flouted fashionable emaciation, full and satisfying in its insistent roundness; the nipples like the pupils of two dark eyes. With continuing surprise, she watched me strip my clothes. Laid a hand behind my leg, in the fold of flesh where thigh meets buttock, and with the other reached for my hand, urging my weight down over her.

"Easy," she said.

Making love with Laura had always been a celebration as varied as the surfaces and textures of the human body, each territory newly explored in each new context. But that morning I just wanted in—and lost it.

"God damn it!" I rolled off angrily. Wildly blaming myself, blaming Laura. But it was deeper. What I had lost was more than a moment's virility. It was the comfort of my hard-won silence and isolation. I knew that in the space of a single day, I had lost it. I had lost it irretrievably.

"God damn it!" I said again.

Laura put her arms round me and kissed my hair and rocked me in her arms.

God damn it.

NINE

◇

"Can I help you?"

It was late morning in the Samantha Dmitri Gallery on West Broadway. I hadn't noticed the young woman approach me. I hadn't even seen the painting in front of me, though I had been staring at it for some minutes. Things had seemed clear enough when I started out from the studio. But now I had only the vaguest idea what I hoped to find in coming here.

"The gallery's closed," she said. "For installation. Perhaps you'd like to come back later in the week?"

To cover my confusion, I turned the Molnar glare on her. She wore her hair in a short brush cut with a streak of turquoise. Loose top, khaki, fashionably ripped. Top buttons open far enough to encourage the eyes to peek in at small, defiant breasts. In any event, she refused to be bullied.

"Whose work is this?"

I nodded at the painting, as yet unhung and propped on its side against the wall for installation. A largish horizontal affair, great balls of arcade color swirling against a background of celestial gloom. A bloody cleaver hurled into space like a tomahawk.

"The artist is Desmond Scott," she said. Her voice expressed barely patient tolerance for my ignorance.

I turned the glare on her again until she decided I might be a prospect after all and launched forth into a lengthy spiel about the artist. It was composed, rehearsed. Nicely trained. As she talked, I thought I noticed a change in her attitude, a movement of doubt in the eyes. A "Shouldn't I know you?" and "Why should I know you?" rolled into one.

"I'd like," I said, "to see some of Patty Drayton's work. I understand this gallery represents her?"

I had decided not to call ahead, to benefit from the anonymity that time and distance would afford. I needed first to see the work if I wanted to know whom I was dealing with. Patty Drayton. Carlos Smith, too—though I knew more about him.

Work had been out of the question in the studio. My fingers had been cold to the charcoal. After the failed attempt at love, Laura had seemed as distant as Mount Fuji. My fault, not hers. After an unconvincing pass at the drawing in progress, I had known better than to touch it. I had tried a number of tricks to relax and renew my concentration, from working up new sketches, loosening up the eye and hand, to simple breathing exercises. For two hours.

I sent her home with a wrenching sense of finality. Drawn to the window, I watched as she walked back to the subway. There were the winter trees, the brownstone fronts, blackpainted railings, the occasional pedestrian, parked cars, patches of snow. Oddly, the familiar scene was charged with a drama I couldn't identify and I worked to commit it to memory, to absorb it as fully as I could. Later, I would bring it all back to the surface in a drawing—a task I often use to train the eye and mind.

"Patty Drayton?" the gallery assistant asked.

"You do handle her, don't you? The estate?"

"Yes, of course. But I just don't know . . . we're so shortstaffed today. One of our artists . . ."

"Killed. I know," I said. "I'm sorry." I put on my gravest look and turned on her. "What is your name?" I asked.

"Me?" she said. She was flustered at the idea that things could take a personal turn. "Oh, I'm Brooke. Brooke Elliott, Samantha's assistant."

"Brooke," I repeated. "In that case you must surely know what work you have in inventory. Patty Drayton?"

"Well. Yes, of course. I think we have something in the back, if you'd like to follow me."

Her pique was expressed not in words but in the

movement of her skinny, indignant backside. I followed it through a glass door at the rear of the exhibition space and on through the offices to the gallery's back room—a huge storage area that housed the stock-in-trade. Usually it's the most interesting place in any gallery. Art works everywhere. Tall racks of paintings lined the walls and aisles, creating a labyrinthine corridor that led still deeper toward the rear of the building. A side spur of this corridor led to another door, almost concealed by stacked art. Brooke led me into a small white room—small enough to seem crowded with just two of Patty Drayton's construction works. A few framed pieces, too, were stacked against the wall in the far corner.

"Thank you, Brooke," I said.

My gaze clearly indicated dismissal and left the girl perplexed. To leave a stranger unattended in the inner sanctum was a transgression against gallery policies and all her better instincts. I made it clear to her that I wouldn't look at the work until she left.

"But," she responded to the unspoken demand, "Samantha insists. I don't know you. I have to stay here."

"I think you know me, Brooke," I said. "At least if you're as smart as I think you have to be to work in a gallery like this one."

I would have laid even money that Brooke was recently out of graduate school, with a glittering thesis on contemporary history. Too much like Cynthia. Somewhere in my wallet I kept an old business card just waiting there for an occasion such as this one. I fumbled through the contents and pulled it out.

"There," I said. "I expect you know the name?"

A blush on Brooke's unshockable cheeks seemed laughable. She stared at the card in her hand, glanced back at me, and stared at the card some more.

"Oh God!" she said. "I'm so embarrassed. Of course I should have recognized you. Your face was so familiar. It's just so totally unexpected. I mean, they say you never come out these days . . ."

There were advantages, I thought wryly, in having made it to the history books.

"Listen," I said, "you've no earthly reason to apologize. Please don't give it a thought. But if you wouldn't mind, I'd really like a few minutes with Patty's work."

She backed out through the open door, still flustered by her monumental gaffe. Maybe I had earned a favor.

Alone, I turned back to the two construction works—the first Patty Draytons I had seen aside from reproductions in a magazine. Here if anywhere I could find out about the woman Carlos Smith had said was murdered. Catch her at home.

While I can indulge my prejudices as well as anyone, I can suspend them when I need to. I walked and touched softly, adjusting my eye to the information Patty Drayton had to share about her experience of the world, listening to what she said.

The work felt better than I would have suspected. Laura was right. There was more to Patty than I had allowed myself to see.

I crossed the room to the small framed works and turned them away from the wall. They were a series of figure drawings, considerably more mature than the one in Carlos's package. There was a veneer of intended cruelty that made them consistent with the larger works. But beyond the veneer, the drawings were crisp and tough and impressed me with their mastery.

It was the same with the three-dimensional work. The real pain of these figures was not in the genitalia. These were bravado, flashy, nicely accomplished, cocksure—and surprisingly right in their anatomical reference. Not in the genitals, though, but in the structure. Eloquent tension borne of recalcitrant materials. The illusion of real, trembling flesh, the essential humanity of a gesture made with rusted wire and corrugated iron, with once-sodden roofing paper, broken tiles, and street debris. The evocation of grace and fragility, of human presence, with a few clumsy rejects of material reality.

For me, one of the litmus tests of an art work is: What does it do to another artist? Only the best can do what Patty Drayton's work had done. It made me question my own. It threw down that ultimate Rilkean challenge: *Du musst dein Leben ändern.* You have to change your life.

Was this the heritage of a neurotic and a suicide?

TEN

◇

"Why, Jacob Molnar! This is an unexpected honor!"

The tiny room was suddenly as overwhelmed with Samantha Dmitri's exuberance as it was with her perfume. She seemed unsure only, when the moment came, whether to risk the familiarity of a hug and kiss between art world celebrities, but was smart enough to read the signals. She reached out a small hand from the folds of black that enveloped her diminutive figure.

"Brooke called to tell me you were here," she said. "I never would have believed it."

Samantha was a powerfully attractive woman, without being the least bit beautiful or pretty. Her dark eyes had a brilliance that seemed the distillation of energy. I was surprised by a Southern accent.

"Yes," I said. Her warmth, real or feigned, left me embarrassed by my own stiff courtesy. "I would have called ahead but . . ."

"Nonsense, nonsense! You're welcome here any time."

She kept my hand clutched in hers and gazed into my eyes with an adulation so intense it left me speechless. Even my well-fed ego balked at believing that my presence was enough to have brought her rushing back to the gallery on such a day. What could Carlos's death have meant to her?

I noticed, too, that she was sweating as though she had covered the whole distance at a run.

"Jacob Molnar!" she continued, her words spilling out so fast and forcefully as to render thought impossible. "A legend! A living legend! I grew up with your work. I cut my teeth," she said, "on Jacob Molnar."

She smiled as though to demonstrate their current efficacy and managed to keep talking. She told me more about myself in sixty seconds than I cared to remember. I would have heard my entire professional career rehashed had I not interrupted.

"Brooke told me you wouldn't be in today. I heard about Carlos Smith."

Her beatific beam converted instantly to an expression of profound sadness. She smoothed the black velour of her jacket, the uppermost of several fashionable layers.

"Isn't that just awful," she breathed as she led me from the Drayton room. "An artist so full of promise! Do you know his work? His recent work?" She waved an arm to dismiss all previous work as insignificant beside the new production. "Spectacular!" she breathed.

On a wave of energy, she wafted me through the gallery's back room to a private office and insisted that I take a seat. I sat, then thought better of it.

Since the moment she arrived she had taken over, dictated the terms of my being here, and had used her surprisingly impressive weaponry to deflect my aim in coming. It was enough. I stood up stiffly, looking down at the seated Samantha and forced her silence.

"I think it's important for you to know the reason for my being here," I started. "I met Carlos Smith for the first time yesterday. I was familiar with his work only through pictures in magazines and had no desire to know it better." She was about to speak but I compelled her silence with the flat of my hand.

"The truth of the matter is that I regarded his work as inferior and still have no reason to change my mind. He called early yesterday, apparently to let me know that he was deeply troubled and to ask my help. I tried to refuse but he wouldn't take no for an answer. He begged for a meeting and suggested yesterday's sale at Sotheby's as a suitable time and place. I went only because I'd found no way to turn him down. You were there also," I said.

Samantha Dmitri only nodded in response. I wondered how much she could have known of my side of the story.

"With heavy reservations, as you can imagine, I did meet Carlos as he had requested. After we left the auction, he stuffed a mysterious envelope under my jacket, pleaded some inexplicable pressure, and insisted that I meet him later at my studio. I agreed to do it. God knows I've regretted it ever since. The meeting never took place. Smith never made it to my studio. He was met by a man who first attacked him, then chased him off. This morning, I discover that he has been killed. I have to believe that all this is some cruel coincidence. But now I feel obligated to know the man. I need to be sure."

I paused, watching. She held her palms to her temples, pressing in, as though to contain an overflow of agonizing thoughts.

"My God," she said. "What am I hearing? This is craziness." And, wide-eyed, she returned my gaze. Nothing. Not a shadow of insincerity. Only, I thought, sheer fright.

"Probably," I said, "it is no more than craziness. I need to know for sure."

"Why you? Why would he come to you?"

"From what Carlos said, I can only suggest that he had an exaggerated faith in my integrity. But it's not so much why as the fact that he did."

Samantha's hands were busy turning a small chrome sculpture on her desk, its smooth surfaces glinting alternately under the lamp and reflecting the violet of her manicured nails. Her office was all business: stark white walls with immaculately framed drawings, a deco walnut desk and credenza from the Thirties, their surfaces clean save a few well-chosen objects. A two-drawer file cabinet. Black.

"Patty Drayton," she asked next. "I still don't understand why you came here asking to see the Patty Draytons. What do they have to do with anything?"

I kept my eyes on hers. "You don't know?"

"I can't imagine. Well, I knew they were close at one time. But that was years ago."

"Close?" I asked.

"Good friends," she said. "I don't think it was much more."

"And nothing else?"

"Nothing that I know of." She shrugged, but she wasn't looking at me. I didn't know whether to trust her.

"Carlos believed she hadn't committed suicide. He thought she'd been murdered. He claimed he could prove it."

So hard to read.

"Murdered? Patty? That's totally crazy. My God!" Her hands left the sculpture, fluttered toward the light, and landed in her lap.

"The package I mentioned," I told her, scarcely knowing what my intention was. "He thought of that as evidence."

"What evidence?" she asked. "My God, what could he possibly have got his hands on? What did he have in there?"

"Photos, clippings. Some documents." I was vague. I had no cause to tell her that I'd barely glanced at most of it. "By the way, where did Carlos live?"

"He had a studio on Bleecker," she responded absently.

"The street address?"

A tiny hesitation?

"Four thirteen. I'll take you there," she added in a new rush of enthusiasm. "Tomorrow. I have a key, of course. Yes," she said, "that's a great idea. Then we can discuss this further. Most of his new work is still down there. He would have had a show next month. Anyway, I'll meet you there first thing. Nine? Ten?"

"Let's make it ten," I said.

I was about to leave when I had another thought.

"Oh. By the way," I said. "Do you have any Worthing Nelsons? For sale, I mean? I heard there were some around."

ELEVEN

◇

It occurred to me as I walked back up Broadway that I was having a good time. Perverse, perhaps. I was astonished by the spring in my step.

My latest impulse brought me to the door of Carlos Smith's studio. Why wait for Dmitri and another day? It was turning out to be a good day for impulse, or so I told myself. I had no way of knowing how it would turn out.

At the street entrance, a row of bell buttons with fading name tags showed that Carlos had lived on the third floor. Beyond the threshold lay the dim entryway of what had been a regular commercial building before its conversion into lofts. Little had been done to improve its outer appearance. The sound of my steps on frigid boards bounced off gray walls and up to a stained ceiling. Faced with the choice between a dilapidated elevator and wooden stairs, I took the stairs.

I had no idea how I planned to get in. But the door was open anyway, and light spilled out to the landing, along with the sound of voices.

I put my head around and was blinded by the transition from the scant light of the landing to the track-lit brilliance of an artist's studio. White on white on white. A single, high-ceilinged space, divided only by rough partitions and dominated by a rack of paintings along the far wall. A dropcloth was spread out under an unfinished work.

It took a moment for the two men standing in the center of the studio to become aware of me. One wore a dark overcoat, the other a light one. They stood as though posed in strange, incongruous isolation, living statues, back to back. They looked as bland and unfamiliar in this setting as those immaculate suburbanites who inhabit the still world of a picture by Magritte.

One of them broke away and strode toward me when they saw me. He fished in his pocket and showed me a badge. Still young enough to be insecure about the authority it represented, he confronted me with an implied aggression learned at the police academy. A little Billy Goat Gruff.

"Officer Callahan," he said. "What's your business here?"

"I stopped by to visit. I'm a friend," I said. "An artist."

My explanation had a hollow ring. The cop looked skeptical.

"You have identification, please?"

I showed him a driver's license that I keep renewed but barely use. The license was carefully inspected and returned.

"No one told you this guy was killed today? The guy that lives here?"

"Well, yes," I said vaguely, not wanting to get caught in a lie. "As a matter of fact, I'd heard . . . it was . . ."

"Stopped by to visit?" he asked incredulously. "What kind of response is that? How did you expect to get in? You have a key?"

Confronted with this remorseless logic, there was little I could say. I swallowed a dose of pride and shrugged.

"Well," I said, "I just stopped by to see if I could help. I was curious to know if anyone had any leads . . ."

"Lieutenant," he called back over his shoulder. "This guy is curious."

The second officer joined us. Black. He carried considerable weight with the grace of a lighter man. Unlike the other officer, he shook my hand. Perhaps to inform me with its impressive size and strength that he wasn't to be fooled with.

"Richards," he said. "Homicide." I had never expected to hear lines straight from the screen, yet Richards's grave presence and his modulated voice deprived the cliché of its absurdity.

"You're an artist?" he asked. "You knew the deceased?"

Artist. Deceased. The way he spoke the words, they might have been synonymous. Deprived of his name, Carlos seemed even more removed from the reality of my life. Who was this man? What was he doing to me?

"Barely," I said. "I barely knew him."

The two officers exchanged a glance, Callahan with an ill-disguised expression of contempt. My eyes wandered to the work in progress. A big figure, clumsily outlined and thickly overpainted with jagged darts of color. Naked expression with nothing to express.

"Anything special you'd be looking for?" Beside his terrier partner, Richards was a Doberman. Formal, restrained.

"Not really, no," I said. "In part, I just don't know what brought me here. It's strange when somebody you know just turns up dead, like that."

Where your friend had done the same, I might have added. After an urgent, strange encounter. After he had handed you a package of materials he'd said were evidence of murder.

"Yeah, well," said Richards after a pause. "I guess there's nothing here to see."

It was intended as a dismissal, and Callahan emphasized the point by ushering me to the door.

So much for impulse. A rising wind bit at my face and ears. The sky slashed down between dark facades, a translucent blue, and the metal fire escapes stood out in crisp relief. I walked home quickly, as though speed could clear my head.

No doubt that Dmitri had frozen at Worthing Nelson's name. Her nervous animation converted into hostility, but this could have been simply a reaction to an implied threat, an accusation.

"No," she'd said. "I never handled Worthing Nelson's work. That was before my time."

As I turned onto Eleventh, the memory of yesterday's chase revived. Carlos alive and running.

I unlocked the door and found the red light glowing on the tape deck.

TWELVE

◇

There were two hang-ups, followed by an unfamiliar voice.

"Mr. Molnar, this is Sergeant Lynch of the New York Police Department. Please contact me urgently as soon as you return. Thank you."

He left a telephone number.

What now? My pulse rate surged as I dialed.

The phone rang twice.

"Police."

"Sergeant Lynch, please."

"Hold the line."

Christ, hurry.

To control the panic, I practiced breathing as I'd learned years ago at a yoga class with Cynthia. In through the nose, out through the teeth with a hiss.

"Lynch speaking."

"Sergeant Lynch, this is Jacob Molnar. You left a message asking me to call."

There was a tiny silence while the sergeant sifted through his memory. Come on, man.

"Oh, yes. Mr. Molnar."

He must have been riffling through a sheaf of papers. I heard them rustling on the line.

"Not good news, I'm afraid. Young woman by the name of . . . Laura Rice."

My God.

"She was the victim of an attack over on Forty-ninth. I have to say she was beaten pretty bad. She asked for you before she lost consciousness. I promised I'd get to you as fast as possible. We found your phone number in her bag. The guy must have dropped it when he ran."

"Where is she now?"

I was cold with fear. Cold with pain for Laura, and guilt that I didn't fully understand.

"St. Clare's. It's over on . . ."

"I know where it is, Sergeant. Thank you for calling. Thank you for the message." I reached for the coat I had just returned to its hanger and was out the door. I avoided thought. The taxi lurched through knots of traffic with excruciating slowness while I sat and drummed my fingers on the vinyl seat and stared without focus at the street ahead.

A receptionist pointed me to Intensive Care.

They had shaved the hair from Laura's head and plastered a thick white patch where the hair had been. Both of her lips were swollen, cracked, and the black threads of surgical stitches, congealed with dark blood, closed a deep cut from the upper lip to the nose. One eye was closed by a massive bruise at the temple. The other was open, fixed and sightless, in a dreadful reminder of Carlos Smith.

Coma.

I sat down by the bed and took her hand in mine. A face whose calm beauty and rich humanity I had contemplated through long days of work and hours of love. Reality, I thought, is unimaginable. The nurses told me she had not only been beaten around the head, but kicked repeatedly after she had fallen to the ground. Beyond the wounds that were obvious and visible, there was extensive internal damage. They still didn't know how much.

What could I do but sit and be with her? After an hour or so her family arrived. A gray father with anxious eyes and the hand of an aristocrat—long, thin-fingered, cool. And Laura's mother, calm, austere, with a graceful body that had run to fat.

From Philadelphia, said Laura's mother. After brief, whispered introductions and a hurried explanation, I fled.

It was five-thirty when I got back home again. A

day since Carlos Smith had arrived on the steps and shattered my life. Routine and habit had always kept its parts together. Without them, time had warped in length and depth. A day?

I unlocked the door and was immediately aware of another intrusion on my private world. Something. A smell? A movement? What?

I snapped on the light, crossed the hall, and kicked open the door to the study. There was no response to the light switch by the door, but reflected light from the hall was enough to see the total destruction. Fury. Books swept from the shelves and scattered on the floor. Pages ripped out and crumpled. Furniture upended, slashed, and the reading light smashed. A stench of piss.

A confusion of ideas and images arranged themselves with sudden, appalling logic.

Carlos Smith. The crowded street, the package. Smith, attacked on my doorstep and later found dead. Laura. The glossies and clippings laid out on the study table. Worthing's slides. Laura arriving the next morning, letting herself in. The keys. The purse torn open, tossed aside. They'd been after the house keys, after the contents of Smith's package.

The reading table in the center of the room was the only object that seemed, shockingly, untouched. Until I realized that the four neat piles of Carlos's evidence had gone. Gouged in crude letters the length of the polished antique surface there were two words: THANKS JAKE. Destruction for destruction's sake. Smith's package had been there on the table for the taking.

The studio!

Good God, if they'd done this to the study, what shape could the studio be in? Years of work were stacked on the open racks. What could be hundreds of thousands of dollars.

I pushed open the connecting door between the rooms. At first sight the contrast was complete. Nothing seemed to have been touched. The racks were undisturbed. The easel was still angled toward the window where the light came in each morning. The couch where I had lain a few hours earlier with Laura still bore the mussed imprint of our bodies. The drawings I had left pinned on the walls were intact.

I crossed to the window where I had stood that morning watching Laura walk toward the subway and stared out into the darkness, remembering the easy swing of her hips. I saw the bag dangling from her shoulder.

When I turned to the easel I found the final obscenity. A childishly crude erection, cock and balls, had been drawn in heavy charcoal and stuck in Laura's mouth. And scrawled across the surface of the picture: ART FOR ART SUCKS!

I picked up the charcoal and blacked out the surface of the drawing, inch by inch.

THIRTEEN

◇

It must have taken me hours to work that surface. I don't remember. What I do remember is the pains I took to make the blackness complete. I slaved for total perfection, the silky texture of a Reinhardt, and dedicated every painful mark to Laura, willing her back to consciousness and life. I worked charcoal after charcoal to a stub until my head throbbed violently.

Not only my head. My whole body ached from the effort to maintain control.

It finally broke down into a sweaty fever. At moments during the night, I found myself kneeling on the white tile in the bathroom, retching, or pacing the hall and studio in the dark. I collected armfuls of ruined books and piled them in the trash. I made eggs and devoured them without appetite. At some point in that dreadful night I found my way to bed and sweated through a couple of hours of delirium.

I woke in bed, still clothed. I don't know how long the phone had been ringing, but it brought me out of a fitful sleep at seven o'clock exactly. I must have forgotten to set the tape when I rushed out to the hospital. I rolled out of bed and swore.

"Molnar."

A voice filtered through to me out of the ether somewhere.

"I'm instructed to tell you that you've had your warning, Mr. Molnar."

It was a mistake to close my eyes. My head took a huge, drifting lunge into space and I staggered against the wall.

"Let's not fool around," he continued, enunciating

carefully. "The message should be clear enough by now. It means simply, get back to your studio. That's where an artist belongs. We'd like for you to stay there. That is all."

Whose bloody butler was this? A polite, anonymous voice, brisk and direct. It seemed the master had told him the message needed no discussion.

A warning? Jesus! Laura beaten half to death. My home and studio raided by animals?

Get back to the studio, he'd said. That's where an artist belongs.

But it was anger alone that took me back there. A surge of energy. Do something, Molnar, I told myself. For Christ's sake, do something.

I slammed down the receiver. Back in the studio, I fought down the nausea and rage as I tore off the blackened picture from the easel, replaced it with a new sketch block, and started out. Finding a rhythm that surprised me with its ease and speed, I blocked in the dark facades of houses, windows, railings, riffling through files of memory for every detail I had absorbed as Laura left that morning. The particular quality of light at noon. The winter's day, still overcast. Cloud cover high and thin, no longer threatening snow but not yet promising to clear. Here was Laura, nearing the intersection. Here there were others, sparse and huddled, hurrying against the cold.

Exercise for the eye and mind. Zoom in. I knew there was something there.

Then I found it. Clearly. A single figure isolated from the rest, different because not moving. Waiting. A deep blue parka. Elbow propped on the railing of the brownstone adjacent to the corner grocery.

I ripped off the first page and began a second, focusing on the single figure, pulling the detail out of memory, seeing what was there. I could read the language of the figure as I conjured it back from mind to paper, stroke by stroke.

Now I could begin to see what it was I had seen. The man was waiting for Laura, a woolen ski cap pulled down around the ears. Now I placed the face.

Prominent cheekbones. Eyes. I could almost feel the hard protuberance of earrings as I molded the shape of the head beneath the ski cap. Brian.

Brian with the Cockney accent. Brian who'd left with Carlos Smith from Sotheby's. Brian who'd wanted to know about me. Who's your china?

Of course. It had to have been Brian who was still with Carlos when I reached the studio.

For several minutes I stared at the sketch I had made, putting things together. Then I did what I should have done sooner. I went to the telephone and dialed the number that I had written down for Sergeant Lynch.

"Police."

"I'm looking for a Lieutenant Richards." I explained where I'd met him.

"That would be a different precinct, sir. Please hold. I'll see if I can locate the number for you."

My head had cleared completely, and nervous energy rushed in to fill the void.

"Will you try this number, sir?"

I wrote it down on the pad and dialed.

"I'll ring the lieutenant's line. Please hold."

He answered after a single ring.

"Richards."

Yes, he remembered me from the previous day. Yes, if I felt it was sufficiently urgent, he could be over right away. Would I mind telling him the nature of the emergency?

"It's my study," I said. "It's been trashed."

A pause.

"I'd suggest you call your own precinct, Mr. Molnar."

"Listen," I broke in. "I'm positive it's the same man that killed Carlos Smith. I think I can show you what he looks like. And there's more—but I need to talk to you."

Richards weighed my credibility. "You mentioned none of this yesterday," he said.

"No," I said. "God knows I wish I had."

FOURTEEN

◇

I called the hospital. No change. Then I called Cynthia.

"Jake, are you crazy? Twice in two days?"

"I just wanted to check on our lunch date."

There was a pause. It was eight o'clock and Cynthia still had her morning voice—she never woke up well, for a farm girl. I could see her draped in sheets, and out of that image came the memory of the most recent time we'd gotten together socially. It ended badly— with me wanting to make love. For old time's sake.

God, she was beautiful. We'd met in some penthouse restaurant overlooking Central Park. A clear night. The shimmer of Manhattan's lights against the velvet darkness of the park. Outline of breasts, a shift of head and hair. The enticement of expensive perfume. Enough to drive a sane man wild.

Anyway, it was taboo. Ex-wives don't sleep with ex-husbands, she said. Her rule, not mine.

"Is someone there with you?" I asked.

Another pause. "It's none of your business, Jake," she said.

"I know." But I had never been able to shake the feeling that it was.

"Listen," I said. "I couldn't wait. This thing's gone crazy on me, Cyn. Yesterday was a nightmare. They half killed Laura for my keys, then trashed the study here."

"Laura?" she asked.

"A model," I said. "And friend. You know her."

"I do?"

"You've met her, anyway."

"What did they want in your study, Jake? I don't understand."

"The slides and the other things Smith gave me. They were out on the table. Listen, I'll have to tell you more at lunch. I had something to ask you."

I thought she'd lost the receiver and was hunting for it in the bedclothes.

"Are you there?" I asked.

"Yes. Sorry. What was it you wanted to ask me?"

"There's a guy called Brian mixed up in this thing. British. Cockney accent. Earrings all around the earlobe. Punk look, with a bony face. I don't know his other name, but he looks like the killer he might be. Could you find out anything about him, through your sources? Who he is, what he does, where he lives—anything?"

"I can try it, Jake, if you think it would be helpful." She was doubtful. "My sources don't cover that kind of circle much."

"He's known in the art world, I can tell you that. What about Dmitri?"

"Samantha? The big time, huh?"

"Just give her a thought. See if you can turn up anything unusual on her. I saw her yesterday and she's showing me Smith's new work this morning. She seems to be right in the middle of this thing, too, with Smith and Patty Drayton. I asked her about the Worthing Nelsons and I could have sworn she was lying when she said she'd never handled any."

"That's it?"

"No. Something was happening yesterday at Sotheby's with Traceman."

"Traceman? Dan Traceman?" She was incredulous.

"Yeah. Your friend and mine. Handsome Dan Traceman and some buyer named Wolff. I forgot the first name. There was some kind of shady deal going down on that Carlos Smith they sold. Smith mentioned it to me when we left. I'd just like to know what was happening there. I don't trust the guy."

"Jesus, you're reaching, Jake. I mean, I know what

you feel about the art world, but isn't the paranoia getting out of hand?"

She could have been right. "Will you do it for me, Cyn?"

She sighed heavily. "Sure, if you ask me. I don't know when I'm going to find the time, but I'll try."

Could I still feel a pang of jealousy, after all this time? She'd found her independence in New York. That's what she'd left me for, she told me, and what she'd fight to keep. "Jesus, Jake, go buy yourself a slave to feed and fuck you," she used to say. "Is that what you want? That's all? I can't do it, Jake. It's not me!"

Trouble was, the madder she got, the more I had wanted her. After we split, I had just shut myself off from feeling about her. Even before, there'd been the groupies. They couldn't wait to get their hands in an artist's pants, so it wasn't hard to find substitutes in the sack. God help me, I screwed everything from freaked-out hippie artists draped in Indian bedspreads to mind-blown heiresses and their blowsy mothers.

For the rest, it was glorious solitude. That's what I thought. Or that's what I thought I thought. From this perspective, it all looked unreal.

FIFTEEN

◇

"Like dogs," said Richards a few minutes later. He surveyed the heap of fallen books that stank of urine.

"Dogs?" I asked.

"Staking out territory," he said absently. "They're sending some people out to go over this."

It hadn't occurred to me. I had imagined somehow that after he'd seen the mess I could have the cleaning lady come to straighten it out.

He looked over the rest of the damage without comment, his large presence dominating the space and seeming more at home than I felt myself. When we reached the easel in the studio, he leaned forward and squinted at my hurried sketch of Brian.

"You knew who'd killed Smith," he asked, "and mentioned nothing yesterday?"

We studied the picture together for a moment.

"Was this him?" I asked.

He turned to look at me.

"We have a couple of reluctant witnesses," he said simply. "If they could draw as well as they can booze, they would have made this picture. Who is it?"

"Brian," I said. "That's the only name I know. I never saw him before yesterday. No, I've lost all sense of time, it was the day before. My guess is he's responsible for the mess in the study, too. And Laura."

"Laura who?"

I showed him the first sketch, with Laura walking down toward the subway.

"Laura Rice," I said. "My model. Here she is. The

bastards beat her yesterday and took her keys. She has keys to the studio. That's how the guy got in here."

"Was this reported?"

"Part of it. The mugging. Not reported, but it was the police that found her. It was a Sergeant Lynch that called to let me know. That was yesterday, around . . ."

"You have somewhere to sit?" he asked, looking around the studio. "I'm going to ask you to go through it from the top. I can write it up as a statement for you later."

We went to the kitchen and sat with elbows on the table, staring across at each other from two different worlds. I could only guess at his. A smart man, self-starter. He exuded a tough street wisdom that had mellowed into controlled intelligence. Yellow whites around the eyes, where anger had long been contained by discipline. His huge hands rested easily on the table.

It was good to talk to him, I found. Good to sift through each detail stored in the memory and stack it out on the table. I must have talked for half an hour before I came to the drawings.

"It's an exercise some artists use," I told him. "A way of training the eye and mind to work together. Often the eye transmits a piece of information that the brain receives and stores before you're aware of it. Drawing's a way of discovering what I've seen. When I met you yesterday, I'd already seen what was there but wasn't completely conscious of it. That's what the drawing achieved."

Richards nodded slowly. He seemed to have made some connection from his own experience and found it convincing.

"And you know nothing more about this man aside from what you've told me?"

"Nothing. Except that I had the impression he knew the people outside Sotheby's. And he did know Carlos Smith . . ."

"Guerrero," said Richards.

"What?"

"Guerrero," he said, rolling the r's. "That was Smith's

name. He was born in Los Angeles, Carlos Guerrero. We were in touch with the family yesterday. They're taking him back there to be buried."

I smiled. Carlos hadn't been above his own share in the hype.

"Anyway, my impression was that this Brian is familiar with the art crowd. If I knew some of those people myself, I could be more help."

"But you don't?"

"I haven't moved with that crowd for years. I'm known as a hermit."

Richards sat for a moment in silence, studying my face. The worry lines deepened in his forehead. "And the young woman?" he asked.

"The one in the picture? Laura. She certainly wouldn't have known him, either. He would have come at her out of the blue." I looked at my watch.

"We'll check with the hospital again soon," he said. "Meantime, come back to Smith's package for a moment. He was trying to convince you that two other artists had been killed. I'm not sure I understand the motivation."

"My guess would be that Smith had been mulling this over for a couple of years—probably since Patty Drayton died. He was bothered by a strategy the art world's famous for. It's the same as marketing any other product, really, but people like to kid themselves that art is somehow pure. An unknown artist gets picked up by a promoter—usually a gallery—and packaged in various ways to stimulate an artificial value for the work. Create a myth and you've got yourself a gold mine. Patty was well on her way to being a myth. Her suicide assured it. She was a bona fide martyr."

"But isn't there a snag in there somewhere?" asked Richards. "If you kill off your artist, you lose the source of your supply, no matter what the demand."

"That's true," I said. "It's possible that Patty wanted to move on. Maybe she wanted to change galleries. Who knows what Carlos thought? But don't forget, a dead artist can be better value than a living one.

Supply's severely limited and demand skyrockets, with a sensational death like that. You could make a killing."

Richards smiled bleakly.

"What kind of money are we talking, Mr. Molnar?"

"For a Patty Drayton? An important piece before her death might have fetched ten thousand. After, I'd guess fifty to a hundred grand, maybe more. Big money, anyway. For the Worthing Nelsons, astronomical. Suppose the works in those transparencies are genuine and available, they'd each be worth well over a hundred thousand, that's three to five million right there, on a single sleeve of slides."

Richards raised an eyebrow.

"Go back again. You said you were surprised that these were paintings you'd never seen before?"

"Astounded. Listen, I knew the guy as well as anyone—his work, I mean. Nelson's last years are referred to everywhere as 'the silent Seventies.' If it turned out he was producing all those years, they'd have to rewrite the history books. And value! God knows! Tens of millions."

Richards absorbed this information calmly, too, as he noted the numbers. He wrote down all the zeros.

"Can you imagine a scenario for Nelson's murder—supposing Smith was right?"

I had given that one a great deal of thought. "Well, it stretches the imagination, but yes, I can. Let's say that, for whatever reason, Worthing had collaborated on concealing his production all those years. I can hardly believe it. It would have gone utterly against his grain as an artist—like any other artist, Worthing needed shows. But let's say he did."

Worthing's famous silence. I had thought so much about it that I had overlooked my own, how sitting in my studio had cut my own communications with the world out there. Talking to others was something different from listening to them talk to you. Where had I been?

"Let's say that he simply changed his mind," I went on. "Reverted to character. Decided the work had to be exhibited, maybe, or used as the basis for a foundation. He often talked about that."

"A foundation?"

"For the work. To make sure it stayed together and out of private hands. That's not unusual for an artist. They hate to have work swallowed up by collectors. For whatever reason, suppose he wanted out of whatever weird agreement he had made . . ."

"It could cost someone millions . . ."

"As I said, if you control the supply, there's nothing better for a dealer than a dead artist."

"The next question is, who? A dealer?"

"Unlikely," I told him. "Not Worthing's dealer, anyway. Too respectable. Too long in the business."

"Can you give me his name?"

"Irving Scully. He closed up shop after Worthing died. I'm not sure what happened to him."

"And?" He picked up my hesitation to continue.

"Listen," I said, "as I see it you have two possibilities. Mutually exclusive. Carlos Smith was either right or wrong. If he was wrong, if this is all nothing but his fantasy, you're dealing with a psychopath who takes delight in blood and violence. God knows what lurks in the mind of a creature like Brian, but it can't have much to do with art, still less the market. But if Smith was right, it's a very different picture. It has to be big business. For one thing, Brian couldn't sell a Worthing Nelson if his life depended on it."

"Oh? Why not?"

"To sell an art work you need credibility. He has none. A punk kid. Collectors are a nervous bunch. They need to be—even the unscrupulous ones. They need to know the provenance of what they're buying, especially if it's shady."

"Provenance?"

"Where it comes from. Dogs have a pedigree, art works have a provenance. Their authenticity is guaranteed in part by who owned them before, what gallery they come from. You don't put out a couple of hundred thousand dollars for a painting unless you're pretty sure of what you're getting. Brian would never even get a hearing from these guys."

Richards barely allowed himself a blink. It occurred to me as I spoke—and I think he had realized too—how much about the art world couldn't be explained in a single session to a man who hadn't lived and breathed it.

"We do have specialists in the field," he said, as though answering a question I hadn't asked. "We'll call them in, I expect."

I nodded, but I had no great love for specialists these days. I preferred my humans large and regular. Like Richards.

"Oh," he said. "And one more thing . . ."

"Ask," I said, as he seemed to hesitate.

"The picture. Brian. It would be helpful if you'd let us have it. We'd have it copied and distributed. For purposes of identification."

A Jacob Molnar on the walls of every police station in New York. What better audience for my first public exhibition in ten years? "But don't forget," I said, "to give it back."

Always the artist.

SIXTEEN

◇

The team of experts came and went. At least I
suppose they went. I left them to lock up. I couldn't
imagine they'd find anything of significance in the
mess and—after a fruitless call to the hospital—I was
impatient to move.

I couldn't say that I hadn't been warned—and not
only by my friend with the butler's voice. The last
thing Richards had done was remind me to change the
locks. For all that, I recognized that my mind was set
on catching up with them. To hit back. To find out
why.

Lacking a specific target, I had no better plan than
simply to stamp around and raise the dust, and the
best place I could think to start was Samantha Dmitri's
corral. Be blunt, I thought. Ask everything.

The Dmitri woman wasn't alone in Carlos's studio
when I arrived there thirty minutes late. One of the
gray-suited foot brigade was hovering at the door.
Behind the Ivy League greeting was an unmistakable
message: Samantha Dmitri did not like to be kept
waiting. Even for Jacob Molnar. I gave him a mock-
sympathetic grin and pushed on past with enough body
contact to rough his suit a little.

"Well," I said. "Samantha! Good morning!"

I'm not sure that I was supposed to catch the end of
an expression of sheer venom. Perhaps. In any case, I
took care to exude a pleasant familiarity that took her
off guard after yesterday. The adjustment crossed her
face like a video wipe. In another moment she was all
smiles and business.

The period of mourning had evidently been brief—or

the wardrobe rapidly exhausted. Yesterday's extravagant black was now replaced by a shimmer of purple silk in loosely falling folds, contrasted with the knotty peasant chic of a woolly coat and sweater and a mother lode of chunky gold. Her walk was a carefully orchestrated cascade of sound and light. I thought of badtime Charlie Baudelaire.

She was good, no question. Not that she completely understood what Carlos had been after, but she knew enough to sell the hind legs off a donkey. Whatever her reasons, she loved the work and made her own unquestioning conviction contagious. Listening to her, I began to understand the source of her power, the reason she'd become a force to be reckoned with in the higher realms of art. The kind of woman you'd like to have as a dealer if you wanted to get to the top. It seemed a shame to interrupt her.

"You know," I said as we looked through Carlos's paintings, slipped from the racks by Samantha's suave assistant, "the more I think about it, the more I'm convinced that Smith was right about Patty Drayton."

She ignored me. "He'd just started looking back to the myths that were buried in his own ethnicity." She waved a hand through several passages in a new big painting. Leaning against the wall, it towered above her, heroic in scale, and epic, at least in its intentions. Brechtian figures out of some morality play pranced nude against ancient pyramids and cityscapes in crudely distorted perspectives.

"Tough," she said. "No?"

"How much have these been fetching?"

A small gesture of irritation suggested that she'd expected better. My dealer used to do the same. I would lay odds that she used it regularly on her clients—and I hope more effectively. Roughly translated, it informed the ignorant that it's crass to mention anything as trivial as money in the presence of great art.

"Twenty, thirty thousand. Until yesterday. He's got a big following now. A feature article in *Flash Art* two months ago. A growing European market. Reviews and articles in all the major glossies. I'd planned to have his show presold before it was installed next month. It's getting to that point."

A pair of sketchbooks lay on a home-built drafting table and I started to leaf through them as she talked.

There was something there. The paintings still didn't make it. Not for me. There was something forced in their scale or subject matter, something that didn't ring true. Set pieces. Here in the sketchbooks there were ideas for landscapes that seemed closer to an individual vision. Palm trees. A recurring lake. Houses set on the hillside. An undercurrent of implicit violence. Flames in the sky.

"Did these ideas ever come to anything? As paintings, I mean?"

"Oh, yes," she said. "I never liked them much, to tell the truth. Small paintings, not his strongest work. Arthur, bring out a couple of those little things. Behind the counter there. The smaller stack."

Arthur did. The paintings were small enough to prop against the wall in a row along the counter top. Intense and highly personal, they were more carefully worked than the large pieces. Lacking the loud social message, they worked on sheer lyrical density.

"You've never showed these?" I asked.

"Could never have sold them," she explained. "Too dinky. Childhood memories, that kind of thing. I always found them sentimental."

I turned one over.

"Echo Park, May 5, 1979." Cinco de Mayo. I had lived in Los Angeles briefly in the Sixties and remembered the small park with its lake a short drive north and west of downtown. Palms and pigeons. Pedal boats. Set in a once fashionable suburb, by that time completely taken over by the Hispanic population—Mexican, Cuban, Central American, in an uneasy mix. A busy, bustling, sometimes dangerous neighborhood. One of the few places in Los Angeles where you still find people walking on the streets.

It was home, I guessed, to Carlos Guerrero.

There it was. These tiny paintings contained the kernel of the vision that had allowed others to make him what he had become. I should have known. Without it, he wouldn't have made it, Samantha Dmitri notwithstanding. This was what Carlos Guerrero had been given to tell the world. He had never needed those big paintings. Samantha had needed those. The market had needed them. Not Carlos.

"Tell me," I said as I held one at arm's length and squinted down at it, "tell me about Brian."

I turned to look at her directly, mustering all the male I could bring to bear. Father, tyrant. Lover. I've learned to do my share of bullying.

She took it. Shook it off with scarcely a blink.

"Brian?" she asked. "Brian who?"

She knew damn well. I knew she knew. She knew I knew. But the moment was hers.

"Brian," I said, "a friend of Carlos. He spoke to him after the auction."

"Brian," she said with a glance at her assistant. "Arthur, have we heard of this Brian? It seems to me we must have heard the name." Arthur was well enough trained to know when he shouldn't hear. He continued silently replacing works in the racks.

"Punk look," I said. "Earrings. British accent."

Samantha's eyes went vague.

"Yes," she said absently. "I may have seen him around. At openings perhaps. There are so many of them now. Looking like that, I mean. It's hard to tell them apart. Why do you ask?"

I held back a moment. I needed to get her rattled and decided to dish it out straight.

"Brian," I said, "was fighting with Carlos on the steps to my house the evening before he died. He was hanging around there yesterday before my model was beaten for her keys . . ."

I couldn't be sure if it was fear or horror in Samantha's eyes.

"Yes," I said. "That, too. I recognized Brian and made a sketch of him. The police have it now. The picture matched descriptions of the man who killed Carlos. There were witnesses. The police are out there looking for him now."

We'd reached the edge and I had the sudden feeling she was about to go over. At least there was doubt in her eyes. She stood there and looked at me, undecided, while Arthur hovered nervously by the door.

Then the spell broke. There was a clatter from the elevator and the studio door flew open without a knock.

It was Traceman.

"Samantha," he said. "Thank you! Thank you so much for waiting for me. So sorry to be late!"

He wrapped an arm round her shoulder and kissed her pleasantly on the lips. Holding her a moment longer under his wing, as it were, he turned to look at me.

"Jake!" he said. "Terrific!"

Even his eyes smiled as he reached a hand for mine and I couldn't be sure if it was friendship he intended to convey, or pleasure at what he might have sensed was a defeat.

"You're interested in Carlos Smith, I see," he said. "Me too." He rested a hand on my back and walked me to the door.

SEVENTEEN

◇

Cynthia's business needed only a tiny space. She had started out years ago on West Broadway with a kind of "trace-it" information service for art works and artists. She'd had the sense to computerize a couple of years ago and tripled her business. Now she was up in the Chrysler Building, light-years ahead of anything that smelled of competition.

I had often reminded her that I had rescued her from the fate of completing a doctorate at the University of Iowa.

That was in 'sixty-four. I had a residency there—a healthy chunk of salary for half a year, a respectable two-day teaching schedule with graduate students only, and a cramped but workable studio in a quonset hut down by the river. The students were reputed to be the pick of the crop. You could have fooled me. Barely a handful of them could draw.

And then I had acquired a model. Lover. Wife. In that order. Chronologically at least.

For her—as she often reminded me—it had meant the end of a career.

'Sixty-four. From the hot Ozark Airlines flight out of Chicago, an old turboprop with its air-conditioning blown, you could see the miles of man's most massive abstract painting: the prairies, alternating brown, straw yellow, dusty green. Each distant intersection of the grid was marked by the white dot of a farm house, barn, and silo. Here and there the dust trail of a speeding car would blur the horizontal or the vertical with a smudge of white.

Perhaps it was here that Cynthia's pitiless logic had its roots, as well as her stubborn independence.

Straw blond, tall, robust, she had become a scholar in art history by dint of obstinate slogging against massive odds: a rural education; dismayed and practical parents; classmates who had left high school for Montgomery Ward's, car dealerships, and fast-food restaurants in Cedar Rapids.

She made it to that moment she had knocked on my studio door one late fall afternoon in search of the living history of American art in the person of Jacob Molnar. Interview with the artist.

The session had ended—as much to my astonishment as hers—with her utterly magnificent breasts, as smooth and tough as corn silk, exposed to the artist's breathlessly admiring eye. Even in the days of Pop I kept my hand in with the figure every day, and managed to sell her on the notion of exposure in the interests of advanced aesthetic research.

God, what a curious fantasy it was, for both of us! How had we ever believed it? Somewhere she kept pictures of our wedding. A dapper Jacob Molnar, erstwhile cosmopolitan and art world celebrity, preening outside the First Methodist church in North Liberty, Iowa, in a row of dark-suited, wedding-gowned, carnationed relatives, anxiously smiling into the camera. And a magnificent Iowa bride, a shade taller and a whole head smarter than her grinning groom.

Later of course she claimed I had ruined her career. Left her undoctored and deprived of the brilliant future she'd planned out for herself in academia. Saved her, I would growl like the voice from heaven in *Faust*.

What she did now, she did well—and loved. Her work brought research skills and solid knowledge to a business that needed honest qualities. There was a growing demand for her exhaustive searches and informed appraisals. She was trusted by private collectors and respected by the museums.

ARTRESEARCH. The letters were stenciled with simple elegance on the glass pane of her office door.

I buzzed.

She buzzed back fast, assuming it to be me. Wednesday. Ginni would not be in today. It was risky, I had often told Cynthia, to buzz people when she was alone in there without knowing who they were.

The suite consisted of two small rooms: an interior office and a tiny display and reception area. The latter held a coffee table, two arm chairs, a single tall green cactus. The image was clean cut, unostentatious, put together in a series of subtly contrasting grays.

The walls allowed no more than the four small pictures hanging now: a series of Hopper watercolors. They were choice, of course. Hopper at his best—bleak American cafés, streamlined, but devoid of the human life that would give them meaning. Windows staring out on abandoned, night-lit streets, distillations of the emptiness of neon efficiency. Cynthia's reputation was based in part on these infrequent mini-exhibitions. No sales. These were just special items she'd stumble on and make available to others. Sometimes she would catch them in transition between owners—works that might otherwise never be seen. Sometimes I couldn't begin to guess where she'd dug them up. She seemed to have an inexhaustible supply of contacts.

The interior office was alive with the white sound and sophisticated energy of the Fortune 32:16 that made her work so attractive to the client who needed answers fast.

It was from the office that she now emerged, perfect as ever. Damn.

"Jake!" she said. I was relieved by her ease and pleasure. I folded her in my arms, cocking my head back to look at her for a long, delicious moment. Then we both laughed and kissed.

"Jake, it's really great to see you!"

"I missed you, too, baby."

She gave me a cockeyed, curious glance as though she might have been tempted to believe me. Then smiled.

"Okay, Jake. I'm yours for an hour. We'll lock up and get out of here for lunch."

I was anxious to check the hospital, and used the office phone while Cynthia put on her coat.

"Intensive care," I told the switchboard.

"I.C.U. Can I help you?"

"I'm calling to inquire for Laura Rice."

"Who's calling, please?"

"Jacob Molnar. A friend. I was in yesterday."

"One moment, please."

She put me on hold with a click. A silence. I drummed my fingers on Cynthia's blond wood desk and watched as she swung the dark coat over her shoulders and shrugged into it.

"I'm sorry, sir, we have no information on that patient."

"But just this morning I was told . . ."

"I'm sorry, sir. It's hospital policy. Immediate family only."

"But . . ."

Bureaucracy! Call back a little later, get a different nurse.

"There's still no word on Laura," I told Cynthia as we left. "Last time I heard, she hadn't come round."

We'd just stepped out from the Chrysler Building into the flow and counterflow of noontime pedestrians. Suddenly I stopped dead and a chain reaction of small collisions took place all around us.

I looked around.

Suppose I was right. If Carlos had stumbled across a big operation, as I had suggested to Richards, they had more pawns than Brian. Having been at such pains to deliver their warning, wouldn't they logically check on my performance? Or was this creeping paranoia?

Moving out into the stream of pedestrians, I tried a guarded look behind us. Nothing. It would have been hard to pick out the familiar face of a friend in the crush of jostling humans, let alone an unknown fellow traveler.

A test, then. Ignoring her surprise and irritation, I grabbed Cynthia's arm and hurried her forward.

"Jake, what. . . ?"

"Stick with me, baby. I'm sorry, I'll explain."

We risked a red light at the run and doubled back on the other side of Lexington. Paused at a shop window and looked back to the intersection.

Kitty-corner across Forty-second, a man scanned the crowd in our direction. He was impatient for the traffic light and led the pack as soon as it changed. Tall and blond, he had the look of one of Samantha's young executive types. He reached the far side of the intersection and peered about uncertainly.

"You'll think I'm crazier than ever, but I have the notion that we're being followed," I said. Cynthia started to laugh.

"No," I said, "seriously."

She stopped to look at me, but my voice alone was enough to have convinced her.

What next? If the man was a tail, the damage was done: The contact with Cynthia had been registered and she'd been exposed. No way to change that—but they could put an innocent construction on it. Nothing more normal than lunch with your former wife—unless, of course, they were in a position to know that Cynthia had as much information on the art world stored in her Fortune as probably anyone in the world.

It seemed better to let him spot us again and check my suspicion. I took Cynthia's arm again and steered her back north. We stood for a minute creating a noticeable eddy—so I hoped—while I went through the motions of debating where to go for lunch. Then we doubled back for a second time and walked straight past. A half-block south we paused at another store-front and I stole a glance. He was not far behind us, idling, heading south, as though unsure of his direction. I still couldn't be sure, but it was clear I'd have to check for him after lunch. If he was still around in an hour, there'd be something more than coincidence to worry about.

"How's this?" I asked. We stopped at the door of an anonymous deli and Cynthia nodded without great delight. I would have taken her in there anyway.

I had been waiting for the explosion. It came as soon as I had closed the door behind us.

"Jake," she said. "Don't think you can do this to me anymore. First off, you drive me crazy with your punk murderers and muggings. You fling wild charges at people you don't even know. And now you go out on the streets and act like some third-rate horror movie. What the hell is this?" She shrugged my hands off her coat. "Grow up, for Christ's sake, will you?"

"Please," I said. "Please, Cynthia, you have to trust me. Let's just sit down and order and we can go through the whole thing again, okay? I know how you feel but . . . please?"

She let me take her coat. We found a booth and ordered and she sat across from me and listened. Asked a question here and there, her eyes on mine as though to measure them for truth. She even allowed me, at one point, to reach across the table and take a hand, folding it between my own to convey the urgency.

"Okay," she told me when I finished, "supposing all this is true and not some flight of Molnar fancy. What more did you want from me?"

EIGHTEEN

◇

"First off," I said, "we're going to make a deal. If it turns out that I'm right, you're out. I mean, if we really were being followed and it's not my paranoia. Okay? This stops at a friendly lunch between old ex-mates." I could live without Cynthia on my conscience as well as Laura.

"We'll see," she said. "Things sometimes aren't so easy." She paused. "You're sure it's not the cops?"

Would Richards have put a tail on me? I looked at my watch. It was three hours since I'd left him at the studio. "I can't think why," I said. The waitress dumped something leafy down in front of Cynthia and a ham and swiss on rye for me. I bit into a kosher dill. "Have you got something for me?"

"I'm sorry, Jake. I haven't had a moment since this morning," Cynthia told me. "Ginni's not in today and it's been hectic. I haven't given a thought to anything you asked."

"I hadn't expected much," I said. "Not in this time."

"Besides, a first name isn't much to go on, is it? Brian? Is that what you said? I have a note of it somewhere."

"Brian," I said. "But listen, there's other ways to track him down. Your time's much better spent on the Worthing Nelsons. Carlos was killed because he'd got something right. It had to be those paintings."

The ham and swiss was a perfunctory job, but the first bite reminded me that I was ravenous. It was days since I had sat down to a meal. Cynthia picked among her greenery with a fork.

"What's happened recently on the Worthing Nelson

market?" I asked. "You have to have all that down on the Fortune. Check anything from the early Seventies—anything that hasn't showed up in the history books or the catalogs. If there's a stash somewhere, it can't stay under wraps forever. They're bound to be showing up soon. Private collections, loans to exhibitions. Does that sound like something you can do?"

Cynthia was thoughtful. She nodded.

"Sure," she said, "I can do it. It'll take time."

"Treat me like any other client," I said. "I'll pay. I don't want you paying out of pocket."

"Some hope," she said. I grinned. My ex-wife was nobody's fool. She'd certainly made out well enough when we divorced.

"While you're at it, watch out for Samantha Dmitri's artists, too," I said. "Any anomalies on the market, investment buying. There's something rotten in that business."

"Oh, Jake, be real," said Cynthia. "You brought this up on the phone this morning. Samantha Dmitri? Dan Traceman, yet? You're talking two of the most successful people in the business. What do they want with bashing people on the head? These guys are millionaires."

It did sound ridiculous.

"They were together again this morning," I told her. "In Carlos Smith's studio."

"So Traceman buys art. So he collects Carlos Smith and buys from Samantha Dmitri. Is that a crime? So he sells the stuff at a profit. That makes him a killer? Then he sets himself up in Carlos's studio with Samantha when she knows you're going to be around? Sounds like old grudges, Jake."

"Okay, so I'm fishing. Remember, Dmitri had to have had a backer to get started," I insisted. "Why not Dan Traceman? Maybe the man has an empire in there to protect."

She shrugged. "I think you're crazy, Jake. But I'll try it anyway."

I picked up the last crumbs of the sandwich with a

fingertip and pushed the plate to one side. Cynthia left enough to feed a hutch of rabbits.

"You remember Sam?" I asked. "Sam Russell, Worthing's friend. Where did he disappear to when he'd broken up with Worthing? And the other guy, Nicholas. Nicholas . . .?"

"Lazarus." Cynthia filled in the name with barely a thought. Then added, "Nick Lazarus, wasn't it?"

"Mind like a floppy disk," I said.

"Hard drive," she corrected. "What do you want with them?"

"Just talk," I said. "I've no idea what Sam would remember, but Nicholas must have known what Worthing was up to in the studio. Can you track them down?"

"I'll try," she said. "So far as I know, neither one has had much to do with the business since Worthing. But I can probably turn up an address through one source or another."

We tried to pay and the waitress told us to take our money to the desk.

"You think she cares as little about the tip?" I asked.

"I guess," said Cynthia. "Try not leaving one."

The guy was still waiting for us, standing across the street. He banged the cold from his chest with crossed arms and blew out long plumes of breath, taking no trouble to be inconspicuous, perhaps because he'd no idea I had seen him. So much the better.

I took Cynthia by the arm and walked her back to the Chrysler Building, arguing with her, but she wouldn't hear of backing out.

"Watch out, Jake. I'm on your case," she laughed.

"Keep the door locked." The memory of my devastated study was too close: I had visions of what could happen to the Fortune. "I don't want you taking any risks."

We stood face to face at the entrance to the building, ready to say goodbye. Looking at her, I winced at the memory of Laura in intensive care. I could go up right then and check in with the hospital. I decided to leave it until I got home.

When I'd kissed Cynthia and watched her through the doors, another thought grabbed me.

I loped across to Fifth, reaching the intersection with barely the time to board a southbound bus. I lurched to the back and watched through the window as my follower flagged down a cab. Okay. Easy enough for him to follow the bus and watch for me to get off.

I found a seat and stared at a deodorant ad that had received the same treatment as my drawing. Cock and balls.

I wondered how it might work. Frank Stevenson was a man I didn't know at all. He was one of Samantha's artists, and for weeks I'd watched him working on a site-specific piece in a storefront down by Parsons. With luck, he would be the first live artist from the gallery I could talk to. Tonight at the opening I could catch a good sense of the public view. From Stevenson, if I could get him talking, I planned to hear the inside scoop.

Stevenson was working in the window when I got there. So was my tail, a quarter block behind me. I watched him pay off his cab and saunter along, still taking little trouble not to be seen. When I reached Stevenson's storefront, he found shelter in a doorway a short way down and across the street.

The work was interesting. Stevenson's idea was to add a second, sharper reflection of the opposing street scene to the one already offered viewers by the reflective window glass. The viewer could stand and, with simple movements, merge or shift the two images in a kind of diorama in which he himself was the central character, sandwiched between three different layers of reality: the wall-sized painting behind the glass, the window itself, and the actual scene behind him. The trick was to invent one's own place in the world.

I stood there for a few minutes, captivated by the drama. There stood Jake, square to the window, gazing in on himself. Shoulders a little sloping, eyes somewhat haggard against the red-gray stubble of beard.

There was Frank Stevenson, the artist, his back square to me, working at eye level to reconstruct the image of the windows in the building behind me. And there, reflected in a corner of the pane, was my anonymous brown-coated escort in the shelter of his doorway. All static—waiting for the next act of the drama to unfold in the multiple proscenium.

I tapped on the glass. No reaction.

Stevenson must be used to that by now and had learned to ignore it. I tapped again, louder, and waved. He twisted his head with a look designed to discourage window-tappers and turned back to his work. I tapped again and gestured urgently toward the door. He shook his head, but squinted more carefully through the window. Then shrugged, set down his brush on a stool, and lumbered round behind the drywall panel.

I stepped sideways out of the picture, out of my own reflection, and reached the door as it opened, just a crack.

"Yeah?"

There was something peculiar about the sound that I couldn't place.

"Excuse me, you're Frank Stevenson?"

"Yeah."

He was watching me closely as I spoke, his eyes a fraction out of contact with my own.

"I've been watching your work the past few days. I wondered if I could meet you?"

"Yeah."

He made it sound like a no. Some artists take advantage of a nonverbal reputation when they simply don't want to talk. He was a big bear of a man in his mid-thirties, broad-faced, lined with what seemed like a cross between good humor and anxiety. His wavy brown hair was thin and had already receded far behind the temples. He risked losing more, the way he ran his hand through it nervously with a lighted cigarette between the fingers. He wore a heavy plaid shirt and brown corduroys, both saturated with acrylics. The same with his blue Adidas.

"I mean, to talk. I'm interested in your work." His

eyes never left my face. "I'm Jacob Molnar," I added lamely.

"Molnar! Jacob Molnar!"

I had it. Stevenson was deaf. The pitch and enunciation were strangely distorted at the edges and words seemed to hang in his mouth like cotton balls.

"Molnar! My God, come in!"

He stood back, opening the door, and invited me in to the storefront. It was stripped of everything but for a large, spread dropcloth with a hundred cans of paint.

"My dealer," he told me. "She rented this space for three months. I'm through in two weeks. Then . . ."—he grinned and grimaced, gesturing broadly to indicate the crowds—"she brings press and cameras. Cocktails! Big deal!"

You could follow him easily enough, once you adjusted to the odd speech patterns and words swallowed or omitted. The sound was unnatural, more a creation than an imitation, and his speech was a song without tune. Emphases fell in peculiar places and subtle distinctions between sounds were lost.

"Coffee?" he asked.

He made some instant from a kettle steaming on a one-ring burner and laced it lavishly with bourbon from a Jim Beam bottle stashed among the paints.

"Sure helps," he said, "against the cold! Welcome!"

The floor was the only place to sit, so we sat there, cross-legged by the electric space heater. Far from inarticulate, the man was animated, eloquent, his eyes and hands in constant motion as he spoke. He was anxious, like the rest of us, to have his work seen right. He had started out, of course, as a studio painter.

"What brought you out?" I asked.

"Same thing, I guess," he said, "as others. I found myself talking to the same folks, over and over . . . and not much to say."

"And now?"

He laughed. "World's my audience," he said. "Everybody gets to see the work. I always liked movies, too."

I wasn't sure I saw the connection, but he read the question before I had time to frame it.

"Sets," he said. "Unlike most people, I always see movies silent." He pointed to his ears. "Figures and their surroundings count for more. It's a little disorienting until you've gotten used to it, and you need to make a constant small adjustment. That's pretty much what you see here, a kind of psychic discomfort."

He gave a big, braying laugh and gestured toward the window.

"Do people look at paintings? Do they?" he asked scornfully. "The average person spends a total of one point six seconds in front of your average painting in your average museum, according to statistics. I want more than that. I get a lot more with this stuff. People stop every day."

I listened to him, aware of the pleasure of talking to an artist about art. I thought again about the exile that I had chosen: Communication was the give as well as the take. Even if I had decided there was nothing worth the taking, how little I had had to give, in recent years. How grudgingly I had passed it out.

NINETEEN

◇

"You have an exclusive with the Dmitri gallery?" I asked. It was an uncomfortable feeling of betrayal, steering the conversation back where I wanted it.

"Samantha? Yeah," he said. "I work with her."

"She does a good job for you?"

Stevenson shrugged. "What kind of job does any dealer do?" he asked. "She wants to sell. That's a little hard, with most of the stuff I do. I give her drawings, proposals. She puts up with me pretty nicely. Gets behind the work. And comes up with a commission like this one when she can. I can't complain. But I guess she works better for the ones that make the job easy—the ones she's known for."

"Like Patty? Carlos?"

Frank looked at me sharply. I'd echoed something that was on his mind.

"Young Turks," he agreed with a nod. "The kind that die young. I guess she did well by them. At least that's the rep."

"Did you know Carlos?"

"I guess I knew them both a little, way back when. Before she died. Before he began to make it. When he and Patty were . . ." He paused and seemed to be searching back into the past. His attention wandered as he sought out the word that put it right.

"When he and Patty were . . . ?" I prompted. He didn't see that I had spoken.

"When he and Patty were together," he finished without looking at me. "They lived together for a while. That must have been three, four years ago."

I remembered the arm around Patty's shoulder in the snapshot. Wincing inside at the memory of the intensity of life in Carlos's eyes, I touched Frank on the knee to focus his attention on my lips.

"Were they still together when Patty died?" I asked.

"No," he said slowly. "She was alone by then. They'd broken up. She died alone." He stopped for a moment, and I lost his eyes again. "It was me that found her. Did you know? I found her. I'd gone to her studio for some damn fool reason. Funny. I've never been able to remember why I went there. That part of it was just blown away. Anyway, I found her there."

There was another silence. He warmed his hands around the coffee mug, thinking of Patty. I thought of Laura. I guess it was a prayer of a kind. Then he took up the story again without prompting, as though it flowed now of its own accord.

It was harder to follow him. There was so much emotion, the words came out less clearly, half of them swallowed in his throat. I had to reconstruct the narrative, sometimes from the tag ends of words, or consonants alone.

"Strung up like a chicken from the cross-beam in her studio," he said. "My God, it was awful! What do you do? I mean, what do you do? Like a fucking chicken, stretched out from the neck. Jesus! And not a stitch on her body. Not a goddamn stitch. That skinny body, dangling there, which scarcely weighed, when I brought it down. And no reason. Such a sweet kid. I mean, I know she did the whole punk number, with the hair and clothes, but she was a sweet kid, let me tell you. Her face, I tell you, with the spiked hair and that makeup that she used, God it was like some godawful mask!"

His body shuddered, recalling the contact with the nude remains of Patty Drayton. He shook his head and looked back up at me, puzzled to have been thrown back into a forgotten nightmare.

"She was unhappy, then?" I asked.

The word seemed grotesquely inadequate. Stevenson evidently thought so, too.

"Unhappy? Jesus, Molnar, what does that mean? Aren't we all? She was pissed. I don't know that she was unhappy, but she sure was pissed that week. There was some story of a show and how Samantha wouldn't release the work. Her own best interests—some such thing. God, was she pissed! Unhappy? Jesus, aren't we all?"

I brought his eyes back to my lips.

"Most people don't hang themselves because they're pissed," I pointed out.

"Who knows?" he said. "Who really knows what's going on in some other person's head? I guess I could never figure Patty anyway. Sweet kid. Good artist. Good head. I wish to God it hadn't happened."

"And Carlos?"

"Carlos? Jesus, Molnar, you got some kind of fetish for dead artists?"

I watched as he found a reason for my being in his studio which wasn't the one I had given. A tiny bud of anger flared in his eyes and blossomed without warning, then exploded.

"What is this? Two dead artists and up jumps Jacob fucking Molnar from the past, sniffing around like a fucking bloodhound in heat!"

He was on his feet, and I with him, backing away from an anger so intense I had lost all contact with the man. It seemed beyond all proportion.

"Listen," I told him. "I can explain . . ." To calm him down, I wanted to tell him I had lost someone, too. I wanted to tell him I had lost Worthing. I wanted to tell him about Laura.

"Get out!" he yelled.

"Wait, Stevenson . . ." I was yelling back, as though I could get him to hear. But I had lost him. I would have told him I hurt as bad as he did, but there was no way I could reach him. I needed his eyes and they were blinded by anger. His voice went strange and wild as he lost control of the sounds he'd worked so hard to master.

"Get out of here, Molnar! Go fuck yourself. I'd always heard you were a fucking fink!"

That's how it sounded, anyway. I opened the door and with a single lunge of his body he sent me spinning out into the street. And slammed the door behind me, leaving the glass pane chattering in its rotted molding.

A fucking fink.

I half-ran home in the dwindling light. Jesus, the man was right. A fucking fink!

By the time I got back to the studio, I was ready to shut myself in for another decade. I might have done it, but the tiny red light was glowing on the tape deck. I played back a single message: "Lieutenant Richards, New York Police. Call me."

I dialed the number he'd left. "Richards? This is Jacob Molnar." Molnar the fink.

Silence.

"Mr. Molnar. There's never a good way to say this, so I'll say it straight. It's Laura Rice. She died in the hospital this morning. She never came out of the coma."

I clenched a fist and slammed it against the wall. I clamped my teeth and jaws so tight they sent back spasms of pain into my brain. I needed to keep control.

"Mr. Molnar?"

"Yes, I'm here."

"Can I do anything to help?"

"No, nothing. Thanks."

I couldn't let go. There was too much to do.

"Listen, I'll be in touch later, then."

Richards hung up and I stood there listening to the dial tone.

TWENTY

◇

    First thing, I turned her pictures to the wall. I wouldn't have gone into the studio at all, but I needed the stack of old *Artforums* I kept on the corner shelf. So I turned all her pictures to the wall and made her a promise that I would draw no more until . . .

    Until what?

    It had something to do with vengeance, but I couldn't quite analyze it. I wanted to avenge her death. To purge myself, as much as anything.

    I called Cynthia to tell her about Laura. It seemed only fair. "I can't let you go through with it now," I said.

    "Don't be ridiculous," she said. "Listen, I feel terrible about Laura. I feel terrible for you. But it only makes you need me more than ever. Let me help, Jake. Please?"

    "Well, for Christ's sake be careful."

    It was four o'clock. I would be at the opening at the Dmitri gallery by eight.

    The study was still a mess, so I sat at the kitchen table and worked back through five years of *Artforum,* putting together a picture of the gallery. The newest issues carried full-page color ads for Smith, Frank Stevenson, and a half-dozen others whose images were now familiar coinage.

    These were the core of the stable. Desmond Scott was installing yesterday, opening tonight. A painter of cosmic ambitions, he specialized in visions of human incursions into space, the violent colonization of constellations with laser weaponry and nuclear bombast. There was Mindy Malheur. Her epic, week-long performances incorporated rock bands, bulldozers, mountains of trash—and a cast of hundreds of unwitting street people. She brought the art set slumming in the South Bronx and the Lower East Side, but her spin-off products included high-priced paintings and construction works, incorporating the debris from performances.

In recent issues, virtually every Dmitri show was covered by a review. You pay for ads, you get reviews. It's never quite so crass, you still can't buy a review. But the more you manage to propagate the image, the more the image sells. The more it sells, the greater the resources to advertise it. Critics are no more immune to the syndrome than buyers.

A 1983 issue carried a feature article on Joan Needham—four full-color pages of rough, organic totems, splash-painted in an outrageous clash of primaries. Great, gaudy pricks. An issue from a year or so back introduced the work of half a dozen new expressionists—four of them represented by Samantha Dmitri. As I remembered, the article had been a catalyst, consolidating Dmitri's position on the market. It was dated barely a year after she'd lucked into the limelight with the meteoric rise and tragic death of Patty Drayton.

Before Patty, there was nothing to speak of. A few small announcements in the advertising pages with now familiar names but no reproductions. These were a quarter-page at most, starting in 1978. In 1977, there was no mention anywhere of the Samantha Dmitri Gallery.

I remembered a piece in one of Andy's *Interviews,* a while ago, and went to the study to track it down. October 1981. The cover showed Dmitri in designer clothes, luxuriating in her converted loft and surrounded by an admiring semicircle of artists. They were all frontally nude, in a parody of the sex press, with splashy stars concealing their vital parts and identifying each by name. How had she pulled that off? Most artists aren't the exhibitionist freaks they're made out to be.

The interviewer was a Harry Dick, and the piece

was long on gossip and life-style but short on information except for one interesting exchange:

HD: And how was it you eventually got the gallery off the ground?

SD: Well, I'd worked for years with barely anything to show for it and then one day it just happened. Like that. A young artist walks in off the street and shows me a portfolio. It used to happen all the time. With artists, I mean. A bunch of slides, a black portfolio. I can't even look at them anymore, I haven't the time. Such a shame. Anyway, here was this one artist who showed me her portfolio and it was just like, wham, this is it. I mean, this is what people are going to listen to, right? They've been listening to it in music and now, wow, here it is in plastic form. Gutsy. Real. I flipped. Turned out the artist was Patty Drayton. I knew right there she was going to make it. And I was going to make it for her. And we did.

HD: Many galleries, I know, have financial backers to get them started. Did you have that kind of help?

SD: Never. I've always retained a controlling interest in everything I've done. Not that there haven't been angels who've come along from time to time and invested heavily—sometimes just in a single artist's work. The trouble with backers is they want to tell you how to run your show. I never liked that idea. Even in bad times, I fought to keep my independence. I like to think that it's paid off in the long run.

Somewhere in the pit of my belly I was convinced that Samantha Dmitri was a liar. If it wasn't Traceman, someone back there was pulling on the strings. Not that it's a sin to lie to *Interview*. That's business.

TWENTY-ONE

◇

I took a catnap before leaving for what promised to be a long evening out. Nothing like a nap to drain the head and body of their tensions. I fell asleep with visions of Laura alive: textures of skin, textures of flesh and hair, movement so subtle it defied the eye. But I woke an hour later to the vision of Laura dying, bandaged and raw, unconscious, and the anger returned.

Six-thirty. I made short work of dinner, devouring a plate of cold cuts. I was tempted by an open bottle of zinfandel, but I passed. There was too much to do, and I needed my whole head to do it.

I shaved and showered and poked about in the closet. I had proved to myself that my name was still a passport, but tonight was a social comeback of sorts and I wanted to have it right. I would need to move as easily with artists as collectors.

The first attempt was a pair of patched blue jeans and a workshirt, with a heavy, embroidered vest—a gift from Cynthia in the days when gaudy decoration was the style. Cowboy boots had been in. Now they looked absurd and dated, Sixties chic. I stripped back down and settled for a black corduroy jacket, maroon shirt, and gray tie. And a heavy overcoat with roomy pockets.

Next, I sorted through the tool box in the hall closet for a small flashlight and a couple of screwdrivers, one light, one heavy. I added a pair of pliers for good measure and stashed each item in a separate pocket to avoid the inelegant clanking that resulted when they were together. Finally, I checked in the mirror, tapping the outside to see if the bulk showed through.

The compleat burglar.

I left the studio for the walk through Washington Square and down across Houston into SoHo. The bitter edge was off the chill in the air, and yesterday's dusting of snow had already vanished from the streets.

My friend was in tow. Good luck, I thought. With four hundred there, he'd never be sure if I had left. How long would he wait in the street?

By eight-fifteen, I was back on West Broadway, walking up the gallery steps for the second time in as many days—a measure, perhaps, of how my life had changed. The transition from the dim blue fluorescence of the street to the brilliant light of gallery tracks evoked both a thrill and dread. The opening was already in full swing. Naively, I had relied on my familiarity with the cast of characters, expecting somehow to recognize and be recognized without introduction as I would have been ten years ago. The first glance was a shocking reminder of those lost ten years. There wasn't a face I knew.

I stood by the door with the stiffness of the novice at a ritual of initiates and looked for a Virgil to lead me into the inferno. There had to be someone. I shouldered a path toward the center of the gallery and scanned the crowd.

Elmer! Perfect. He was nodding frequently in the direction of a solid sterling woman who shouted to make herself heard above the din. He sloshed a little wine from his glass with every nod.

"Well, Elmer, hi!" I clapped an arm around his shoulder and grinned at the silver lady. Elmer lost the thread of his argument and looked at me over drooping half-moons. It seemed odd that he'd choose to wear them at an opening.

"Jake?" he said. "Again? This is getting to be a habit, isn't it? My God, it's been at least a day!" He stuck out a stubby hand in my direction.

"Elmer," I shouted over the din. "I need some help!"

The woman he'd been talking to was swallowed into the crowd behind his shoulder. We stood and faced each other.

"Help?" he yelled. "What kind of help do you need?"

"Listen," I said. "Don't ask me to explain, it's just too crazy here. I need to know some of the artists, some of the new crowd. Kind of a guided tour. I'm ten years out of date and I don't recognize a soul. Can you do an old friend a favor?"

Elmer could be an irascible fellow. He looked at me quizzically a moment, then smiled broadly.

"Jacob," he said. "Anything. For you, I'd be delighted. Stick with me, baby, as they say. But only if you'll promise to show me some new work. And soon, okay? Good God, the art world's missed you! Anyway," he said, "I'd like you to meet . . ."

He hadn't realized that the steely blond had left until he turned to introduce her.

"Well," he shrugged, "I'd like you to have met Lilian Marley. Relatively new to the art scene, obviously. She didn't recognize your name or would have stayed. That sort. Buys modestly, and mostly from Samantha. Safe. Husband's a vice-president in some publishing outfit. Simon and Schuster, I think. Rats, the lot of them."

I grinned at Elmer's cheerful vindictiveness. A blend of solid information, gossip, and perceptive observation. He'd do just fine.

There was Samantha, glittering. I had the notion she was less than thrilled—and perhaps curious to see me with Elmer. Worried? We came upon her in a small clearing near her office door. She flashed a smile of breathtaking insincerity and turned back to her conversation.

"From that," said Elmer, "I take it you've run into our Samantha before. You know the man she's talking to? Stan Burwood? He's been around a good number of years. Dates from your time, I'd say."

"Seems familiar," I nodded. "The name and the face—but remind me anyway."

"Curator at the Whitney. Been climbing the ladder there these past few years. He's a power to be reckoned with. Popular with the artists. That's quite a trick. Visits their studios, shows up at openings, that sort of thing."

Burwood glanced quickly in our direction, then kissed Samantha on both cheeks and strode toward us, hand outstretched. An older version of the smooth, gray-suited gang, I thought. Corporate cool. The light gray suit was nicely tailored to his tall and slender frame, set off with a striped tie.

"I'd like to introduce myself," he said, smiling. "Again, in point of fact. Samantha had to remind me who you are, I'm ashamed to say."

Burwood presented a business card. He was correct, respectful on the surface, while managing to convey a clear intimation that he was above the crowd.

"We'd love to catch up with your latest work," he said. We, the museum, I wondered? Or we, Stan Burwood? "You are still working, I believe? Any chance we'll be seeing it somewhere soon?"

I shook my head, smiling regretfully. "Not ready for a comeback yet, I'm afraid. Perhaps someday. Do you work with Samantha?"

"Do I . . . ?" The ambiguity of the question caught him off guard. Museum curators have been known to swing a deal. It was worth a shot, even a cheap one. "Oh, you mean, have we showed any of her artists? Well, certainly, we showed a number of them last spring in the biennial. And then two years ago we had a big Patty Drayton retrospective in the spring. Posthumous, sadly."

"Carlos Smith?" I asked.

"Carlos? No." His focus seemed to fade and shift. Perhaps he didn't like the questions. Perhaps he'd simply decided my interest was exhaustible. He seemed to be eyeing another prospect somewhere behind my shoulder. "No," he said absently, "we never worked with him. Sad, isn't it? Listen, excuse me, I must get on. Elmer, good to see you, as always."

His next port of call, I noticed, was Dan Traceman. Elmer raised an eyebrow, remembering that I had met him at Sotheby's.

"No," I said. "I can live without that."

"I'll never forget the Marlborough affair," yelled Elmer. "Great moment!"

Traceman had asked for a discount. He had approached me directly, at an opening, wanting fifty percent—I suppose for the privilege of being in his collection. He offered me ten thousand cash. On the spot, behind my dealer's back. Pressed ten brand new thousand-dollar bills into my hand. "No questions asked," he said. Back then I could certainly have used that many tax-free dollars. It would have meant a half year free to work. After all these years, I could still feel them there in my hand, stiff and new—the dreadful green of money.

"He was treated to your celebrated Molnar glare, as I remember," Elmer said. "That hideous silence as you tore the bills up one by one and dropped them on the floor. And then stalked off without a word. Poor Dan was left to pick up the pieces. He never lived that one down."

Elmer laughed at the memory as he steered me to meet the artist, Desmond Scott.

"Congratulations!" I said, vaguely waving an arm around the gallery. "Terrific show!"

"Well, thanks. Knowing where that comes from, I take it as high praise."

I didn't disillusion him. I had barely looked at the work. Scott was with Joan Needham, and I supposed from their natural intimacy that they were a couple. Remembering Needham's gaudy phalluses from the *Artforum* piece, I chuckled at the thought of strange May rituals around the Scott erection. He was dressed in her colors: a vivid blue shirt with artfully spattered paint, and baggy purple pants. Both young, attractive, full of each other, they were talkative and genuinely pleased to meet the fabled recluse.

"We loved your work," yelled Needham with a grin. Past tense, I noticed.

"Loved it!" agreed Scott.

"We always hoped we'd have the chance to meet you."

"Always," said Scott. "We never expected to see you here," he added. "At my opening."

"Never," said Needham.

I tried to find the easy, natural moment to bring up my agenda, but none occurred, and finally I went at it simply and directly.

"I've been anxious to find out about Carlos," I said. "He was sort of a friend. Did you know him well?"

"He was a friend?" said Elmer.

"Poor Carlos! I just can't believe it," said Needham.

"Doesn't seem real," agreed Scott.

"We spent the day with him," said Needham. "Before he was killed."

"The day before?" I asked. "You weren't at the Sotheby's sale with him?"

My heart did a double rebound off the inside of my chest. Could it be so easy?

"That's right," said Scott. "Sotheby's. They sold his piece. Seventy thousand dollars! It was unbelievable!"

"You didn't see Brian there," I asked, "by any chance?"

Not even a pause.

"I think Brian was there," said Needham casually. "Was Brian there?" she asked.

"Brian?" said Elmer.

"I think he was," said Scott.

I could have hugged them both.

"Listen," I said. "You've got to tell me about this Brian. I've heard so much about him, but who is he? Where does he come from?"

They looked at each other and then both looked at Elmer. The exchange of glances made it clear that Brian was nobody's favorite.

"Brian," said Elmer, "is a performance artist. To be accurate, I guess I should say he was a performance artist. So far as I know, he hasn't done anything in years—for which we can all be thankful. He came over here from England in the early Seventies as part of a team. They called themselves Brian Brain and Barry Body. You don't remember this, Jake?"

I shook my head.

"You probably suppressed it," Elmer said. "It was pretty sick stuff. God knows, it seemed legitimate to some of us at the time: body art, right? Mutually inflicted pain. The art world flocked to see it, God help us. Blood and bandages. Well, Barry died— somehow the result of one of their numbers. Big scandal, soon forgotten."

"And now?" I asked.

"Now Brian just sort of hangs around, I think," said Scott. "You see him all over, grinning like a death's head. He's one of those characters that thrives on violence." I knew about that. "You get the feeling he's probably on dope."

"Was he Samantha's artist?"

"God, no. I've seen him around here quite a bit. Odd jobs, that sort of thing. But Samantha would never be interested in his art."

"I don't think anyone is," said Needham. "He hasn't done any for years. I hope we've all grown up since then."

It was time for the final plunge. I took a breath.

"Has anyone seen him here tonight?" I asked.

No one had.

"Curiouser and curiouser," Elmer remarked as we moved on. "Jake Molnar surfaces after a ten-year absence, and only the day before his newfound friend Carlos Smith is brutally murdered. He asks strange questions about Brian Brain. By the way, did you know that Carlos had just got back from Los Angeles? The day before Sotheby's, I think. I don't know what he'd have been doing there."

"No," I said. "I didn't. Thanks."

"You're welcome. Now can you tell me what the hell this is all about?"

"Later," I told him. "When I know what it's about myself."

I waved hello to Warhol. Andy peered at me quizzically through those glasses, as though he might once have known me.

He had. But I saw nothing to pursue in that direction. It seemed improbable that Andy would feel the need to murder artists. He had already done a first-rate job of murdering art.

And time was getting on.

TWENTY-TWO

◇

The opening had been announced for seven to nine. By a quarter to ten, the crowd had begun to thin. Even allowing for late-comers and late-leavers, the gallery would likely empty out by quarter- or half-past ten and close down, certainly, by eleven. With Elmer's help, I had already managed more than I had thought possible. I was almost back on the circuit.

"Elmer," I said, "how can I thank you? Don't tell me, I know how to thank you. An exclusive. But if nothing else, I owe an explanation."

"Lunch," he said, "tomorrow? Breakfast? Supper tonight?"

"Soon," I told him. "Not tomorrow. Let me have a number where I can catch you."

I took his number without leaving him more time to argue.

I had noticed that you had to go through the offices into the storage area to get to the men's room. Brooke was now casually in charge in the office. She had kicked off her shoes and her feet were propped elegantly on the desk. Four or five friends had drifted in from the gallery to share a joint, and I wandered into the back without attracting special note.

In the storage room, it was easy enough to find a corner where I could prop a painting up in front of me and create a small space to sit and wait. It was hardly comfortable, but short of a thorough search of the gallery's back room, I could expect to survive the end of the opening without being found.

The thought of the other alternative—a well-known artist in ripe middle years found hiding in a gallery storeroom late at night—was too embarrassing to contemplate. Instead, I closed my eyes and concentrated on the sounds that reached me from the office and, more distantly, from the gallery.

I was reassured to hear the joint was taking its effect. The laughter grew louder, looser, and more frequent. Conversation gave way to an exchange of exclamations, muffled by walls and only occasionally understandable. A pattern of footsteps and the repeated flush of water confirmed a thorough covering of my traces. Nobody would notice that a single guest had beaten the path and not returned.

In time the background noise receded. Most of the guests had left. I breathed more carefully now, controlling the rhythm in an effort to relax. Despite myself, my pulse had quickened.

Burglary was not my strongest suit.

There were new voices in the office. I thought I recognized Samantha's, irritated, short. The laughter broke off. I had the impression Samantha disapproved of the marijuana.

"I'll put these lights out, shall I?"

I had kept my eyes closed, and Brooke's voice was suddenly clear and loud as she stepped into the storeroom. She paused for a moment, perhaps to glance around, and then flicked the switch. I could feel the change in light.

The door closed. I looked about me, for the first time in maybe thirty minutes. Everything was darkness, except for a diffused glow at the bottom of the door.

The silence was nearly complete. Intermittently, a voice was raised in the office, still less audible with the door closed. Perhaps ten minutes passed. Fifteen. Another door closed, inside. Samantha's office? Then the remaining glow was suddenly extinguished and simultaneously a last door closed, between the office and the gallery.

Then silence. Total darkness.

I pressed the light button on my watch to check the time. Ten-forty-five. I waited, eyes closed again, relaxed. Immobile.

What seemed at first to be silence turned into another range of sound. I was aware of the sounds I made, the friction of clothes, the whisper of breath. Beyond, there was the occasional, regular drip of water from the plumbing. Finally, muffled to the barest level of audibility, detected more as vibration than as sound, there was the passing traffic on the street outside.

Eleven-oh-five. Eleven-ten.

At eleven-fifteen I took the flashlight from an inside pocket and tentatively pushed the switch, creating a sudden flood of light. I switched it off and waited, aware that my precautions were excessive. After a minute, I switched it on again and took the time to relocate myself.

Movement came hard, after an hour of immobility. It was noisy, too, with the rustle of clothes and small collisions with surrounding objects. My joints were locked in. It was painful just to get to my feet. I rested a while, standing and listening, before I started slowly, picking a path with the flashlight beam toward the office door. I waited there with my ear to the wood surface.

Nothing.

I directed the beam to the handle. I'd noted earlier that the door was key-locked from the other side, leaving a thumb key to open it from this side. I switched off the beam, to be safe, and fumbled for the gloves I had in my pocket, then turned the handle carefully and pushed the door ajar. I waited again.

Nothing.

Opening the door slowly, I moved through to the office. The darkness assumed a sudden volume around me, palpable. Somewhere there was a window to the main gallery. It, too, was dark, and there was no light from Samantha's office door.

Decisive now, I put on the flashlight and crossed the room. Samantha's office door opened outward, with the business end of the hinges left this side. With the larger screwdriver, it was a simple matter to knock the bars of the hinges up and out, using the palm of my hand as a hammer. No alarm system there. I knew there was one on the front door to the street, but I would deal with that later. Meantime, I wasn't concerned to cover traces in the office, so long as I wore the gloves and left no fingerprints.

My flashlight beam picked out the black two-drawer filing cabinet in Samantha's office. There were tall files in the main office, but I reasoned that if any of the files had useful information, it would be these. They were locked. With screwdriver and pliers, I bent some metal and snapped the lock out of its socket. Both drawers slid open easily.

The number of files was relatively small. The ones she kept in her own office were presumably preferred—the clients she'd made special efforts to cultivate over the years. Repeat buyers, or the big-bucks spenders. The faithful.

She had the clients on top and the artists down below. I took the clients first. My finger stopped at the silver-plated Lilian Marley's file and I pulled it.

The record bore out what Elmer had suspected: The Marley collection included several of Samantha's artists. Handwritten notes—scribbled, perhaps, at a dinner date—sketched the rest of the collection. There wasn't much there, but I could imagine the information was useful for a dealer to have on hand.

There was a handful of newspaper clippings, too—mostly social events where Lilian Marley had been seen, with whom, and why. Some names were underlined in red, along with references to a handful of charities, the opera, the Met.

Samantha did her homework well. What she had in the file was a detailed portrait that had multiple uses. It was good, for example, to know which Joneses the Marleys kept up with. Good to know who the Joneses' friends were, in case they'd want to keep up in turn. Cross-referencing quickly, I found that a number of the underlined names had their own files. The picture was of a strong and developing public for the gallery.

One section of the client files was labeled with the names of institutions. I pulled the Whitney and checked through a stack of invoices. Samantha had done quite well with the Whitney. There were clippings, too, and press notices of exhibitions that included gallery artists. Some correspondence, mostly formal confirmations of exhibition arrangements and purchase orders. Many signed simply "Stan." Stanley F. Burwood, Curator. I leafed through similar files on the Modern, the Walker, and the San Francisco Museum of Modern Art. She'd worked with university art museums in the Midwest and the East. I was impressed by the quality as well as the quantity of clientele.

I had already closed the clients file and opened the artists when a thought crossed my mind. I turned back to the clients and leafed through to the end of the alphabet. Curious. There was no file for Dan Traceman. Surely he must have bought from her.

Puzzled, I turned to the artists again.

Smith, Carlos. I pulled the file and laid it on the desk, leafing through every separate item. Announcements. Consignment papers, copies of invoices. Newspaper clippings. There were some handwritten notes from Carlos and copies of responses on gallery stationery. I read through a couple of recent notes. Nothing to suggest problems, let alone a cause for murder.

Patty Drayton's file was thicker than Carlos's, and the sales more impressive. Most of the recent sales had been to museums, here and in Europe. The prices confirmed what I had guessed, ranging up toward six figures. I checked some invoices against the collectors files, and found that everything seemed to match. Patty's letters were typed on an old machine, its typeface inky and irregular. Reading through some of them, I was amazed that the relationship had lasted as long as it did. She must have been a "difficult" artist for Samantha—emotional and erratic, with frequent, outraged complaints. Her prose was seamy, unsparing of its recipient's feelings.

I checked under N for Nelson, though I couldn't imagine she'd have a file.

She did. At first I found nothing of value: a few pages Xeroxed from catalogs with small marks checking off prices, and a single invoice—a drawing she had sold some time ago. A penciled note explained it had come in on a trade and she'd sold it within hours to a Jeremy Sanders, upstate, with a single telephone call—a call that netted her a nine-thousand-dollar profit in two minutes.

Then, clipped to the back of the file, I came on a Polaroid snap of one of the pictures I'd found in Carlos's package of slides. On the blank strip at the bottom, it was dated 1974, with an exclamation point and an annotation: "Conner, Bev. Hills."

I knew the collection. They had a couple of my own. I checked in the collectors file under Conner, but there was no cross-reference. I searched for an invoice for the painting, or for some reference to any of the others. There was nothing anywhere to suggest it was anything but a fluke.

Yet the Polaroid alone would have made my burglary worthwhile. I was about to call it quits when I stumbled on the clincher. It was a folder so thin that its tab had lodged behind another under the B's. Brian Brain. Even in daily reference to the files, Samantha might have missed it there herself. I pulled it out.

The only contents were a number of payment records for "services"—all dated two or three years earlier. And a single half-sheet of paper, torn from a yellow pad. "Sammy, you luscious bitch. Call me or else. BB." It was dated 11-11-81.

In an act of reckless malice, I left this last file open on the desk. The drawers I left open too, and picked my way out through the office into the gallery.

The pinpricks of red and green alarm lights played through their coded sequence by the door. I checked over the system of locks and bolts with my flashlight, unlatching them one by one and leaving till last the double bar mechanism that triggered the alarm.

Bedlam broke loose as I pulled the last lever down, pushed open the door and stepped into the street.

It was just past two o'clock, and even my tail had given up on me.

TWENTY-THREE

◇

Somehow the minuscule red light on the tape deck had become the indicator of the state of things in my life. I turned the key to the studio at two-forty-five in the morning with lingering thoughts of Laura, and found it glowing malevolently.

It could wait. There was nothing now that couldn't wait until morning.

I was bone-tired, confused, alone in the studio again. Laura's absence filled it with an aching emptiness. When I got my head down on the pillow, mercifully the lights went out.

But the tiny glow from the answering machine must have burned inside all night long. It was with me first thing in the morning when I woke, struggling between the need for hours more sleep and the will to be moving on.

I got up, sloshed water in my eyes, and looked at the time. Six-thirty. Damn.

The tape screeched out a backward message and a couple of hang-ups as I went through the fast rewind.

"Jake, this is Cynthia," the message said. "Not much, I'm afraid. I haven't had any luck with the Worthing Nelsons yet. One quickie, though: Sam Russell's living in California, has been for eight years. No contacts with the art world. Here's the address." I wrote it down. "That's it. Be in touch tomorrow."

I sat by the phone and made a decision in two minutes that would have taken a month of agony before. I could see through the door to the studio, where Laura should have been today. The morning light flooded it as it always had, leaving the frames of the windows outlined on the floor. But now the light no longer seemed to fill the room: It emptied it, and the space was left unoccupied.

It was time to leave.

I dug out a dog-eared telephone book from the old days, picked up the phone, and dialed.

"Jake! I'll be damned!"

Some people you can still call after a twelve-year silence. This was Dick Corman, an artist I had known and worked with many years ago. Our last project had been Art and Technology, at the L.A. County Museum.

"Dick, listen. I'll be in L.A. by this evening. Any chance I could stop at your place for a night or two?"

"Love it. Any time."

"You're still on Santa Monica?"

"Still the same studio, yeah. Just west of Highland, north side of the street. You'll know the building when you see it."

"I remember. I'll try to get in late afternoon or early evening and rent a car."

Six-forty-eight. I dialed American Airlines and made a reservation on the next flight out from Kennedy.

It was good to close down the studio and bang the door behind me as I had done in my younger days, without knowing when I would open it again. There was nothing and no one to say goodbye to.

There was even a little thrill in noting that my tail was back. I had a moment's pleasure imagining how long it would take him to realize I was headed out of town and figure out what he was going to do about it. I hailed a cab at the intersection and shoved the valise ahead of me onto the back seat.

"JFK."

"You got it, buddy."

It was new, a whole world of clichés. Follow that cab. I watched through the rear window as he hailed his own.

Who was he? Was it possible that the police had assigned a man to watch out for me? It seemed un-likely that Richards would not have told me. I made a mental note to call him from the airport. At least I owed him a word about Brian Brain.

More likely he had been sent by the other side. I had been explicitly warned off and had made it equally explicit that I didn't plan to be scared. They'd have little doubt after the gallery files.

What was their next step? Try to kill me? The smartest strategy would be to divert me. I assumed they knew of my contact with the police and realized that another death could be one too many. I assumed that, Brian's sadism notwithstanding, their motive was financial gain. The smart money would keep an eye on Molnar and be sure he didn't get his hands on any hard information.

It was thirty minutes to flight time when I reached JFK. I picked up a ticket and made for a pay phone.

" Lieutenant Richards, please."

"He won't be in before eight-thirty. Can I take a message?"

I looked at my watch. Better to leave word than wait six hours and call from the coast.

"Tell him that Jacob Molnar called," I said. I spelled the name."Tell him the last name of the man he's looking for is Brain . . . right. Brian Brain."

"Is there a number where Lieutenant Richards can reach you?"

"Tell him I'll get back in touch as soon as possible. Thank you."

I hung up. My tail was waiting at the ticket counter and I wondered for a moment if he was going to buy a ticket. How would he know where I was going?

But he left the line and followed me to the boarding gate. I showed my boarding pass at the ramp and turned back to find him staring at me. I gave him a cheery wave.

The man turned on his heel and headed for a phone booth.

TWENTY-FOUR

The 747 lost height as it crossed the mountains and powered down toward the airport. In axonometric perspective, the housing tracts and clustered city centers, freeways and cloverleafs, glittering high-rises, the endless blocks and relentless parallels of streets rolled by in a continuous, brilliant canvas. Someone, I thought, has yet to paint this landscape from the air—and find its depth, not the surface.

I took the rental car shuttle and picked out a Buick Regal. It was solid, square, and black. Automatic. It boasted power brakes and power steering, power windows. Power everything.

Just my baby. It had been more than five years since I last drove a car, and I was thankful that the streets were busy and slow. Content to avoid the freeways, I felt my way gently back into a habit I had been happy to unlearn.

Sepulveda, the rental agent told me with relish, north to Santa Monica, maybe five miles, then east on Santa Monica. Angelenos, I remembered, love the sound of their street names. They sure beat numbers.

I drove past the sad, reflective monoliths of Century City—a film lot in my day—and on past the green lawns and cactus of Beverly Hills. Dream or nightmare, I had never been able to decide. The west end of Los Angeles had been a haunt of mine in the old days. The galleries had been here—Ferus on La Cienega, Nick Wilder's on Santa Monica. Barney's Beanery, too. There was new lettering on the old Wilder gallery, I noticed, announcing the Koplin Gallery. Whoever that might be.

It looked like gay heaven here now. I remembered hookers, massage parlors. Further east, where I slowed to watch for Dick Corman's, rows of bare-chested teenagers, jeans resting loosely on slim hips, hooked bored thumbs at passing cars.

The studio was as easy to pick out as I had thought: a high, curved roof behind a deco facade with mock Egyptian detail. If I hadn't remembered the building, I would have recognized the outline of the massive old Mk.VI Bentley drophead coupé parked in the lot at the side. Dick had owned it a good deal longer than the fifteen years that I had known him.

It was soon after one-fifteen when I rang the bell at the side door to the studio.

"Jake! Jacob Molnar!"

Dick was skinnier. He had a little less hair on top and a good deal less hair in back than when I had last seen him. There was a good deal of gray. But the eyes were unchanged, still brilliant and laughing. Extraordinary! The familiar grin, the warmth of a hand whose friendship hadn't changed in twenty years.

"God damn!" he said. "It's good to see you." He grinned and flung big, hairy arms around me. Then he stood back and looked at me, grinning some more. "God damn!"

"Hey, Yumiko!" he yelled over his shoulder. "Come on out here! You never met this bastard. Jake, meet Yumiko. Yumiko, meet Jacob Molnar, great painter. Paint the ass off anyone around."

He put his arm around her and they stood side by side in the doorway. Yumiko can't have been more than half his age. Tall, I thought, beside other Japanese women I'd known, she carried herself with the delicate gawkiness of a long-legged bird. Yet her face was surely as beautiful as any face I've seen and the delicacy, I thought as I took her hand, was no more than a guise. With Dick, she'd need all the toughness I felt in her hand and her eyes.

Dick had converted the interior of the building—a silent movie studio in the twenties—into home and studio. The high ceiling was supported with wooden beams and struts, all painted white. There were sky-lights and rows of paned windows high in the walls, which created an incredible ambience in daylight.

I'd known Dick as a painter—and a good one—back at the start of his career. He was one of those artists whose work, in the critical time of change, simply dematerialized. While the astronauts were up there charting outer space, Dick had become the pioneer of inner space. His strength was to be able to define it and humanize it in the subtlest of ways, through barely audible sound waves or patterns of light.

Dick and Yumiko led me through to the living area, separated from the studio with drywall partitions, but sharing the same soft brilliance, white on white. The furniture was sparse, Japanese in its pleasant economy, its center of gravity low: Nothing seemed to reach above the waist.

"Have you eaten?" Dick asked. "We just got through, but there's salad in the icebox."

"I could sure use something," I said, "after airline snacks."

They left for the kitchen and came back, Yumiko with niçoise salad in a huge glass bowl, and Dick with ice and a bottle. "Glenfiddich," he said. "It's not too early, is it? We need something to celebrate with." He arranged himself, in a single easy movement, to sit lotus-style on the floor.

"You've changed," I told him as I lowered myself gingerly and grabbed at my protruding knees. "I remember a lumbering bear on a barstool, swilling beer."

"Goddamn East Coast intellectual!" he grumbled. "Jesus, look at you. Forgot how to move your body."

He poured us a generous half tumbler each.

"Here's to you, Jake! What's left of you. And welcome back!"

"It's good to be here," I said.

Yumiko sat close to Dick, and they glowed with that peculiarly Californian air of health and well-being. I'd almost forgotten how it was.

"Listen," said Dick, "don't overdo it on the salad. We'll be eating out later. Sushi. Great place, you'll love it. And we have a date for you. I couldn't imagine you'd object, and I think you'll really like her. It was one of those curious coincidences that aren't quite coincidences. Must be karma. Anyway, she just happened to call."

"Not an artist?" I asked suspiciously.

"She's an artist," he said, laughing. "But she's okay, smart. You'll see. Anyway, for Christ's sake, what brings you to L.A? You never leave your studio, even in New York."

"You ready for a long one, Dick? It takes a while, and I have to tell you it sounds crazy, even to myself. I was hoping maybe you could help me make some sense of it."

Three thousand miles from the devastation, I reconstructed the story for him, piece by piece. The distance allowed perspective. And Dick was no Lieutenant Richards. Decades of involvement in the art world and its marketplace allowed him fast, accurate insights and conclusions that reinforced my own.

"Bastards!" he muttered in the silence after I had brought him up to date. "Those bastards!"

He sucked an ice cube from the bottom of his glass and chewed on it thoughfully.

I knew who he meant. The direction his work had taken, so different from mine, resulted in good part from the same historical crisis: no product, no market. No market, no manipulation.

Dick shook his head slowly and poured more Glenfiddich over melting cubes of ice.

"So what do you think, Jake? They aced a decade's worth of work out of old Worthing and then did him in. And used the profits as working capital to set up a front?"

"That's what I think Smith was trying to tell me. And the front's developed into something more than a place to launder dirty money. From what I can tell, the Dmitri operation turns a whopping profit."

Dick nodded. "So what's your best bet? What do you hope to do here?"

I'd had plenty of time for that one on the airplane.

"Find the source of the Worthing Nelsons. Everything goes back to that. If I can find out who has them, I'll know who's behind the whole operation. The Guerreros might help. Or the Conners. And Sam's out here, as I told you. Good old Sam. He might know something about what was happening in Worthing's head, around that time." I looked at my watch. "I should give Cynthia a call," I said. "See if she has anything for me yet. Can I try her now?"

Six-thirty, East Coast time. I dialed her apartment number, and let the phone ring unanswered for a while.

"Try later," Dick said. "But listen, what about the cops? You can't just give them what you know and leave it to them? It's some risk that you're taking, Jake."

I'd weighed that risk. It came up short beside what Laura had been worth.

"Now that the Carlos Smith material is gone," I explained, "there's not enough hard information for me to hand them. It's all soft stuff—a gut feeling, an instinct. Besides, I've given them what I know. It's not enough. For me, I mean. I'm involved. It's the first goddamn thing I've been involved with in the past ten years. They invaded my life, Dick, and they killed a friend. What would you do? I can't explain it any better. It may sound absurd, but I feel like they called me out."

TWENTY-FIVE

◇

" 'They' who?" asked Nicki later in the evening. We had agreed to avoid the subject at dinner, but inevitably came back to it and Nicki was left in the dark. Dick had introduced her as Nicole Girard, recently arrived from France. The fresh red meat of a tuna sushi drooped between her fingers. Angling her head down, she bit off half and looked up, smiling, over the remaining morsel. A fragment of rice had caught on her lower lip.

Her particular quality was elusive. I would need to get her down on paper before I could begin to define it. Her hair had an obvious beauty, though. She wore it long and heavy, so that it fell half forward, half back over her shoulder.

"They," I explained, "the people who brought me here. I don't think they meant to, but they did."

Nicki's eyes clouded, puzzled. Expressive eyes, they were by turns serious and doubtful, credulous and skeptical.

Artists had thrived on chili with beans in my day in Los Angeles. Sushi was better, with hot sake and cold beer. Paned paper screens with sumi brushwork separated the tables, set between miniature gardens with smooth black pebbles. The blond woods were inexpensive, but finished with attention to detail and love for their intrinsic natural qualities. The ceramic ware was handmade, chunky and irregular, with simple blue calligraphy.

"When did you come to the States?" I asked.

" 'Seventy-nine," she said.

"Maybe you wouldn't know," said Dick. "But long

before that, our friend Jake was a superstar. You're talking to a national monument."

"I know, I know," she said with an impatient little shrug. "You think I don't know who Jacob Molnar is? What I want to know is why he went underground? He had everything going for him. Money . . . celebrity . . ."

"It didn't mean much," I said. "When I started out as an artist, I was looking for something that asked more of me than what people came to expect. Wham, bang, slap it on canvas, sell it at Marlborough. That's the kind of stuff I was doing. I didn't like it, and I didn't like what was happening around me."

Nicki nodded slowly. She was young, I guessed less than thirty. She knew that I wanted her and I still wasn't sure if the feeling was mutual.

"And what do you like?" she asked. "For art, I mean, of course."

Dick laughed loudly.

"No, I mean seriously, for art," said Nicki.

"What else?" said Dick. "Tell us, Jake, what have you been doing in your garret?"

"Drawing," I said, looking at Nicki. "Figures."

Dick roared with laughter again. "Don't tell me, for God's sake, you've got hooked on this so-called expressionism?"

"No," I said. "Real drawing. Real figures. I'm thinking Leonardo. Goya. Degas."

In the silence that followed, I had a vision of Laura. I guess the hurt showed on my face. Dick looked at me thoughtfully.

"Hasn't that," he asked, "been done?"

I knew him well enough to know that it was parody he intended, not the question itself. But I answered anyway.

"Not well enough."

Dick sighed. "I guess nothing ever is."

It was later, with an ease that seemed natural and right, that Nicki and I found ourselves alone. We sat across from each other drinking beer, long after Dick and Yumiko had left. A party of Japanese businessmen were drinking themselves into loud and belligerent drunkenness at the sushi bar, where the air was heavy with the smoke from their cigarettes.

It was close to midnight. Close to three in the morning, New York time. Nicki told me about her childhood. Her father had been a doctor in Nantes and had died of a heart attack when she was fourteen years old. Her mother was an ambitious, domineering woman who took a load of social and sexual loneliness out on her teenage daughter. That was how Nicki saw it. As soon as she reached eighteen, she fled to Paris to become an art student. She had lived there for more than five years.

"Why did you leave?" I asked.

She shrugged. "I was not happy there, I suppose," she said.

"A man?"

Nicki looked at me, nodding slowly and playing with her beer glass on the table. The Japanese business party were leaving in rowdy disorder, fighting for the check.

"Partly," she said. "It was partly that."

"Tell me?"

"There's not much to tell," she said. "He was an artist, who'd already made it. I guess I thought somehow that his success might rub off on me. I thought I loved him."

We were the last ones left. A waiter fussed nearby to remind us of the time.

"What was his name?" I asked.

"Roger Fourchet. You've seen it in art magazines." I had, in articles covering 1960s French abstraction. I had the vague image of Matisse-like color fields, but without their substance.

"Were you married?"

"He was, to someone else," she said. "We had this, what you call, relationship. I hate that word. He kept telling me that he was going to leave his wife. I suppose I believed him—I was very young."

A tear appeared unexpectedly in the corner of her eye and she wiped it away with a finger, licking the salt. I reached across to touch her cheek and she held my hand there, turning to kiss the inside of the palm.

"I've no idea where that came from," she laughed. "Must be a five-year-old tear. It's nothing to me, really. He was a terrible man. I don't know why I put up with him for so long."

"How long?" I asked.

"Years," she said. "Three years. It was hard to leave."

"Then what?"

She sniffed back another one and laughed again.

"The man was desperately insecure. And a real cliché," she said. "He drank. He got violent. He took all his frustrations out on me. It made him feel like a man. But I think he really hated me. Besides," she added, smiling, "he had a little dick."

She held her thumb and forefinger an inch apart and squinted at me through them. I studied the space between them.

"Looks pretty big to me," I said. "What makes you think mine's any bigger?"

She giggled and gathered up a monstrous tapestry bag, which looked as though it carried the jetsam of a lifetime.

"Let's go take a look, shall we?" she asked.

The waiter expressed his relief in a thousand little bows as he locked the door behind us.

It was a fifteen-minute walk through deserted streets to Dick's studio. The night passed there with barely another word between us, yet not without tenderness—though I found myself waking in the middle of a dream to call her Laura. Despite the fatigue—perhaps because of it—I lay awake for hours after that.

We woke together in the morning.

I should say that Nicki woke me. Starting from the head and with what seemed incredible slowness, she dragged her hair the whole length of my body. I lay back, naked and still in the California morning light, exhilarated by the barely perceptible massage of that weight of hair, and by the subdued brilliance of the white, reflected light.

"You lied," she said thoughtfully, examining that item we'd discussed the previous night in the cold light of morning.

"No," I said. "I only asked the question."

She took the tip between her lips and ran her tongue around it. Spreading over my face and body, long strands of hair seemed to reach every part of me, mingling with the tough, short curls of my own chest hairs and bringing each follicle to life.

"So this," she said, wagging the stiff article from its matted roots, "is the real Jacob Molnar."

I laughed.

"That's pretty much the sum of it," I said.

She raised her body up over mine, easing me into her and grasping my thighs between her legs. And sat erect a while, teasing my eyes with the immaculate contour of her breasts.

"Will you draw me, Jake?" she asked.

replace for an abstract. Unlike Laura, her mood could shift from moment to moment. And unlike Cynthia,

TWENTY-SIX

◇

Friday at breakfast, Yumiko conjured magic with eggs and scallions in a wok. Dick made coffee while Nicki snorted contempt for the galleries section in the *L.A. Times*. A call to Cynthia's office from Dick's studio only gave me the opportunity to leave a message that I had called. For a while longer, I sat quietly in the studio, enchanted by the quality of light.

"Jake!" Dick called me back from the studio and waved a section of the newspaper at me. "Listen to this: 'Rites Set for Artist. Funeral rites are set at eleven o'clock today for artist Carlos Smith at Funeraria Goldman–Hernandez on Sunset Boulevard in Los Angeles. Smith died Tuesday in New York as a result of injuries received in a mugging incident. Born Carlos Guerrero in Los Angeles, Smith had resided in recent years in New York. He had achieved prominence as a representative of the young generation of neo-expressionist painters. Smith is survived by his parents.'"

"I'll go," I said, checking my watch. It was nearly ten. "It could give me a good start. I was planning on meeting the parents anyway."

"It may not be a good moment," Dick suggested.

"No, but at least I can check it out, and get some sense of what they look like."

Nicki reached across the table and put her hand on mine. She looked serious, suddenly, confused.

"This is the reason you came to Los Angeles?" she asked. "He was a friend, this Smith?"

"It's one of them," I said.

She rested her chin on both hands and looked at me, her eyes troubled, as though she were searching my face for an answer. Unlike Laura, her mood could shift from moment to moment. And unlike Cynthia, she allowed the passing mood to surface in her eyes.

"Then I'll go with you," she decided. "No, no" —she waved away my objections with the flat of her hand—"no, no, I'll go with you. Besides, who knows how long you'll be here. I want to go."

She came to me and laid a hand behind my head. The loose green T-shirt she had borrowed from me glowed against the soft brown of her skin. Why not? One thing I needed was to learn to trust my instinct over reason.

"Relax, Jake," said Dick. "It's good for you."

"I'll drive," said Nicki.

It was an offer I couldn't turn down. Maybe I should have. Nicki turned out to be a true Parisian driver— the kind who likes to turn to the passenger and comment on other people's driving while accelerating into traffic.

At least she knew where she was going. We hurtled east on Santa Monica, scattering pedestrians at crosswalks and bullying other drivers with hair-raising precision.

"Not to worry," Nicki told me. "I'm a fantastic driver, the best!" Her tender assertiveness in bed was more than matched by her devilish abandon on the streets.

There wasn't anything to do but laugh. "Nicki," I said. "You must be some kind of artist!"

"Oh," she said, "I am. Will you come to see my work? Jake, will you?"

After the bored indifference of so many women I had known, her bubbling energy was seductive and contagious. I chuckled, admiring how she looked. She had borrowed a loose black jacket from Yumiko for the funeral, and she wore it with at least two scarves over my green T-shirt and her own blue jeans. The best she'd been able to do with Yumiko's jacket was drape it across her shoulders. She wore it with a freedom I envied.

"Will you?" she asked.

"Of course," I said. "But later. I've got problems to take care of first."

Funeraria Goldman-Hernandez turned out to be a square concrete block, set off with a line of dark cypress trees and a doorway of elaborately modern stained glass. Inside were crimson carpeting and plush-lined walls. The doorways were draped in heavy folds of velvet, intensifying the claustrophobic hush that swallowed the whispered conversations of parties in search of their respective dead. In the small chapel to which we were escorted, the light was so subdued that it was difficult to find a seat.

A reconstructed Carlos Smith was spotlit, propped— somewhat jauntily I thought—in an elaborate, silk-lined casket, staunchly holding his own against an encroaching flood of flowers. A bearded, brightly painted Christ stood benevolently above him, arms outstretched.

Nicki and I sat near the back. A number of family and friends gathered at the front, and scattered further back, about an equal number of others who, to judge from unorthodox tastes in funeral dress, were artists like ourselves. They were those, perhaps, who had known and worked with Carlos before he left for New York.

The service was in Spanish. Nicki knew the language and whispered fragmentary phrases of translation in my ear: " . . . this great tragedy . . . an artist whose talent was honored not only among his own people, but throughout the nation and throughout the world . . . God in his great wisdom . . . those who have known the departed, his friends, his loving family, his parents . . ." The sonorous language flowed from hyperbole to hyperbole, crescendoing to a climax and decaying into a last few melancholy phrases.

Carlos took it all with apparent equanimity, surrounded by his flowers. I remembered his first words to me at Sotheby's and thought he would have accepted these as eulogy enough: The man could paint.

To the muted sound of an electronic organ, we were

invited to pay last respects beside the open casket. I would rather have stayed seated. Later, I was grateful to Nicki, who was at once more sanguine and wise in her understanding that farewells are meaningful. She grabbed me firmly by the hand and led me to the front.

Carlos looked much more at peace in death than he had in life, but I supposed that to be normal. His pale face had been overly made up, a touch of rouge in the cheeks giving him a faintly Anglo appearance as though this, in the mind of the mortician, was the desirable condition for the last call. Improbably, he held a paintbrush in his right hand, and a palette in his left. It was probably the first time in his life he had ever done so.

We left the casket and joined the line to present condolences to Eduardo Guerrero and his wife. The mother's perfect white hair glistened in odd and touching contrast to her husband's perfect black. Their faces, too, were a study in contrast. His features, dark brown-complexioned, seemed drawn in tense unison toward a point between the eyebrows. His figure was bunched and muscular. Her lighter features fell softly away from the same point between the eyes, easing into smooth pockets of the fleshiness of age. They greeted us strangers with the same courteous gravity they extended to each of the mourners.

As we returned to our seats, an usher handed us two small cards. The first was an image of the praying Christ in a crown of thorns, with stylized, tear-shaped drops of blood adorning cheeks and brow. A prayer was printed in elaborate lettering below. The second was a printed card with the message in Spanish and English: "Private interment. Mr. and Mrs. Eduardo Guerrero invite you to a reception in memory of their son following the interment, at 2:30 P.M." An address was printed in italics at the bottom of the card.

"We'll go," I told Nicki as we moved from darkness into blinding sunlight.

"Let me see?" she said. She took the card from my hand and looked at it. "Two-thirty? Okay, we'll go. But first I have to make a telephone call, you know?

There's someone expecting me this afternoon, a little later. A few seconds only, okay? Wait."

She dodged the traffic across Sunset to a public wall phone on the south side of the street. I watched from a distance as she dialed and waited, her fingers playing on the aluminum acoustic panel at the side, and chuckled to myself as she broke into richly gesticulated conversation. There was a staccato burst of explanation followed by a frowning silence, finger in ear, to listen. And finally there was a Gallic scenario of flying wrists and shrugs whose meaning, even from this distance, seemed clear: Can I help it . . . well, what do you expect . . .? Forget it!

She banged down the receiver.

"Is he mad?" I asked her, when she came back.

"Who? Is who mad?" she asked.

"Your friend."

"Oh, it's nothing," she said. "Believe me, nothing."

But she avoided my eyes, and was silent and unresponsive to my touch when I took her arm. I returned her silence while we walked back to the Buick and wondered where to spend the time until two-thirty.

"Are you ready for lunch?" I asked.

She took a moment to focus on the question, and suddenly was bright again.

"Burritos," she said. "We'll get machacas and eat them in the park. Did you ever have a machaca? Fantastic, you'll see."

This time I drove. She guided me a half-mile west on Sunset to the corner of Alvarado. Burrito King turned out to be a take-out stand that looked unpromising but made, Nicki insisted, the best burritos in town. We drove back to the park and walked across the green lawn to the lake's edge.

Here was the origin of Carlos's special vision. From the paintings, I recognized a fleet of bright paddle boats, herded against a jetty with a network of retaining ropes. Noisy brown children clambered over swings and slides and nearby a bag lady sprawled inelegantly under a tree beside her rusty shopping cart. Palm trees poked their heads into an azure sky and, east and west, facades of pastel houses lined the hills in Mediterranean serenity.

Nicki was right about the burritos. The tortilla was filled with hot, spiced beef, beans, onions, and chunks of green pepper. Juice dripped everywhere.

"Tell me about your work," I said.

"I paint."

She seemed less anxious to talk about it now.

"I know you paint," I said. "But what? How?"

"Oh. This and that." Her shoulders gestured a dismissal of the subject and her eyes were remote again.

"You have a gallery?"

She glanced at me briefly.

"Perhaps," she said. "Some ones have shown interest. It's not important. Besides, you ask too many questions."

She smiled and came closer, pressing my shoulders down against the grass and leaning forward to rest her weight on my chest. Her hair fell forward and she brushed it away from my face, kissing me lightly on the lips and cheeks. Feeling her breasts pressed up against me, I laughed from sheer pleasure, reflecting how little I had had cause to laugh in recent years.

Yet her eyes were serious, searching mine. "You still haven't told me, Jake, what is with this Carlos Smith."

"Later," I said. I pushed her gently back from me. "Where next?"

"Where?" she asked, puzzled.

"You have the card," I said.

TWENTY-SEVEN

◇

We were still early, finding the address before the family returned from the cemetery.

It was a small wood-frame house, set twenty feet above the street. A decaying concrete stairway led past a side door to the next street up the hill. Flowering pink hibiscus bushes lined the side of the house. A small green terrace lay to the lake side of the porch. It seemed a peaceful house, more freshly painted than its neighbors—a result, I thought, of Carlos's recent affluence.

We sat in the car and waited. There was little traffic in the hills, this early Friday afternoon in January. A pair of mourning doves glided down from the fronds of a palm and paraded on the Guerreros' roof with serene propriety. A neighbor called to a child from an open window. It was a scene of such tranquillity that what followed took on the polished, celluloid unreality of a Hollywood movie.

The entire house billowed suddenly, silently, and with graceful elegance into a coral bloom of flame. The visual effect was followed instantly by sound, the suck and roar as of the lighting of some unimaginable, giant gas burner.

I was stunned. Nicki, too. She sat beside me, gaping with disbelief.

A second later I was aware of the blur of a running figure, leaving the side gate at the steps and turning up the hill, away from us.

"Nicki," I yelled. I fumbled for the unfamiliar door latch of the car. "Nicki! Get to a phone! Get help!"

I sprinted across the street to the concrete stairway.

The man ahead of me reached the last steps of the flight as I reached the first, and I barely caught a glimpse of him. He turned downhill on the street above. Taking the steps three at a time, I blasted through a wall of solid heat and reached the top no more than twenty seconds behind him.

It was twenty seconds too many, and I was already out of breath. Coasting, I turned downhill and saw that he'd passed the next bend in the winding street. As I ran on, I heard the slam of a car door and the burst of a starting motor ahead of me, and rounded the bend myself in time to catch the tail end of a small red car accelerating into the next bend. It roared on down the hill, and there was a squeal of tires as it turned into the cross street down below.

I stopped, doubled over for a second, winded by the effort. Then I turned again and raced headlong down the steps. Nicki was running too. She emerged from a neighbor's house and ran across their lawn toward the fire. Others were pouring out of their houses to the street, yelling.

"Help! Get help!"

"Call the fire department! Did anyone call?"

"Get the hose!"

And one of them did find a hose, directing its pitiful dribble toward the flaming roof.

Within seconds we heard sirens and the blare of horns from down the hill. As I reached the bottom step, the first of the fire trucks lumbered to a halt, its load of men and equipment spilling out over the roadway. Several of them headed first for the onlookers, driving us back and out of the way. I shouldered past one of them and dodged the unraveling hoses to get to where I thought Nicki had to be.

She was. Somehow she'd got a smudge of dirt across her face, as though she'd fallen.

"You okay?" I yelled at her above the din.

She stood there, shaking her head as she gazed up at the house. Her eyes were tearing with the heat and smoke and she rubbed at them with the sleeve of Yumiko's black jacket.

"I can't believe it," she said. "I can't believe it."

Putting an arm round her shoulder, I pulled her in close.

From down the hill to our right, the funeral party arrived. Access to the street was blocked by fire trucks and equipment, but we could see where they'd left their cars further down the block. They advanced in slow, dazed ranks, dark-suited, impassively silent, like a delegation. The Guerreros themselves led the procession.

When they reached the scene and had stared for a few numb moments at the burning house, Eduardo Guerrero took his wife in his arms with strange formality, and they both wept as they watched the fire crews work.

Yet Guerrero was back in control when we stood outside on what remained of the green terrace some time later. It was a junkyard of charred timbers and debris. Everyone had left but the fire chief, whose car was parked down on the street behind the Buick, its red light still revolving. The neighbors and funeral guests had left soon after the fire crews, and the quiet that earlier had seemed delightful had settled on the neighborhood again.

Amazingly, some of the house had been saved, perhaps only by the moments gained by our accidental presence there at the moment of conflagration. Much of the roof had gone, and much of the interior was ruined by smoke and water.

"Is that all you can tell me?"

The fire chief's question was directed to me, and I nodded, staring steadfastly into the ruins of the house to avoid his eyes. We had already covered the funeral, our early arrival, the start of the fire. I had told him about the chase up the steps and the red car. The rest was my business for the moment.

"Will you be all right?" the fire inspector asked, turning to the Guerreros.

They nodded. "We have neighbors . . . and family . . ."

We stood in an awkward little group and watched

the fire chief reverse across the street into a driveway. There was still unfinished business. I hadn't exchanged a word with old Guerrero, but he made it clear that he knew we had to talk.

He urged us with gestures and brief phrases back into the house, leading us to the kitchen in the back. It was the only room to have survived the worst of the damage. Even here, a smell of gasoline pervaded the air, mingling with the powerful odor of burned wood and fabric.

We sat around the kitchen table. Guerrero ceremoniously opened a bottle of tequila set aside for the reception that had never taken place.

"Now," he said in Spanish, taking the seat across from me, "you knew my son Carlos?" He took command naturally under his own roof and looked to his wife to make the translation.

"Yes," I said. "I knew him briefly in New York." Nicki broke in with a translation and the old man acknowledged her fluency with a brief smile.

"Why do you come to Los Angeles for his funeral? It's a long way from New York."

I looked at him directly as I answered—but I was aware, too, of Nicki's reaction as she listened and translated. "I came," I said, "because I believe that Carlos was not mugged by a stranger on the street. The night before he was killed, he was attacked in front of my house. He was coming to tell me about what he believed was the murder of a friend of mine, many years ago."

Guerrero swallowed the contents of his shot glass and stared at me. I reached out to touch Nicki's hand, wishing that I had taken the time to tell her sooner.

"Why you?" asked Guerrero simply.

I shrugged. "He chose me. He knew me only by reputation."

Guerrero seemed to accept the answer.

"If all this happened in New York," Nicki translated, "why do you come to Los Angeles to find answers to your questions.

"Carlos was here only last week," I said, "and I

think he may have learned something here. It's possible he told you something, or left something in your house. What happened this afternoon makes me think that I was right. What other explanation do you have for this?" I gestured toward the ravages the fire had left behind.

Guerrero gazed at me for a few moments, his hands clasped on the table in front of him, searching my eyes as though to gauge their honesty. Then he poured himself a second glass of tequila and raised it.

"To Carlos," he said.

This time we drank together.

"Carlos told us nothing," he said. "And I think he left nothing here. But a man was here yesterday, a man from New York like yourself. Elegant. Expensive. But a man I would never trust. He told us that he came from Carlos's gallery, that he would represent the estate of Carlos Smith."

Guerrero turned to his wife with a grin and patted her hand. "Smith, my son had chosen to call himself! Business, he told us. What kind of business is it where you're ashamed to use your own last name? Anyway, the man from the gallery gave us money he said belonged to Carlos."

Guerrero gestured to his wife. She opened a kitchen drawer and brought back a stack of hundred-dollar bills. They were sodden with water from the hoses, but miraculously they had survived the fire.

Guerrero seemed neither impressed nor relieved. "Ten thousand dollars," he said. "Of course, I asked the man for an accounting. Even an old Mexican is not so stupid as he wanted to believe. He promised that everything would be accounted for—the paintings, the possessions, everything. Soon, the man said. He claimed it was complicated: Carlos had not left a will. Well, we shall be patient, I told him, but we, too, will have our representative. I asked him for his business card, where our attorney could reach him in New York. He gave me this."

He reached into his wallet and handed me the small white card. Samantha Dmitri Gallery.

"His name's not on the card," I pointed out. "Did he mention it?"

"He said his name, too, was Smith," said Guerrero. "A Brian Smith. No relative, he said—but he laughed when he said it. He was lying. I pride myself on knowing when a man is lying."

It sounded like a joke of Brian Brain's, but there was no way he could look elegant and expensive. Who, then, was Brian Smith?

"Did he ask any other questions?"

"No questions, but a lot of talk." Guerrero dismissed it with a gesture. "Then he wanted to check Carlos's room, to see what work was there, he said. perhaps some drawings or paintings."

"And did you show him?"

"Show him, yes. I wanted to see what he was looking for. But I stayed there with him because I didn't trust him. He asked me, would I leave him there alone for a while. I told him no, my son's business is now my business—there's nothing here to hide." Guerrero grinned. "He seemed annoyed, our friend, and stayed only a few minutes after that. He found nothing other than a few old notebooks. He looked through them carefully anyway, and left."

"He didn't take anything with him?"

"Nothing. I would have known."

"Do you mind if I look?"

He shrugged and led me back through the devastated sitting room to a small room leading off it, overlooking the park and lake. From the stench of gasoline and the condition of the room, it was obvious the fire had started here. Not only that. Like my study, the room had been searched and trashed before the fire had started.

I had the impression of a rushed job. Even from the charred remains and the ashes, you could tell that books had been swept down from the shelves and drawers simply pulled out, their contents dumped. Chairs had been ripped apart, the mattress slashed and tumbled off the bed.

I picked up a small framed picture where it had

fallen from a shelf and rubbed it clean with my fingers. I had seen it before—or half of it: Carlos with Patty Drayton, his arm around her. Patty was still a little plump and jolly, and Carlos barely recognizable in a beard, his hair below the shoulder.

There was a small painting left hanging on the wall. It was blackened by the smoke, but still obviously one of the Echo Park series. I stepped through the rubble and reached over to take it down.

The back was sealed clumsily with strips of wide aluminum tape, bulky and uneven. On impulse, I began to peel a strip away, and sensed immediately the old man's bristling disapproval. I looked at him.

"May I?" I said.

He hesitated, looked at the backing, and then nodded yes. I peeled some more, uncovering the clear corner of a sheet of transparencies. Pulling the tape away, I stripped the entire sheet from its sticky covering and held it up to the light through the broken window frame. But before I looked, I knew what it had to be.

The Worthing Nelsons. Duplicates.

TWENTY-EIGHT

◇

"What's bothering you, Nicki?"

We were driving back slowly to Dick Corman's studio. She'd been silent for at least five minutes, staring out of the car window, fretful and distracted.

"Oh," she said, "I'm sick to my stomach. I think I have a migraine coming on."

She did look pale. It was hardly surprising—the afternoon had drained me, too, and left me feeling nauseated.

Ten thousand dollars. I guessed they had thought it was enough to win the Guerreros' cooperation, yet not so much as to make them greedy and suspicious. They had counted on a stereotype of the Mexican immigrant, not on the shrewd man they'd run up against. The result was another example of the savagery that had been their trademark in New York.

"Nicki," I said. "I hate to see you suffering like this. Why don't you go home? Get well." Back at Dick's studio she barely had the energy to climb out of the car. "Or you could rest here for a while."

She nodded dismally and I put an arm around her.

"I'll go home," she said. "It would be easier."

She stopped long enough to exchange Yumiko's black top for the sheer vinyl motor jacket she'd worn last night at dinner.

"I'll drive you home," I said.

But she wouldn't have it, and I went to the door and watched her back her little silver Honda into the alley, knocking a trash can on its side.

"Call me," I shouted after her.

Exhausted, I lay down for an hour of solitude and

silence in Dick's guest room. I must have dozed, for I drifted back to consciousness with Nicki on my mind. Things seemed so right between us—up to a point. But I hadn't been able to get beyond a deep reservation that I sensed in her.

It was six o'clock, Friday. Not that it mattered. I had missed so much sleep since Carlos's call that I had lost all track of time. Now, to complicate things, jet lag was catching up with me and I found I'd lost my sense of space as well. Despite the rest, my mind and body went through their motions in a kind of limbo.

Nine o'clock, then, in New York, on a Friday evening. Cynthia still had no idea where I was. She'd be worried.

Dick must have heard me stirring: I found him in the studio, loading the Worthing Nelson slides into a cartridge.

"Too bad," he said, "about the migraine. Yumiko told me."

"Too bad," I said. "How long have you known her, Dick? Does she often get these things?"

He paused to look up at me and frowned, searching back in his memory.

"Let's see," he said. "We've known her since she came to L.A. That must have been in the summer of 'seventy-nine. Someone in Paris gave her my address. We've seen a good deal of her, on and off, since then. And no, come to think of it, Yumiko just told me she'd never seen her look so awful. What's on your mind?"

"Nothing. Just something I haven't figured out. It's been a tough day. Do you mind if I use the phone?"

I stood behind Dick and dialed, watching him squint up through the slides before loading them. Back in New York, Cynthia's home phone rang seven times. No answer. I could see the white telephone in her apartment kitchen, ringing under the row of copper pots she never used, ranged in descending sizes on the wall. The neat white countertop. Nothing if not perfection.

Would she be in the office tomorrow, Saturday? I

guessed she might. If not, she'd be bound to pick up messages from her answering service. I dialed the office number. Fortunately, Ginni was working late.

"Ginni? Hi, it's Jake. Is Cynthia there?" She was out at a meeting somewhere. "Could you tell her I'm in Los Angeles? Right. Los Angeles. And Ginni? Give her this number to call." I read Dick's studio number off the dial.

When I tried the Wallace Conners, the collectors who—if Samantha Dmitri's files were to be believed—owned one of the new Nelsons, I got through right away to Babs Conner. She was thrilled to hear from me. Could I, I said, stop by the following morning? I was trying to review some old ideas and needed to see some paintings I had done in the Sixties. I apologized for the short notice. Of course, they would be delighted, she said. Come at eleven.

Sam Russell was home, too. Well, this is a surprise, he said. Good old Sam. Yes, he had been living here for nearly ten years now. And yes, he'd be in this evening and of course I could stop by. If I dared, he added, with a saucy chuckle. He gave me intricate directions up into the hills.

"Jesus," said Dick. "Good Christ!" He had doused the lights and flashed the first slide on the studio wall. "I thought maybe you'd been exaggerating, Jake."

I hadn't. It was the same series of paintings, all twenty of them. Without the pink receipt, could I find the photographic shop on Sunset where Carlos had made dupes? Would it be worth the time and effort? The slides themselves might be useless, unless I could track down the paintings, and by now they could be scattered in collections throughout the country—or throughout the world.

But I was getting closer. Excitement tugged away at me as I traveled east again on Sunset after dinner, following Sam's directions into the hills at the far east end of Hollywood.

His house was cantilevered over the slope of the hill below the road. A few steps led me down through a neat rock garden to the green glass door, where a wrought-iron fixture shed patterned light over the building's peach exterior. I pushed the bell.

For all the years I had known him, I would not have recognized the man who came to the door to greet me. For a moment, I thought this must be Sam's new lover, until he smiled and I caught a particular movement in the eye, a glimpse of gold in the mouth. And was kissed firmly on both cheeks in a familiar embrace.

"Sam?" I said. "Sam?"

He laughed, delighted.

"You wouldn't have recognized me, huh?"

The Sam I had known had been flamboyant. Always immaculate in silk shirts and ascots, he had been delicate, not to say frail. He had sported long, wavy hair that shimmered from endless brushing from the forehead to the shoulders. The new Sam wore a plain white T-shirt, tight around the biceps, and a pair of jeans. His features bristled with a brush cut and mustache. Always shortish in stature, he was now swarthy, bronzed. He stood on the doorsill, grinning some more at my astonishment.

"Come on in," he said. "Come on." He put an arm around my shoulder and led me through the hall into a beautifully proportioned Spanish living room, opening out through glass doors onto an extraordinary vista of the city. On this clear night, the glitter of lights reached out in cobwebs of vertical and horizontal strings from the rim of the basin to the ocean. On a neighboring hill, the white walls and copper rotundas of the Griffith Park Observatory stood out in floodlit contrast to the dark contour of the mountain range, outlined in turn by a glow of lights from the valley beyond. Only the stars were missing, outshone by the man-made universe below.

"Breathtaking, no?" said Sam. "On a night like this, I can barely imagine how I spent all those years in New York."

He insisted on escorting me through his domain, from a deep brown, designer-perfect bedroom to the spartan chrome and cast-iron palace of his exercise room—Sam's pride and the source of his new image.

He must, I reckoned, be well into his sixties and looked immensely more fit—younger, even—than in the days I had known him.

We carried Napoleon cognac in huge snifters back from the kitchen to the living room. It was dominated, I saw now, by two large paintings. An unusual Worthing Nelson from the 1950s, splendid in its serenity. Those had been his early years with Sam. And next to it was a painting of my own, a gift to Sam and Worthing on some occasion that must surely have seemed important at the time, but subsequently had escaped my memory. Seen this way, hung together, the paintings stirred memories of our closeness in those days. Sam watched me, picking up on the sudden range of feelings.

"I know," he said. "Sometimes they make me feel that way myself. But I've always kept them. Most of the time they just bring warmth and pleasure into my life. I loved the guy. It just took me longer than most people to grow up. And I don't think Worthing ever did."

We sat down, gazing into the fire in the hearth, and I was amazed again what distance Sam had traveled from New York. The old Sam couldn't have laid a fire to save his life.

"I came to ask you about Worthing," I told him. "Worthing's death."

"I figured that," he said. "Two visitors from the New York art world in as many weeks would have been too much coincidence."

"Two?" I asked.

"Young man, the painter, I forget his name . . ."

"Carlos? Carlos Smith?"

He snapped his fingers. "That's it," he said. "Carlos Smith. I've no idea how he found me. Anyway, he was here with some cockamamie idea about Worthing having been murdered." Sam leaned back comfortably in his easy chair, crossing his feet on the ottoman in front of him. He wore big purple woolen socks without slippers.

"Did you know that Carlos had been murdered since he came to see you?"

"You're kidding?" Sam, once so excitable and easily upset, seemed unperturbed. He barely raised an eyebrow. "No," he said, "I didn't. I scarcely ever read a paper nowadays. What happened?"

"It could have been taken for a mugging," I said. "In New York."

He shrugged and ran a hand through the soft brush of his hair.

"Why not?" he said. "I hear it happens all the time."

"For one thing, he was found in the exact same spot as Worthing. For another, it was me who found him. He'd been to see me with the same story that he'd told to you."

He watched the clear brown liquid swirling gently as he nursed his glass. The new Sam seemed happy to accept things as they were. He offered no comment.

"What else did he tell you?" I asked.

"He told me very little, honestly," he said. "And I'm afraid that I asked even less. Let's see. He wanted to know about me and Worthing, cheeky little sod. He wanted to know when we'd broken up and who Worthing had hooked up with after that."

"Did you know Nicholas?"

"Oh, yes," he said. He eyed me with a curious little grin. "I knew him. He was sort of hanging around when Worthing and I were still together. Waiting in the wings for his moment in history, I suppose. I couldn't stand the guy. And it wasn't," he emphasized, pointing his glass at me, "it wasn't jealousy, I can promise you. No. Worthing had far more reason to be jealous than I had." Sam's grin broke into a coy giggle at the memory.

"Can you put your finger on why you didn't like him?" I asked. "By the way, I agree. I couldn't stand him either."

"Well," said Sam. He drew out the word as he tried to focus on the memory. "I always had the feeling he was a user. He went after Worthing not because he was Worthing, but because he was the famous Worthing Nelson. Cold. A real calculator. I don't think he gave a tuppenny damn for anyone but himself. Listen, I'll show you something that I wouldn't have shown your friend."

"Your friend" came out with an emphasis that conveyed a tolerant contempt for Carlos—perhaps for the combination of his youth and sexual preference.

"I did meet Worthing one time after we'd broken up for good. It was late in the Sixties, as I remember. I just called him on an impulse and we had a lovely, civilized lunch." Sam got up and crossed the room to a small writing table, opened the drawer, and searched in it for a moment. He came back with a single sheet of paper.

"He wrote me after our meeting, and it was the last I ever heard from him. It's kind of pathetic, really, you'll see. It's short. Worthing was never much on writing. But it gives some insight into Nicholas."

I read the note. "Sam, old dear," it started. "I can't tell you what a joy it was to see you Thursday—I've been thinking about almost nothing else since then. We did have some good times, didn't we? Thank you—thank you for calling. We shouldn't do it again, though. I hadn't meant to tell Nicholas, but he dragged it out of me—and he took it rather hard. He's such a taskmaster—a bit of a bloodsucker, really! And yet I love the little bastard—you can see that, can't you? Of course you can. And I suppose he has my interests at heart. Couldn't tell anyone but you—you always understood me better than anyone. Love—as ever—Worthing."

I looked up to find Sam sneaking a tear from the corner of his eye.

"Is he still around, do you know? Nicholas?"

"I've no idea," said Sam. "No idea at all. The last I heard, he was still living in New York with Worthing." He stood up and gazed through the French doors, out over the city, scratching the top of his head.

"Anything more that Carlos said?" I asked.

"Not really." Sam looked back at me. "He blathered on a bit about some slides and Worthing's work in the early Seventies. Of course, I knew nothing about that. When I left Worthing, I left the art scene. Period. I've never had any interest in it since and I can't say that I've missed it."

"Did Carlos tell you where he'd got the slides?"

"Yes. I do remember him telling me. I guess it stuck because he said he'd stolen them. Literally stolen them. Some gallery downtown, I think. Damned if I remember the name—though I seem to recall that he mentioned it. It would have meant nothing to me anyway."

"But it was here in L.A.?"

"Oh yes, it was certainly here, the way he talked about it."

We talked on further into the night. About Worthing and Sam, and Sam's new life in California. We drank his cognac slowly and with pleasure, and basked in the radiance of Worthing's painting, subtly suffused with light against the rough-plastered wall of Sam's Spanish living room. A more different circumstance, a more different time and place from its origin could scarcely be imagined. It possessed the extraordinary ability to accept change about it and remain insistently the same.

"There's one thing you can do for me, Sam," I said when I finally put down my glass and stood to leave. "Check through the gallery listings in the newspaper, just on the off chance that you'll recognize a name. It could help me a great deal. The only reason I got into this thing in the first place was Worthing. Help me out if you can, for his sake, will you?"

TWENTY-NINE

◇

Back at Dick's place, I found that Dick and Yumiko had already gone to bed. I used my spare key to the studio door. The reflected light from the alley allowed me to cross the studio without turning on the lights.

Once in the bathroom, I stripped and doused my face and neck with a splash of water from the cold faucet, then padded naked to my room. In the dim glow from the skylights, I felt my way to the bed and clambered in, to find it already warm and occupied.

It was Nicki.

Stirring and barely awakening, she turned toward me. I took her in my arms and brought her close, easing her body to fit warmly and intricately with my own.

"Jake," she said sleepily. "I'm sorry."

"Sorry? For what?"

"For everything. My head . . ."

"How is it, Nicki?"

"Better now. Better for having you back."

I felt for the soft hairs at the base of her belly and we eased her sleepy conscience into sleepy passion, falling asleep still joined in the ageless, irreplaceable, ecstatic, and endlessly futile remedy for all human woes.

THIRTY

◇

I found the driveway to Wallace Conner's house just north of Wilshire on Beverly Glen. It was closed off from the street by a wall with a formidable array of spikes. A closed-circuit camera tracked my progress to the gate and peered at me as I drew up. A squawk box sputtered before I'd had time to ring its bell.

"Good morning," it said.

"Good morning," I said back. "Jacob Molnar. I have an appointment with Mr. and Mrs. Conner."

There was a pause, perhaps to allow the voice to consult its appointment book. "Thank you," it said finally. "Please park by the front door." The heavy gates rolled open noiselessly in front of me.

An off-season vine thrust sculptural stems up the wall of the Italianate facade. A Chinese butler in white jacket and white bow tie waited to greet me at the entrance. This was a large double door faced with copper, beaten unevenly and aged to a blue-green patina, embellished with scored patterns whose references were at once ancient and high-tech contemporary. Inside, I noticed, the copper was unaged, glowing with cleanly etched detail.

I was escorted through the hall and down a few broad marble steps into the formal sitting room.

"If you wouldn't mind waiting a moment, sir. The Conners will be with you directly."

I wouldn't, I said.

It was a huge room, painted in the palest shade of peach to give it an edge of warmth. Archipelagos of large, muted furniture were staggered at intervals around the pegged wood floors. A grand piano glinted in the corner, with a tall vase and a single stem, elegant as the David Hockney on the wall behind it.

There was art everywhere. A long, low Lichtenstein bronze that looked like a bar rail. A Jim Dine screen. Both were designers' dreams—the perfect demonstration of how an environment can bring out the worst potential of abstract art: its decorative qualities. On the walls, a large Motherwell elegy piece managed to look absurdly pretty; nearby was a Jasper Johns target. I glanced around further, taking stock: Rothko and Clyfford Still, Poons, Noland, Ellsworth Kelly.

And a Jacob Molnar, over the fireplace.

"Jacob, how very good to see you!"

Wallace Conner's voice boomed out across the empty spaces between me and the door. Wally was the complete California businessman. He seemed as easy with the personal power of his physique as he must have been with the exercise of corporate power in the board room. He wore a navy track outfit as though it were a three-piece suit. He shook my hand and held it firmly in his own, laying a comfortable arm around my shoulder and leading me to the door.

"I see you've found one of your own already. A handsome piece! Handsome! One of our favorites, needless to say. Sorry to have kept you waiting, fella. Telephone. These days they can't leave you in peace, even on Saturday. Let's go find Babs. Last I knew, she was out by the pool."

She was. Reclining elegantly on a chaise, she absorbed the January sun into an already brown, smooth skin. A magazine cover girl, she retained in her fifties that extraordinary youthfulness of the affluent Californian. Babs was desirable, comfortable in the unselfconscious display of her still radiant sexuality. The top of her bikini allowed the occasional glimpse of strong brown nipples.

Though we had met no more than a couple of times, she kissed me easily on the lips and wrapped a robe around her.

"You'll stay for lunch, of course?" she asked.

"I hadn't planned on it. But yes, I'd be delighted to," I said.

"Why don't you look at the art, then, while I get some clothes on. Wally can show you where they are."

The chief executive seemed to have no problem with his marching orders. In a swirl of bathrobe, Babs disappeared up the stairway to the second floor and Wally started me on the tour.

"I wondered," I said, "if I could look at your Worthing Nelsons, too. The newer ones. He was a good friend of mine, you know, before he died."

I proposed it guilelessly and Wally responded with equal spontaneity.

"Of course," he said. "I'll show you where."

He led me into the dining room, across the hall from the sitting room, and left me there with the second of my paintings in their collection—and the two new Worthing Nelsons.

With a noticeable shiver, my skin contracted into goose bumps. I recognized one from Carlos's sheet of slides, and both were works I had never known existed. They were relatively small in scale, compared with earlier works—forty, perhaps, by thirty-six. But for that they were all the more intense.

Yet it was a markedly different intensity from the Worthing Nelson that I knew. The remarkable range of passion that he'd commanded, from rage to lyrical tenderness, seemed to have turned inward on itself. The work had become more ironic in its vision, hard and self-reflective. The paintings were less generous in spirit, darker in tone and color, almost painful. "Tortured" would scarcely be too strong a word.

There was no question, though, that they were genuine. It was a Worthing Nelson changed by time in a way I neither understood nor felt entirely comfortable about—but unquestionably Worthing Nelson. His mark was on each of them in the gesture and brushwork, the texturing of the paint. The powerful, instinctive command of composition, the authority of image, and its continuity with earlier work.

I took them down from the wall to check the back

sides, not for the signature I knew I would find there, but for a possible date and label. Galleries and dealers like to have their imprimatur on anything that passes through their hands.

There were no labels—not a hint of the provenance. But there were dates that confirmed an impression I had gleaned in looking at the two together: There seemed to be an increased emotional intensity in the three years that separated them. From the point of view of Worthing's emotional balance, the difference suggested a deterioration. 1969 and 1972. The later painting conveyed an anguish so strong and eloquent that I wondered how the Conners and their dinner guests could bear to sit and eat in its disturbing presence.

Whether from the unaccustomed California warmth or from the strange dread that the confrontation with these paintings had left in me, I was sweating unpleasantly by the time I joined the Conners on the patio for lunch. It was a modest affair with thin whole-wheat crackers, alfalfa sprouts, and tiny shrimp hidden among assorted lettuce leaves. The food could explain, at least, how the Conners kept their youthful waistlines.

Babs wore a loose white shirt unbuttoned far enough to show more breast than had her bikini. I was surprised to be distressed by the implied provocation.

"Where," I asked unceremoniously, "did you come by the Worthing Nelsons? The recent ones, I mean?"

There was a moment of awkward silence. The two of them exchanged a glance and I chattered on, anxious to fill the silence and avoid their clamming up completely.

"Such powerful work, don't you think? You see," I added confidentially, "I have a few of the earlier works in my own collection—mostly gifts and exchanges, of course, nothing like yours. But I don't have a thing from the later period. I've really been anxious to get one."

They nodded doubtfully and exchanged a second glance, this one a little less guarded than the first. "The problem is," said Wally, "we got them on this confidential deal."

I raised an eyebrow and looked at him, knowing the message would be clear without elaboration. He would know how much the value of an art work is determined by its provenance. Good pedigree, good price. Poor pedigree—or worse, none at all—and the value is at once suspect. "Confidential" means no pedigree at all.

One rotten apple taints the whole damn barrel, too. It wasn't just one painting but the whole collection I could put in doubt with a single well-timed smile. And my smile was the smile of Jacob Molnar—something that Conner was smart enough to understand.

He got the message, but he couldn't resolve the quandary. He wasn't giving up without a fight.

"Well," he said, "I'm not sure we can tell Jake, can we, Babs?"

Good old Wally. Tough businessman. Deflect the heat, she can take it.

Babs shook her head. "You see," she said, "we were offered the paintings by a private dealer. The provenance checks out: They come directly from the artist's estate via a reputable New York dealer. The only thing we don't know is his name. Besides, you can tell they're not phonies just by looking at them. We're not worried about that."

I allowed the silence to speak for my skepticism while I speared the remaining couple of shrimp and doused them in lemon juice.

"Forget their quality for a moment," I told Wally. "Let's take a look at this thing from the business angle. What you have here is a pair of thoroughbreds without sire or dam—a couple of paintings, one from 1969 and one from 1972. They're both from the so-called 'silent' years. I don't think I've ever seen another painting from those years, and I know the work well. You put them on the auction block, you'd be lucky to find a buyer—let alone at the price you paid for them."

Conner was weakening.

"How much?" I asked, with brutal frankness.

It wasn't so much that I expected to get an answer,

but at least to get what I needed by looking in his eyes. They rang up at least a hundred grand for the two of them. Bargain basement prices. The "confidential deal" had been an offer they couldn't refuse, costly enough to numb their ethical reserves—and cheap enough to activate their greed.

"We don't plan putting them on the market," Conner said. "Besides, there are others."

It's not often that you get to enjoy the spectacle of simple knowledge prevailing over wealth. Conner, for all his affluence and power, was cowed. He knew it. So did Babs. And neither of them liked it.

"We did see others," Babs added. "We picked the best of the bunch. Besides, there's a rarity value."

"Don't count on it," I said ruthlessly. "Prices are set by the investment buyers, not by the connoisseurs. Do you watch the auctions? Of course you do. Take last month at Sotheby's. Remember the Monets? They had a brilliant landscape, unlike anything he'd done before or since. It went for chicken feed. A third-rate lily piece went out at a million. Lilies are okay because they're recognized, typical."

They knew I was right.

"From the investment point of view," I told them cheerfully, "I'd say your Worthing Nelsons aren't worth much more than the canvas they're painted on—unless, of course, you can fix up a historical context for them, and set the public record straight. Can you do that?"

Babs looked at Wally doubtfully. Wally glared angrily at me.

"I'd like to help you do it," I told them, smiling. "And I think I can."

I knew I had them. There's always a bottom line. If you're smart enough to afford it, you don't put a hundred grand into a painting without a reasonable security that you could liquidate. Authentication and public recognition could easily triple overnight what the Conners had invested in the paintings. I was offering Wally a way to ease his conscience and make an attractive profit all at once.

He jumped. "What can you do?" he asked.

"I think I can find a significant number of paintings from the silent years and bring them out into the public eye. Imagine, let's say, a retrospective at the Guggenheim. A whole new reassessment of the Worthing Nelson oeuvre. Think of the critical reaction."

"Where are these paintings?"

"That," I told him, "is where I need your help. I know that a number of them exist. I've seen reproductions of twenty of them, but the ones I've seen include only one of your two. That suggests more. Maybe many more. Knowing the way Worthing worked, perhaps twenty, thirty a year for a period of five years. There could be more than a hundred paintings. You ask me where the others are. I ask you where you got these two."

Wally rapped knuckles on the glass top of the patio table, weighing alternatives. He wanted to be sure there was enough protection built in for himself.

"Listen," he said finally, "I just want you to know that if there's anything shady involved in these paintings, we were definitely unaware of it. Our collection has been based on honesty and integrity from the word go. We bought these two paintings from a dealer we believed to be honorable, and we still have no reason to think otherwise. Period. We believed we paid a fair price for them."

So much, I thought, for honesty and integrity. But he didn't flinch when I looked at him.

"Where did they come from?"

He shrugged, floundered a moment longer, then flopped up on my beach with a baleful glare.

"We bought both paintings at the same time," he said. "It was a couple of years ago. We had a call from a dealer by the name of Burke Chung about some Worthing Nelsons. He'd already established something of a reputation around town as a private dealer and we had no reason not to trust him. He knew we were looking for a Worthing Nelson and called to say that he'd unearthed a couple. Would we care to look at them?"

The maid brought out fresh glasses of iced tea and Conner sipped thoughtfully, gazing at me over the rim.

"What could I say?" he went on. "Of course we wanted to see them. Although we'd heard of him, we'd never done business with the man before, so before he brought them over, we checked him out with a couple of friends. They gave him a clean bill of health. Then he showed up with half a dozen paintings in the back of an old station wagon and we fell in love with two of them. It was as easy as that."

"Surely you asked him where he'd found them?"

"Of course."

"And?"

Conner hesitated for a moment. "I have to admit he was a little vague," he said. "But he did say they came directly from the estate through a friend of the artist's. For us, the point was that the pieces were signed. Even if they hadn't been, there's a good chance we still would have bought them—we like to think we can tell a genuine painting from a fake. Even so, we kept them on approval for a week and had them checked out by at least three experts, including Fred Aaron at the museum. They all agreed the paintings were genuine. Unusual, but genuine."

Aaron was curator of contemporary art. He came out of somewhere in the Midwest and I remembered having met him a couple of times before he came to L.A.

"But why the confidentiality? I'd have thought the dealer, this . . ."

"Chung. Burke Chung."

". . . this Chung would have wanted it known that he had Worthing Nelsons and that he'd made a sale to the Conner collection. And you! And Aaron! Here you make an important discovery, two new Nelsons, previously unknown, not mentioned in any of the books or catalogs."

Watching the color in Wally Conner's cheeks turn to a deeper shade of brown, I knew I could easily overplay my hand if I crossed the delicate line between a collector's public spirit and his eventual self-interest. I couldn't blame him. It was his money. But I could admire the control with which he turned his anger into banter.

"And what business is it of yours, Jake Molnar, how I spend my money? Thanks for the thought, but no thanks. We're not buying any secondhand advice today. We're happy with our collection, Jake. We'd like to keep it that way."

"Burke Chung, eh?" I was inclined to settle for what I'd got.

"Burke Chung. Look him up. Ask him your questions. He just opened a new gallery downtown. And don't tell him I sent you—we might just want to do business with him again some day."

Wally Conner clapped a fraternal arm around my shoulder and escorted me firmly to the door. Babs waved vaguely from afar.

THIRTY-ONE

◇

I stopped for gas and used the pay phone at the corner of Wilshire and Robertson in Beverly Hills.

"Dick," I shouted above the traffic. "Did Cynthia call?"

"Yeah," he said. "She called mid-morning, soon after you left. She said to say sorry she missed you."

Damn! Mid-morning would have been early afternoon, New York. I had been ringing her home and office numbers all morning until I left.

"She said to tell you she was sorry not to have called earlier. She didn't have anything exciting or different to report. No trace of the Worthing Nelsons on her computer, she said. And everything at Samantha Dmitri looks just fine. She wonders if you're crazy."

"What the hell's she talking about, crazy? With Carlos killed? And Laura? Did you tell her about the fire? And the slides?"

"Sure, I told her."

"And?"

"She said she'd like to see them, and when were you planning to be back?"

I couldn't see further than the next two hours.

"Dick, can you take some time this afternoon to help me? I'll be downtown." I asked what he knew about the Burke Chung Gallery.

"Name rings a bell somewhere," he told me. "But I'm not sure where. There's so many galleries opening up down there, you can't keep track of them."

"Meet me anyway?" I asked.

"At the gallery?"

"No," I told him. "I've arranged to be at Nicki's first, on Traction."

"I've been there," said Dick. "It was a while ago, but I think I'll find it. What time are you thinking of?"

What else? There'd been something on my mind to ask him. Damn thing had slipped.

"What time do the galleries close?"

"Generally around five."

"How about four? At Nicki's."

"Oh, and Jake," he said. "I almost forgot. Sam Russell called. Excited. He wanted you to call him back as soon as possible."

I fumbled in my pocket for the slip of paper where I had written Sam's address and phone.

"Hello."

"Sam? It's Jake."

"Jake, I did what you asked me. Looked through the gallery listings. I came up with the name you wanted. It's such an odd combination, I'm surprised I hadn't remembered it."

"Burke Chung," I said.

"You'd found that out already?" he asked.

"A guess," I said. "But listen, Sam, thanks anyway. I much appreciate it. The confirmation really clinches things. I'll be in touch."

"Yes, let me know—whatever happens, okay?"

I had my finger on the touch dial to get back to Cynthia in New York. Instead, I called Nicki, to let her know I would be later than I had expected.

"How was Babs?" she asked. Babs's figure was evidently famous in the L.A. art world.

"Not bad," I said. "I stayed for a nearly naked lunch."

She giggled.

"Did you see the paintings?"

"Yes, I did."

"How were they?" she asked.

"They were quite extraordinary," I told her. "What are we talking on the phone for? I can be there in less than half an hour."

"Did you find out anything else?" she asked.

"Not much," I said. "But something."

"Something? Tell me?" she said.

"Tell you when I get there."

"Oh, Jake, I can't wait," she pleaded.

"You can," I said. "Bye-bye, my lovely."

She squealed a protest as I hung up, and I gave that some thought as I drove the twenty minutes to her downtown studio.

It was in a commercial building whose entrance was the loading bay of an industrial print shop. There was no traffic on a Saturday and the main doors were rolled down, leaving access only through a small side entryway. Beyond it, massive drums of paper were stacked in the huge loading area like children's blocks, making monumental sculptures in the gloom.

Unlike New York, where even an industrial warehouse is crammed to the last usable square foot, space in L.A. is everywhere in luxurious excess, characterized more by its emptiness than by its use. You could see where Dick's work came from. It made good sense. To an easterner, the stairwell here seemed more like a museum than commercial property.

I found Nicki's name at a heavy fire door on the fifth floor. I beat my knuckles against solid metal and waited. After a moment, the door moved four grudging inches back along its steel track and then stopped.

"Oh *merde!*" I heard Nicki say. "Again!"

I slid my fingers in the crack and heaved the door back some more. With effort, I managed to make the crack wide enough to squeeze through. She stood inside, examining an injured hand.

"I broke a nail," she explained. "Damn door. I'm always doing it!" She kicked it without visible result.

"Why don't you fix the counterweight?" I asked. "It'd slide much easier."

"It's the landlord," she said. "He won't do a thing for artists. Anyway, come in."

Nicki's hands were an incongruous mixture of business and pleasure. Her nails were polished, but shortened, broken with use. The skin was sensitive, but the lines that marked it were far too emphatic for a woman of her age.

She gave me the damaged finger to make a fuss of it.

"What else," I asked, "do you have to show me?"

She laughed.

"Art," she said. "Or life? You get to choose."

Despite the injured nail, she managed to unbutton her loose blue workshirt as she spoke and the choice was taken from my hands. Closing the fire door, I fastened the latch behind me, then helped the shirt from her shoulders and stood back to lust after the result. Her breasts were pale, light brown at the center.

"Art," I decided quickly, "is short. Life's getting long."

She laughed again, dodging my grasp and leaving me to chase her through an unlit storage room into a brilliant space that ran from end to end along the west side of the building.

I captured her at the far end, where she had built her bedroom, and we both fell noisily to the mattress on the floor. Afternoon sunshine poured through the rows of windows, melting our bodies to butter.

Making love was almost perfunctory. We both wanted it, we'd both been waiting for it since that morning. Yet there was apparently something else on both our minds. Something withheld or hidden, a powerful, unwilling doubt that lingered in her eyes as she looked at me afterward. Something I myself was unwilling to believe, the more I thought of it. . . .

Her paintings came from the French school of post-war abstraction, but with five years of California light and color blended in. Her technical fluency had been learned in the schools, but the self-obsessive, lyrical energy came from Nicki.

I held an arm around her waist as we looked.

"I've heard," she said, "that you don't like abstract painting."

"It's not abstraction I don't like," I told her. "It's what abstraction has done to painting. It seduced everyone to the surface. Painting got to be decoration, a way of making a living. Its real job is to dig deep, to be looking for the truth—even when truth is ambiguous and difficult. You've got stuck on the surface."

"So this is decorative?"

I nodded.

"But for one thing," I said. "A sense of humor. A touch of human warmth that creeps in through the formal issues. Here, for example. Here." I touched the canvas at a couple of points, and she smiled.

"Otherwise? Worthless?" she asked.

"Not worthless," I said. "They're very good paintings. But misguided. Nicki, what single historical event is the most important of this century?"

She looked surprised by the context of the question, but she responded immediately, without reflection.

"Hiroshima," she said.

"Funny," I said, "I would have said the Holocaust. Not that it matters. Same difference. Your answer is as good as mine, and almost any answer would have made the point. For years I painted as though the Holocaust didn't exist. You paint as though Hiroshima hadn't happened. I came to a point where I couldn't live with myself as an artist and ignore the simple facts of presence and absence. Life and death. Six million people gone. Poof! Like that. I think about it almost every day."

She turned away from me and walked to the window. She looked out over the hulks of downtown buildings in silence for a moment, and then turned back to me.

"It's the same thing with Worthing Nelson?" she asked. "And Carlos Smith? And Laura?"

"I guess in a way it is," I said. "Except that it's not quite art anymore. But I need to understand. That's what my work is all about. Some artists say they can still address these issues in an abstract work. I say not—beyond the noble failure of the Rothkos and Motherwells. They produced great empty monuments to absence, elegies."

She was silent again, and stood looking at her paintings through my eyes.

"You prefer the scrawlings of the new expressionists?" she asked. "I find those cheap and shallow."

"Because so much of it is abstract painting, thinly veiled. It's still painting about painting. It still looks for an internal truth in shallow beings and cheap emotions, instead of looking for the indispensable truth. Body or carcass. Look at Soutine, look at Bacon. The new stuff's a cheat because it pretends to be about what it's not about and not to be about what it is about: art. And the artist. That's the whole game, right there."

"No one ever spoke to me like that before."

"I know."

I went to the window and we stood side by side. Below, in the street, one of the derelicts had parked himself in a doorway and slept quietly in its shade, his world in a paper sack under his arm.

"Nicki," I said. "I need to know the truth from you, and now's the time. You have to trust me. Sooner or later you're going to have to tell me. Whatever it is you've been lying to me about, you have to tell me what it is."

THIRTY-TWO

◇

She wanted to tell me. I think she had already decided. She would have told me then, had the silence not first been broken by a loud knock at the door.

"I'll get it," she said.

"I'll go," I said. "It's Dick."

I saved her another broken nail and brought Dick back into the studio. By the time we got back, she had the water on for tea and the moment had passed. Later, I thought.

"Well, I did some research for you, Jake," said Dick.

We sat at the table in the kitchen niche and Nicki brought us tea in mugs.

"And?" I asked.

"I found out some more about Burke Chung," he said.

"He's just a few blocks from here," said Nicki. I knew she wanted the remark to sound casual, but it came out with an edge of tension that was subtle enough for Dick to miss. I looked at her and found her avoiding my eyes.

"I told you the name rang a bell," Dick went on. "So I searched through a drawer full of old announcements and browsed in the past few months of *Artweek*. Here's the story: About six months ago, Burke Chung, a former self-styled private dealer, went public with a brand new space downtown. To put you in the picture, Jake, he was following the famous downtown rehabilitation script. Maybe Nicki's told you about it."

She gestured no.

"Go ahead," I said.

"Well, it's an old story," he said. "The artists moved in first among the bums and made the district safe for the galleries. East of the high-rises, that is. Then came plans for a new contemporary museum, and more galleries got the message. It wasn't long before the place got fit for businessmen, people started driving over from the west side—and rents began to go up. The artists are going to have to migrate again soon. That's the short version. Does it sound familiar?"

I nodded, watching Nicki stare out through the window, wishing she were somewhere else.

"About three months ago," Dick continued, "a card went out announcing the Burke Chung Gallery's association with Samantha Dmitri in New York . . ."

"Our Sammy," I said. "Well, well."

"Yeah. Well, he listed a few big names with works available in L.A. It raised some eyebrows at the time, including mine—it seemed like a heavy gun for a little new gallery to be shooting off. I never heard any follow-up, so I guess it just slipped my mind. Who knows what could have happened since?"

"Let's go find out," I said, standing up.

We had finished our tea and Nicki had collected the mugs. She was rinsing them at the sink.

"Is that where you're going now?" she asked. She looked back over her shoulder.

"Right," I said.

"Then I'd better not go with you." She turned away again. "They know me there. Burke, I mean."

There was a pause.

"They may be showing my work," she said.

Dick flashed a question across the table at me with his eyes, and I simply shook my head.

"You didn't tell me that you knew him," I said.

"Why would I?" she asked. "I only just heard you mention his name two minutes ago."

"How long have you known him?" I asked.

"Oh, not long," she said. "Three, four months. I went in soon after they opened. It's normal, no? A gallery just down the street, an artist looking for a gallery?"

"What kind of man is he?"

"A man." She shrugged. "Nice enough. Half Chinese, half American, I suppose."

"You trust him?"

She went back to the window, set her backside against the sill and rested her weight against it, folding her arms across her chest. God knows, I hadn't put her on the defense. It came from her.

"Why not? I've had no reason not to. He's just a nice, quiet guy. Anyway, I'd rather not go. I have no quarrel with the man."

It was my turn to shrug. It amazed me, how fast our communications could be cut. Less than an hour ago, we had been a single piece of flesh. "That's fine with me," I said. "Why should you need to? Maybe Dick will drive me there. We'll come back later to pick up my car."

We took the steps down to the loading bay and crossed the street to the Bentley, its polished elegance a startling contrast to the crumbling stucco wall behind it.

"Problems?" Dick asked me, pulling away from the curb.

I nodded. There were problems, but were they hers or mine? Or had hers been made mine?

What came to mind was the moment before departure in New York. The tail at the boarding gate. My last, smug wave as he headed for the pay phone. He knew where the plane was going. After taking the trouble to keep me under observation in New York, would they abandon me in Los Angeles? Of course not. They had simply changed tactics. They had used Nicki.

Goddammit, it explained the ease with which she'd slipped into my bed. The moments of silent distance.

"Jake . . . ?" Dick started.

"Drive," I said.

It explained the telephone call from across the street at the mortuary. And, good God, the timing of the fire at the Guerreros'. A call from Nicki, a half-hour for response. Rather than risk my finding what they'd missed, they had burned the whole damn place down.

Judging from her response, the devastating result shocked the pants off her. Her disbelief at the scene of the fire seemed genuine enough, and the physical reaction, the migraine, surely wasn't faked. She had looked terrible.

But why?

"You want to tell me about it, Jake?"

We'd arrived outside the gallery. Dick was watching me, worried by my silence. The Bentley's engine was still running.

"Later," I said. "We'd best get on with it, or the gallery will close."

We parked alongside an abandoned building site, whimsically covered with a coat of turquoise paint. Nothing had been left untouched, from the fragmented asphalt pavement to the chain-link fence and the brick wall at the rear. Bottles and cans, debris, an abandoned baseball cap, even small pebbles and clumps of grass had been painted. Only, in contrast, a new growth of weeds and grass had begun to sprout, and a recently abandoned Smirnoff bottle had shattered on the turquoise concrete.

"An artist?" I asked Dick.

He nodded.

"I forget her name," he said. "She's done some interesting work."

Burke Chung announced the entrance to his gallery in simple black letters stenciled on the white wall. A flight of wooden stairs led directly to the second floor of the two-story building.

Before the daylight had begun to fade, the gallery's skylights would have suffused it with the flood of natural light that seems omnipresent in Southern California. Now, at dusk, the track lights superseded daylight. It had a simple pine floor that glowed with a touch of pink and, to our right, a counter enclosing a secretarial area, presently unoccupied. This led in turn to an inner office, whose glass-paned door was partially open.

We took a look at the current show. Amorphous, vaguely anthropomorphic shapes were outlined in thick paint on enormous canvases: a meteor cloud of gigantic, garishly colored spermatozoa invading the cosmic womb like wet dreams.

"Stunning, aren't they?"

The man had approached us silently from behind and smiled engagingly. From the look of expectant uncertainty in his eyes, I gathered he was unsure whether or not he knew us.

"Burke Chung," he said. "Thank you for stopping by to see the show. Is there anything I can help you with?"

Not tall, and lightly built, he carried himself with a slight, deferential stoop. He looked from one to the other of us, hands joined lightly in front of him. I returned his gaze with no more than a perfunctory smile.

"I'm looking," I said, "for a Carlos Smith. I understand you might have some to show me."

"Smith," he repeated. "Carlos. Yes. There's not much available at the moment. You're aware of course . . ."

"I'm aware," I assured him.

The phone rang in the office. With a flutter of nervous fingers, Chung invited us to continue our tour of the main gallery and hurried back to his office.

I glanced at Dick. "Nicki," I said quietly. "I'm afraid they got to her. Watch out."

"Nicki?" he said. "But why? I don't understand."

"I'm only just beginning to understand myself," I told him. "But watch out anyway."

If I had needed confirmation, it was written on Burke Chung's face when he came back to join us. It was chalky white. The easy smile he attempted turned into a grimace, and his hands were pale butterflies that could find no place to settle.

"Carlos Smith," he said, glancing at his watch. "Yes, I think I can show you something if you wouldn't mind waiting for a couple of minutes. I think I'll close the gallery first. It's close enough to five and I have no one at the desk."

"It's only twenty of," said Dick. "Isn't it still a little early?"

"Well, normally, yes, it would be. But if no one's in by a quarter till, I don't expect anyone will arrive before closing time. There's not much walk-in traffic. You're from out of town?"

I nodded briefly.

"I thought I recognized you," he lied nervously. "Jacob Molnar, isn't it?"

If he had expected a pleased response, he was disappointed. I gave him another nod and looked past his shoulder at one of the atrocities on the wall.

"And you'd be Richard Corman?" he asked Dick. "We've met once or twice before—at openings, I guess." He laughed without any sign of pleasure. "Anyway, it's a privilege to have you here. Most welcome."

He gave an awkward little bow, ill-suited to his thoroughly westernized demeanor, and his footsteps echoed as he hurried down the stairs to the street door. Dick and I exchanged a glance as we listened to the jangle of keys, the click of a Yale lock. He locked the door to the main gallery, too, and returned to us with another dismal attempt at a smile.

"Now," he said, "if you'd follow me."

He hurried us into a second, smaller gallery where we found a Patty Drayton isolated on the hardwood floor—a pair of interpenetrating figures, male and female, assertive, painful, and erotic. Chung didn't give us time for a second glance. He continued through to a storeroom in the back and started to pull a six-foot canvas from the racks.

"Not those," I said. "I don't like those. It's the small ones I'm interested in. The Echo Park series."

Chung looked genuinely surprised.

"Echo Park?" he said.

"Small paintings," I said. "I saw some in Smith's studio in New York. They're by far his best work."

I sketched the proportions with my hands, but Chung shook his head.

"Funny," he said. "I've never seen such a thing. That's a part of his work I'm not familiar with at all. I'm amazed."

"Perhaps, then," I pursued without a pause, "you could help me with some Worthing Nelsons. I heard you've been showing some around town."

For the moment he stalled, glancing back as though praying for help to appear suddenly. Failing that, he started to back away. "Worthing Nelsons?" he asked. "Who told you that?"

"The Wallace Conners," I told him. "Among others." I wasn't about to spare the Conners' reputation at the cost of my advantage.

He backed slowly round in front of me.

My mistake was to leave him time to slip through the door. It would have taken physical action to stop him, and I wasn't ready to be the first. I should have been. By the time I had crossed the threshold after Chung, with Dick behind me, he was running past the Patty Drayton toward the entrance. We burst into the main gallery behind him.

On the far side of the room, the door from the entry stairway crashed open, and Nicki half-stumbled, half-fell through the opening, shoved from behind. She tripped to the floor, where she landed with a yelp of pain, knee first.

Behind her, with a grin I remembered from a cold day on a New York street, was Brian Brain.

THIRTY-THREE

◇

I had built him in memory into something more villainous than he now appeared. Skinny and frail, he seemed more like a child acting out the villain's role. His sleeveless leather vest hung open to reveal a bony white chest, remarkable only in its pattern of overlapping scars. A sickening clump of tissue replaced one nipple and an elaborate black rose was tattooed on each of his shoulders. His chest and arms were a maze of cliché symbols of violence and death.

The juxtaposition of his puny presence with all the insignia of terrorist power would have been laughable but for the memory of Laura, kicked and beaten. Carlos, with his head caved in.

"Well, well, well," said Brian, surveying us with feigned surprise.

He had brought a friend with him, armed with a switchblade, bigger and more powerful than himself, yet somehow less threatening. They stood at the gallery door as though challenging our movement. Nicki squirmed on the floor, and Brian used the heel of his boot to shove her down again.

"So our knight in shining armor finally arrives. Just in the nick to ride off into the sunset."

Brian cackled, digging his friend in the ribs with his elbow. Burke Chung looked pained and awkward, unsure whether to remain among us victims or to join the villain.

"Come on now, old pal," Brian told him. "Don't look like that, all wan and weedy like. Better help me get this mess cleared up. I have it on good authority the old geezer himself is due to get here any minute now. He likes to find things nice and tidy, right? You got a shit-house here, mate?"

Chung nodded miserably.

Brian grabbed the switchblade from his friend and pulled Nicki up by the hair, holding the blade to her throat. A hairline of blood appeared suddenly and Nicki yelped. The blood made a pair of parallel lines that ran down under her shirt.

"Oh, so sorry, my dear," said Brian with cheerful irony. "I wouldn't hurt you for the world. Now would I, Jake, old chum?" It was the first time he had spoken to me directly, happy to have the chance to taunt me with what he'd done to Laura.

I said nothing.

"Right. Old Stone-Face, then," said Brian. "Okay, into the shit-house with the lot of you."

I didn't move, hoping there might be a way to grab Nicki away from them. With the knife to her throat, there was nothing we could do.

"Move!" Brian made it clear he wasn't about to let her go. He grabbed her chin and forced it back toward him, exposing the throat. "Get going!" he said.

We went. Powerless, we followed Chung through the storeroom to the back of the building. He brought us to a tiny room without windows, no more than a closet with a sink and toilet, and barely the space for one to turn around.

Chung opened the door and Brian herded us in, shoving Nicki in last. Then he slammed the door closed with his shoulder and yelled an instruction to his friend. In a moment, we heard something being propped against the door. I fumbled quickly for the handle in the dark and turned it, while trying to get some pressure against the wood with my shoulder.

Nothing. Before I could get the angle to apply some force, the door was firmly barricaded.

"You lot stay quiet now," Brian shouted. "You'll live longer. Maybe not much, but longer." He cackled again. "I'll be back to fetch you, rest assured." Through the door, we heard the three of them walk back through the storeroom, closing the door behind them.

I found the light switch. Dick pulled a length off the toilet roll and silently passed it to Nicki to stanch the blood from the scratch on her neck.

For a while, we said nothing. By dint of cautious maneuvering, we found that Nicki could sit on the toilet seat while Dick half-sat, half-leaned against the sink. That left me standing, my back flat up against the remaining wall, my rear end jammed uncomfortably against the door handle. Meantime, the movement of three bodies in the tiny space combined with the glow of the single unshaded bulb to create a suffocating heat.

"The light," Dick told me. "Switch it off. It'll make it that much cooler. It's not doing us much good in any case."

I switched it off and we sweltered for a while in darkness, each listening to the others' breath.

"Jake," said Nicki. "I should have told you. I was going to tell you. Jake, I'm sorry."

We sweltered a while longer.

"Jake?" she said.

"Why?" asked Dick. "What made you do it, Nicki? I don't understand."

Nicki snuffled in the darkness. She fumbled for the toilet roll beside my leg and tore off another length.

"I was only thinking about the gallery," she said. "Five years I've waited for a place to show my work. I couldn't blow the chance. Besides, it just seemed harmless."

More silence.

"And then, I didn't know Jake," she said. "I'd never do anything to hurt him."

"Why you?" I asked. "How did they get to you?" There was no one in New York who had known where I was going to stay when I reached the coast.

"It started with just plain chance," she said. "Well, maybe not quite. I was in the gallery—when was it, Thursday? Friday? The days are all mixed up together now, I can't remember. Thursday, maybe."

"That was the day I arrived," I told her.

"Thursday, then," she said. "I've been coming in

regularly, to stay in touch and bring some slides. Well, Dick had called me a little earlier about the dinner. So I happened to mention—no, really, I wanted to impress Burke . . . it was the only reason I came in. I wanted him to know I was having dinner with Jacob Molnar. He didn't say much right then, but later that afternoon he called and said could I do him a little favor? How could I say no? You know how it is, when you need a gallery."

The air was stifling now, hot and reused. My shirt stuck uncomfortably to wet flesh.

"What exactly," I asked, "was the little favor that he asked of you?"

"Just to hang around as much as possible while you were in L.A. and let him know what you were doing, who you were visiting, what was on your mind. That kind of thing."

"Did he give a reason? Or were you so anxious to help that you forgot to ask?"

"Lay off her, Jake," said Dick.

"No," she said. "He's right. But it seemed so harmless. He said he'd heard you were doing some new work and that he was dying to get it for the gallery. He said he hadn't a chance without some inside information. I guess I just wanted to believe him. I know it sounds stupid, now that I tell you."

"Did he suggest you climb into bed with me too? Or was that your own idea?"

It was an ignoble question and met, more nobly, with silence.

"Listen, Jake," she said a moment later. "I'd no idea there was anything else involved until I heard you talk about the killing. And then, with the fire, it all seemed so unreal, I went into a panic. That's when this Brian came around, the afternoon I had the migraine. God, was that yesterday? Burke must have told him where to go. He showed me where he'd cut his nipple off, and said he'd do the same to me if I told you anything."

Nicki shuddered.

"He tore open my shirt and grabbed my nipple with

his finger and thumb. Then he pulled it out and stuck that knife against me. I really thought he'd do it, Jake! He looked at me like I was a piece of shit or something, like he could have raped me. But he just said, 'Keep up the good work,' and slapped me hard across the face."

Despite the heat, I reached out to find her hand and pressed it to me. She put a hand over mine and I heard another snuffle in the dark.

"Did you call Chung again?" I asked.

"Not Burke," she said. I could feel her head shake against my belly. "This Brian left me another number to call. He called me once this morning. I told him you'd gone to the Conners. And I called the number this afternoon, after you'd left the studio with Dick. I was scared not to do it, Jake. It wasn't Brian I spoke to, but he knew who I was right away."

"Did you know the voice?"

"No," she said. "It wasn't the English accent. More like American, cultured, a little soft. Then Brian came by just a few minutes later. He must have been right close by."

I shifted my weight and tried to find a new position. One leg was going numb.

"Relax, save your energy," said Dick. "I have the feeling you're going to need it."

"What will they do with us, Jake?" said Nicki.

The question on my mind was, rather, what could we do for ourselves? For the time being there seemed to be a simple answer: very little.

THIRTY-FOUR

◇

I pushed the light button on my watch. It was nearly eleven—six hours since we'd been locked in. From his cramped position by the sink, Dick had tried several times to force the door with his feet or smash it away from its hinges, but eventually we had simply given up. The only result was more heat and more discomfort.

It soon became useless, too, to think of conserving energy for a rush when the door was finally opened. With each passing minute, the heat and cramps sapped more from our dwindling reserves of energy. Slumped across the others' arms and legs and over the hard, protruding angles of porcelain fixtures, I reached the point where I couldn't distinguish limb from limb or self from other in the darkness. It was all one dreadful, communal ache, where movement and lack of movement were complementary agonies.

When sounds returned to the storeroom, it was a toss-up between relief and sick anticipation.

The footsteps sounded like cavalry: Numbed from the hours of deprivation they'd been subjected to, my senses registered new information with almost painful intensity. In a moment, whatever they had used to barricade the door was kicked away and the handle rattled and turned.

I was instantly blinded by a flood of light, and Brian's voice jeered at us cheerfully.

"Wakey, wakey, show a leg. Nothing naughty going on in there, I hope."

Nicki and Dick had the same instinct I had. From exhaustion, muscular rigidity, or fear, none of us moved.

Brian looked in and prodded me upright with the tip of his boot. I took my time, adjusting to the light, allowing the influx of oxygen to restore some energy and thought.

Burke Chung was hovering behind Brian. He held a gun, looking as awkward with the thing as I might have felt. I had never held one in my life.

Was the friend out there, too?

"Out, out, out!" yelled Brian. "You lot are going for the proverbial ride. Get out of there!"

Grabbing hold of Dick's arm, Brian yanked him forward and shoved him against the wall outside. The third man was out there, I saw now. He moved forward and pinned Dick to the wall with an outstretched arm.

"Just watch him, mate," said Brian. He reached forward again into the semidarkness for Nicki, and suddenly yelped with pain, lunging forward, scuffling with her briefly before dragging her out and kicking her to the floor. He pulled his right hand away and looked incredulously at the fleshy part, dripping with blood.

It was a moment before he understood that she had bitten him. Then it hit him suddenly and released a torrent of fury.

"You fucking bitch!" he screamed. "You bleeding cunt!"

I've seen tempers lost before. I've lost my own, and have some sense of what happens when the mind slips out of gear and you lose control. But I've never seen anything quite like the squall that whipped this man into a white-hot frenzy.

I already knew that Brian could kill. What I saw in that instant was a man about to kill.

There's a point at which the body simply forgets its fear and weakness. It just reacts—at least mine did. There was no thought or plan—let alone courage—involved. I sloughed the painful inertia that had paralyzed me and launched myself headlong at Brian.

I landed with my head dead center in his chest and drove him backward, yelling, crumpling under the force.

But while Brian stumbled backward toward Chung, I was the one who hit the floor.

At the moment of my impact, I was shocked into immobility by the sound of a gunshot. It was deafening, followed immediately by silence, then a thud as one of us went down.

"Shit!"

In the first stunned moment after the chain reaction, we all looked around to check our bearings. Chung must have been aiming the thing at Dick, but it was Brian's friend who had been hit.

"Shit!"

Shaking, inordinately pale, Chung stood looking from the thing he had fired to the thing he'd hit as though it were some other person, not himself, who had pulled the trigger. Dick clutched at his shoulder as though he had been hit. He hadn't.

It was Brian who recovered first. He laughed. Cackled almost as uncontrollably as he had been moved to anger. And then the hiss and metallic snap of his switchblade focused our attention. The action seemed to have put him in reverse and he was cool again, taking control with the ease of a man whose ruthlessness is beyond question.

"You all right?" he asked Chung.

Chung nodded. He was pale, but he still held the gun on Dick.

"See what you fucking did?" Brian yelled at me. He held the knife to my throat and dragged me over to where his friend lay bleeding on the floor. The man could have been alive, but I doubted it. To judge by the blood, he'd been hit somewhere in the chest. Brian poked at him with his boot.

"What'll we do with him?" asked Chung.

"Do with him? Do with him?" said Brian. "We'll fucking leave him, that's what we'll do with him. Bloody moron." He left it unclear who the bloody moron was.

"What about the gun?"

"You better hold on to that, mate. Never know when you might need it, do you?"

He chuckled again.

"Right, then," he said. "We'll do this a little different, shall we?" He jabbed at me with the blade and
brought us all to our feet, herding us back together.
"You lot got a car, right?"

I nodded, thinking absurdly that we shouldn't have
got Dick's Bentley into this. "Where are you taking
us?" I asked.

"None of your bleeding beeswax, mate," he said.
"Get moving. You'll find out a good lot sooner than
you want to."

That was it, then. I had left them no alternative but
to kill us. If I had been smart, I would have held back
some cards, but from the start I'd played everything as
it was dealt. I was left with nothing. Worse still, I had
got nowhere. I was no closer than I had been four
days ago, and I had left a trail of disaster. Laura was
dead and other lives destroyed. And now three further
lives at risk. For what? For Jacob Molnar's ego?

An oddly tight little group, we walked back through
the gallery and down the stairs. At the front door to
the gallery, Brian stooped to pick up a stained red
gasoline can—perhaps, I thought, the same one he'd
used at the Guerreros'. There could be only one purpose for it. Fire. I knew that Nicki was looking at me,
but I couldn't meet her eyes. Instead, I put an arm
around her shoulder.

"I'll take these lovebirds in their car," said Brian to
Chung. "You take the other guy in yours. Where is it?"

Chung nodded toward a dark blue Pontiac parked a
few yards further up the street.

"You take that one, then," said Brian. "You can
follow us."

It was a mistake, I knew. And from the glance he
threw me, I knew that Dick knew too. Brian was
counting too much on the weapon, and too much on
the man who held it. Chung knew it too, by the look
of him, but couldn't come out and say it.

"Why don't we stick together?" he suggested.
"Wouldn't it be safer? There's room in my car."

Brian's mind was working forward, distracted from
the dynamic of the here and now.

"We'll need both cars," he snapped. "How do you think we're going to get back? Have the bastard drive and hold the gun on him. Get on with it, for Christ's sake. Here, Molnar, drive your girlfriend and me. Where did you park?"

"I'll need the keys," I said.

"The keys?"

"It's not my car," I said. "It's his."

It didn't take much to follow Brian's thinking. If one car was needed to get back, the other was going to be left behind. Burned out. With us inside it. I was offended for the Bentley.

"Give him the keys, then, Corman," said Brian shortly. He was impatient to be moving. Good. Impatience could be made to work for us.

Dick grinned as he passed me the keys.

"Take care of my car," he said.

"Oh, fuck the bleeding car," said Brian. "Get moving."

As we approached it, the Bentley's elegant mass seemed wildly inappropriate to its present mission. Even Brian couldn't repress a whistle.

"Jesus H. Christ!" he said. "Some meat wagon!" Shoving Nicki in the back, he climbed into the passenger seat and wrenched her forward with a fistful of hair. He pinned her face to the back of the seat and held the blade to her neck while I climbed in. From what I could see, she had to be half-kneeling in the well.

"Okay," said Brian. "Now drive. Nicely."

After years in New York without a car, it had been tough enough to manage the automated Regal that I had rented. The Bentley was too much car. I fumbled with the ignition, remembering that I had seen Dick work the throttle. The high-performance engine thundered alive and growled at me while I studied the gear shift. Dick must have been cringing for his immaculate machine.

I shifted into first. We jerked forward a few feet and stalled.

"Jesus, Molnar, can't you fucking drive?"

I grinned at him malevolently and turned the ignition key.

"Not one of these," I said. "Can you?"

"Better bloody learn," said Brian.

I tried again. This time I made it into second and changed up to third.

The late night streets on the east side were deserted, abandoned by all but the hardiest derelicts. I managed to maintain a more or less steady course, following Brian's directions to San Pedro, where we turned left. It could have been no more than four blocks south to Fifth, where we made a right and slowed to be sure that Dick was on our tail.

Around Broadway, I nearly lost him in the burst of activity. It was like walking down an empty corridor and finding an open door to a party: a sudden explosion of Hispanic life—people and lights, music blaring from still open radio stores. And the door was closed again as we followed Fifth past Pershing Square, and dropped down the short hill by the library into the affluent high-rise business area on the west side of downtown, as desolate in its way as the deserted east side.

Dick was still with me. The changing play of our head and tail lights made magic on the canyon walls of reflective glass. At the western perimeter of downtown, we started up the ramp where the westbound lane of Fifth sweeps up in a long curve over the Harbor Freeway. A sudden switch to brights in the rearview mirror warned me that Dick might make a move.

I glanced at Brian. He still had a handful of Nicki's hair, with her head pinned forward. But he was moody and distracted, his mind still moving forward, rehearsing whatever he had planned for us.

Dick's headlights made a sudden leap.

THIRTY-FIVE

◇

The lights swept sideways up the ramp, across three lanes, accelerating forward. Chung's Pontiac flashed past the Bentley. Brian's head twitched to watch as it went by. At first it didn't register.

"Fucking maniac," he said. "Bleeding road hog."

Then, half turned in his seat, he realized that it was Dick who had just sped past us in the far right lane. His hold on Nicki's head was tightened and she shrieked as he pulled the hair in like a rein. He sat there, tense and ready.

I drove on slowly up the ramp. From up ahead, slightly beyond the curve, came a sudden confusion of lights, a din of metal in collision, the squeal of brakes and tires. The next thing I saw was the blinding glare of headlights as Dick came back round the bend, accelerating the wrong way down the ramp straight for us.

Reacting automatically, I slammed my foot down on the brake and cut in to the left. We bounced up on the curb, crushing the Bentley's nose against the freeway parapet. Dick swerved, too, and skidded down the ramp, broadsiding the Bentley on the passenger side. Brian caught the brunt of the impact and flung his hands up to protect his face. His body was catapulted up and over mine. Nicki was free, rattling around and screaming in the back.

I grabbed for the door handle and wrenched it open, half falling out into the street. I heard the Pontiac's engine gunned again as the car crunched forward furiously, spinning wheels and tearing metal from the Bentley's fender. I caught a glimpse of Dick as he fought with the steering wheel, and Chung beside him, dazed in fright.

I reached back into the Bentley, grabbing Brian by a boot. He kicked viciously as I dragged him out, then struggled to regain his balance on the street. Taking a good step back, I lunged with the full weight of my body and drove my fist into his face. Blood spurted from his nose and he staggered back toward the parapet. One more and I could knock him over. I sprang to let him have it.

It wasn't necessary.

Backed into the narrow angle between the Bentley and the parapet, he glanced at me, then back over his shoulder. He wiped the blood from his face with the length of his forearm, then clambered up, half on the Bentley's hood, half on the parapet.

My first thought was that he was trying to climb across the car, to escape on the other side. But he simply stood there for a moment, reeling slightly, and looked down at the freeway with his familiar death's head grin. Then he turned to me with a look I won't forget—it came from some strange place between rage and triumph.

I couldn't tell then and have never been able to decide whether he actually stumbled over in a daze or whether he jumped. I believe he jumped, trying to show me something in that moment—if only that this was the final satisfaction, the act of self-destruction, the consummation of what his life had been about. The ultimate orgasm. A work of art.

"Fuck it," he said. He was already falling. I had the strangest feeling he was trying to wave goodbye.

In any event, he went over and landed in the path of a northbound semi whose driver didn't have time to touch the brakes before it hit him. It carried him two hundred yards and lumbered to a stop, beyond the next bridge.

"Jesus!" Dick was beside me now. We stood silent for a moment, watching the chain reaction on the freeway. Then he laid a hand on my shoulder and showed me Burke's handgun. "Does my car start?" he asked. I shrugged.

He climbed in the Bentley and turned over the engine. It started. He left it running and climbed out again, checking to see if the wheels were free. "What next?" he asked.

I still couldn't find the words or the will to act. Chung sat in the passenger seat of his own car, staring ahead without moving. No wonder Dick had left him: The man was a zombie.

Nicki was in the back seat of the Bentley, clutching her head between her hands. I stood at the parapet and gazed down the freeway to where the truck had stopped. Its trailer had jack-knifed across three lanes and traffic was already beginning to back up. A couple of cars had pulled into the emergency lane, their drivers running forward, caught in the headlight beams.

Strange, the physical dislocation between effect and cause. It was as though we had had nothing to do with the scene below and beyond us, on the freeway.

"Well," asked Dick again. "What next?"

I glanced at him, then back at the distant scene. A minute, not more, had passed. No police yet. Aside from the four of us, there were no witnesses up here.

There was a certain justice, I reflected, in the way Brian had died. But the feeling of satisfaction I had somehow expected was absent. The sense of unfinished business was still stronger than the sense of business now complete. It was after midnight.

"Home?" I said finally.

He nodded.

"Is Chung's car working?" I asked.

Dick nodded again. "It'll make it," he told me.

Nicki was fine but dazed. It was pointless to move her from the Bentley. I left her there to return home with Dick. Chung was still stupefied when I opened the passenger door of the Pontiac. I pulled him out to the street.

"You're going to drive," I said.

He looked at me as if he had never seen me in his life before.

"It's your car. Drive," I said.

I watched him walk obediently round the car. He seemed not to notice the wrenched metal. Once in, he drove without question, following my directions. It was hard to tell if he was even aware that we were following Dick. The man's mind seemed to have crashed to a halt on the freeway overpass. Okay. So long as we could bring him back later.

Chung's silence gave me the chance to think. I had never much believed in the spirits of the dead, and talk of their restlessness would have struck me as romantic, sentimental. But now I imagined I could actually feel them—the spirits of Worthing, Laura, Carlos, Patty Drayton. Even of Brian Brain. Not fanciful, but painful, real. They needed to be laid to rest.

Chung was a good place to start. He wasn't much in himself. But he had to know more about the source of the Worthing Nelsons he had sold to the Conners and might know where he could find more.

It was a twenty-minute drive to Dick's studio. We found the building lit like an ocean liner in the surrounding dark. Yumiko was already at the door before the Pontiac pulled in beside Dick's Bentley, out of her mind with anxiety: Dick must have left eight hours ago, expecting to be gone no more than a couple. Her English was lost somewhere between anxiety and rage. Language exploded in torrents of confusion.

Dick put a hand across her mouth and reached the other arm around her shoulder, wrapping her firmly into his own large body. "It's okay," he said.

He led her indoors with Chung, while I reached in the back of the Bentley to help Nicki.

THIRTY-SIX

◇

Together, Dick and Yumiko made coffee while I poured whiskey into tumblers and set one each in front of Chung and Nicki. Chung remained stolid and silent, but there was evidence of life returning, a reaction in the eyes.

"It's not what you'd expected, no?" I asked him. Chung was a man, I sensed, who would respond better to a quiet approach than to anger or aggression. He shook his head and reached for the whiskey glass.

"At least he may have helped to save our collective skin," said Dick, bringing coffee. "His friend Brian would happily have rubbed out the lot of us if Chung hadn't let us make a move on him."

All of us knew there wasn't more than a grain of truth in what Dick said, including Chung, but it showed him a way to save some face. We let him chew on that for a while, and I tried to encourage Nicki to take a shot of whiskey. She had been savaged by more than the trauma of the past few hours, and barely found the energy to respond.

"You want to get off to bed?" I asked her.

She shook her head, but then got up and left the room without a word. I let her go, turning my attention back to Chung.

"For now," I told him, "I'm going to ask your help—in exchange for whatever help we can give you, when that time comes."

Chung nodded and Dick and I sat watching him for a while, allowing him time to work out all the options. He didn't have many, as he must have realized. We had him by the balls.

"First off," I said, "I need to know where the Worthing Nelsons came from."

"New York," he said. "What I told the Conners was the truth: They come directly from the estate. They're genuine." He reeled this off effortlessly, but his mind was elsewhere. He could afford to tell me what I already knew.

"I know they're genuine," I said. "But where are they? The rest of the collection, I mean. Who has them? Ten years of work, Chung! One of the major artists of the century. Brian Brain didn't have it in him to pull that one off."

Chung looked up at me slowly and I knew he had reached the conclusion that there was more to lose by silence than to gain.

Dick filled the whiskey glass again and Chung took another swig, shaking his head as though in disbelief.

"I'll tell you what I know," he said, "for what it's worth. It's probably less than you expect."

"Let's give it a shot," I said.

Chung leaned over toward me, elbows on his knees.

"The first contact I had," he said, "was from a New York collector, Leo Wolff. I guess you know of him?"

I nodded.

"Wolff called to let me know he had a couple of Worthing Nelsons he wanted to sell. Could I help him? It had to be outside New York and it had to be confidential. For personal reasons, he said. No publicity. He'd heard I was a reputable private dealer and that I had good contacts. Could I handle the paintings?"

He could, of course, and did—he had no reason not to. The reputation he'd established was still relatively slight and the attention from a major collector in New York was flattering. The chance to sell a Worthing Nelson was a huge boost for his career.

"And then?" I asked.

"A couple of weeks later I went to an opening at the museum and ran into another collector from New York. He was here on other business, but he found time to come around to my office—this was before I even had the gallery. He said he'd heard good things about me from his friend Leo Wolff and would I be interested in handling a few more Worthing Nelsons? Same terms. Confidential."

"Did this collector have a name?" I asked.

Chung hesitated. This was to be the final hurdle. Everything else would be easy. I nodded encouragement.

"You might as well tell me now," I said. "I'm going to find out sometime. You'd do better to let me hear it from you."

"Traceman," said Chung. "It was Dan Traceman."

I glanced across at Dick, who shrugged and leaned back on the sofa, crossing his heels on the coffee table.

"And it was Traceman who Brian referred to as the 'old geezer' before you locked us in the bathroom?"

"It was supposed to be," said Chung. "But he never showed up. I've no idea what happened between him and Brian. Brian left after a telephone call, and didn't show up again until you saw him."

I remembered the moment and shuddered at the thought that we could all of us be dead by now.

"Back up a bit," said Dick. "It didn't occur to you there might be something underhand going on when you first met Traceman? You'd surely have known enough about Worthing Nelson to be shocked when paintings from the Seventies started showing up."

Chung looked from Dick to me and back. "I'd picked up twenty thousand on the first sale," he admitted simply. "I'd never made so much on a single deal before and I couldn't turn it down. I guess I had those questions, but I didn't want to ask them."

Dick sighed. "Who was it said you couldn't cheat an honest man?" he asked.

Chung looked at him, puzzled.

"Go on," said Dick.

"Well, I sold the next couple, and a couple more— that's when the Conners bought. Traceman kept coming back again, and it wasn't long before we had a working relationship. Things went so well that he proposed the idea of a gallery here and helped to work out a deal with Samantha Dmitri. He invested the capital himself."

"You didn't object to being a front for Traceman's operations?" I asked.

"I guess I just didn't see it that way. It seemed like a miracle. You know how hard it is to make it in this business. I was making money for the first time in my life and I've been working at it for the past twelve years."

"Back to the Worthing Nelsons. You never asked Traceman how he'd acquired his supply? He never let on how many of them he had?"

"I had the impression the source was Nelson's lover— though Traceman never told me this directly."

"Nicholas?"

"Was that his name? Anyway, Traceman told me there wasn't very much of it, but what there was had been left to Nicholas in Nelson's will. The guy needed money."

"And why the confidentiality? Why not tell the world?"

"Business, Dan said. To help control the supply."

"And you never had second thoughts about Traceman's operation? You never thought there could be a connection between the Worthing Nelson profits and the capital he used to float the gallery? You yourself could never have considered it without those sales."

"That's true. But I never had reason to believe the sales were illegal."

"No gut feeling, no instinct, nothing?" I insisted.

Chung looked at me.

"I never felt completely comfortable with Traceman, no, if that's what you're asking," he said. "I'd have preferred to do without his help. But it wasn't hard to swallow something a little less than perfect, to get the gallery going. Everything was fine until . . ."

He lapsed into silence, frowning, trying to fit things back into a pattern. I allowed him a few moments before prompting him.

"Until?" I asked.

"I guess you already know that Carlos Smith came

in, a couple of weeks ago. At first I thought it was just a courtesy visit—one of Samantha's artists stopping by to check out the gallery in L.A. I was kind of flattered to have him in there. But then he saw the Patty Drayton in the back room and went crazy.

Chung's eyes went wild and he started to gesticulate as Carlos had done. Then he realized what he was doing and stopped, suddenly self-conscious.

"I don't remember how we got on to the Worthing Nelsons," he went on. "I've no idea now how he knew about them. The guy just ranted on, accusing me of everything from fraud to murder. It got so bad I had to throw him out. It was after he'd gone that I discovered one of Dan Traceman's sets of Worthing Nelson slides was missing."

"Did you tell Traceman?"

"Of course. I called him right away and told him the whole story."

"And?"

"He sent Brian out a couple of days later. That's when it really hit me, what I was involved with. Whatever else, Dan had always been a pleasure to work with, he's an intelligent, sophisticated man. I couldn't believe he'd have anything to do with this Brian. The guy was just a . . . just a . . ."

Chung couldn't find the word for it.

"A killer," I said.

"I didn't know that," he said sadly. "Not until tonight."

"And when you heard that Carlos Smith was killed?"

"I was relieved," Chung admitted. "I guess I was satisfied with the easy answer—that he'd been mugged. It wasn't until Brian got here, looking for you, that I couldn't pretend to myself any longer."

"And now?" asked Dick.

"Now," said Chung slowly. "Now it's a nightmare. All I want is for it to stop. God knows, I wish I'd never got involved."

THIRTY-SEVEN

◇

The first storm of the season hit Los Angeles that night. It was long overdue, Dick told me, and seemed to come down the heavier for that. Even before we turned Chung loose in his damaged Pontiac, we heard the rain battering at the studio roof. Dick lent him a plastic sheet to get to his car.

We stood together at the door and watched Chung's rearranged headlamps highlight the continuous diagonal lines of rain as he backed across the parking lot, splashing black puddles into dirty foam. It was three in the morning. The incredible fatigue that had earlier knocked out Nicki had hit both of us.

"Shouldn't we call someone?" Dick asked, yawning.

My head reeled at the idea of getting on the telephone. With Brian dead, it seemed pointless to call the police in Los Angeles in the middle of the night. But there was the fall from the ramp they should know about. Did we need to call the fire chief, to put them straight about the Guerreros? The police in New York? It was impossible to know where to start.

"Let it wait until morning," I said. "I'll catch Cynthia at the office. She'll take care of things at that end. We'll worry about the rest of it then."

Nicki was sleeping in the guest room when I got there. Had nothing changed? I climbed in, careful not to wake her.

Sometimes, no matter how tired, you can't fall asleep for the thoughts that crowd in on your head. Sometimes, more rarely, the thoughts are so many, so diverse, so overwhelming that the mind obliges by just blanking out. It must have happened that way. All I remember was waking with Nicki in my arms, the right one numb from the weight of her head. She woke, too.

We found ourselves wearing rumpled clothes, appropriate somehow to the shyness that had come between us. Unlike yesterday's brilliance, the white room now reflected the gray tones of the rain and we lay there, watching each other, lulled by its soft monotone.

"Nicki," I said, "I'm flying back to New York today. I need some time . . ."

I didn't say what I needed time for. I thought she knew.

First I had to change my life. What Carlos had brought into it would churn until I had found its resolution. It was more to me than Carlos Smith or Patty Drayton. More than Dan Traceman or Leo Wolff or Samantha Dmitri. More than Worthing Nelson, more, even, than Laura. I knew it was myself at stake.

Carlos's call had asked me a question that was very specific, very personal. It said: Are you dead, Jake Molnar, like these other artists? It said: What is this bullshit? You claim the role of the last great defender of humanity in art, and you shut yourself off in your studio and communicate with no one. And finally it said: Here's an issue involving life and death—resolve it. It was not something I could leave to others.

Could I explain all that to Nicki? It hadn't been easy coming to understand it myself.

"Will I see you again?" Nicki asked. She reached out to touch my face.

"I don't know," I said. There were too many conflicting emotions for us to be able to go through explanations, I decided. Too much guilt and betrayal, on both sides. Too much need, too little thought or patience. She must have known as well as I did, for she didn't press the point.

It was a curious irony that the first and only time I reached Cynthia from Los Angeles was that Sunday, when I was about to board the plane back to New York. I called from Dick's telephone in the studio while Nicki was helping with breakfast. This time, I caught Cynthia in the office. I gave her the short version, sticking to the facts—the fire at the Guerreros', Sam and the Conners, an edited account of the Nicki saga, the Burke Chung Gallery, and last night's climax on the freeway bridge. Then Burke Chung's capitulation.

"I was right," I told her, "about Traceman."

After a moment's silence she said, "I still find it hard to believe. Maybe there's some other explanation."

"Cynthia, facts are facts."

"There's always different ways of looking at them," she said.

"Not in this case, baby. Listen, will you do a couple of things for me while I'm in the air?"

"Of course. What are they?"

"First, give a call to Lieutenant Richards at this number." I read it off to her. "Just bring him up to date with what happened here in L.A. I'm afraid if I get on the phone with him, he'll want me to go in and make statements here. Tell him I'll check in with him first thing in New York, and he'll get everything I know."

"Okay. What else?"

"Find out where Traceman is . . ."

"Christ, Jake. I've got a reputation to protect . . ."

"No, seriously. Screw the reputation. This isn't some art world game. This is murder and mayhem."

"If you say so."

"I say so. Just ask around. Whatever it takes. Supposedly he was here in L.A. last night, as I told you. Something tells me he's headed back for New York, and somehow—soon—he's going to have to drop out of sight. Things are starting to come apart—too many people know too much, at this point. The irony would be to find him on my flight."

He wasn't. Dick and Nicki took me to the airport and we said goodbye, not at the boarding gate but at the loading zone, down among the taxis and the shuttle buses. A hug for Nicki and a hug for Dick. I watched them drive away in the rain, the battered side of the Bentley the only reminder of an event that seemed so remote.

The rain streaked the windows of the 747 as it lumbered toward takeoff. We climbed and burst through the cloud cover into canyons of brilliant angel stuff.

Who knows what I would have done if he had been there, but I checked the rows for Traceman anyway, after the seat belt sign went off. He wasn't there.

I returned to my seat and toyed with a newspaper, trying to turn away thoughts of Nicki. The image that kept returning was her hands—the traces of paint and the broken fingernail.

The jet made a big sweep out over the Pacific and turned back east, over the coastline and the city. The freeways glittered below us with the flow of traffic. By now Dick would have joined it, heading downtown to drop off Nicki at her studio. I had left all the chores to him. When he got back home, he was planning to check in first with an attorney and then with the police. We hadn't been able to figure out if we'd broken any laws.

We crossed the Rockies and flew into dusk over the Midwest. I passed on the movie and instead looked down on the expanse of unchanging landscape. I thought of Cynthia. As darkness grew, the ordered rows of pinpoint lights, remotely spaced, defined the distances between villages and towns. Somewhere down there, North Liberty was hibernating under a layer of ice and snow, awaiting the brief release of spring and the swelter of steaming summer. I remembered her sweet, guilty passion in the cornfields, could taste the saltlick of her creamy body.

I settled back in my seat and slept till I was awakened by the pressure of descent.

THIRTY-EIGHT

◇

The plane nosed up to its boarding gate soon after seven New York time. I heard a small voice trying to tell me something, but I had too many ready explanations for my nerves to bother listening. I wasn't sure I was ready to be home. From this distance, L.A. looked like a summer paradise and Nicki like its angel. I pulled down my winter coat from the storage bin.

We inched forward to the bottleneck at the single exit by the cockpit. The flight attendants waited with the usual flutter of smiles and thanks, but this time they had company: I recognized the man from the morning I had gone alone to visit Carlos's studio.

"Callahan," he reminded me. He showed me his badge again. "Lieutenant Richards asked me to meet you here, Mr. Molnar. He needs to talk to you at once."

It was just a flash, but for a moment I was puzzled, on my guard. Did Richards not trust me to check in with him, as I'd had Cynthia promise? Why would he send a man out to the airport? But with a press of curious passengers at my elbows, I wasn't about to stand there arguing with the man. I turned and led him up the ramp.

Freed from the bottleneck in the aircraft, the herd's pace quickened, lumbering through the concertina passage into a blast of artificial heat as we emerged into the reception area.

Foolishly, I'd allowed my guard to drop. A figure stepped out toward me in the crush of passengers and welcomers with a smile and a hand extended. I was the perfect patsy. I had already started to smile back as you do when someone greets you and you're not sure who they are, but you don't want to offend them. I had started to extend my hand when I placed him.

I had seen him before, and in the same context. It was at Kennedy Airport, when I had waved goodbye.

In the second it took to recognize him, I picked out another detail: the gun grasped easily in the palm of the extended hand.

He counted on surprise and the confusion of the crowd. A moment's hesitation and I would have died, but instinctive reaction saved me. I took advantage of my forward motion, throwing my weight behind it, bringing both the valise and the winter coat forward and up toward him, releasing them as they made heavy contact with his body. And pushed on, directly into him, spinning him out of my path.

I wasn't sure at what point the gunshot came, but I felt its heat and smelled the burned cordite. I pushed on, faster, farther, leaving Callahan in the thickening crowd among screams and panic. Coatless and caseless, I was already gone.

I ran through the airport corridors. Bullied my way past others in the taxi line and had the driver head downtown while I took time to think.

What next?

I checked my pockets. Nothing.

Of course. For comfort on the flight, I had transferred the wallet from my hip pocket to the side compartment of the valise. Now that was gone, along with my cash and credit cards. I was left with the change from a ten-dollar bill I had stuck in my shirt pocket after buying a beer. There was no way now I would dare risk a stop at the studio, not even for the time to pick up clothes: I had set myself up too many times already.

Callahan was at the airport when they had tried to kill me. Had he been there to lead the lamb to the slaughter? Could Richards be in Traceman's pocket? Why not? Traceman could afford it. With a start I remembered that Richards was the only one other than Cynthia to know I had returned from Los Angeles.

I needed shelter and warmth, for a night at least.

Before that, I would need the money to pay off the cab driver.

Cynthia? She was too obvious, too dangerous—for her and me.

One by one, I checked through all my old contacts in the art world and crossed them off the list. I hadn't realized that I had let things get this far, to be left with no one to turn to in an emergency. Elmer? He was a possibility. I didn't know where he lived, but he might be listed in the phone book. An even more improbable solution occurred to me, though, and I leaned forward on impulse to give the driver new directions.

It was after eight and the downtown traffic was light. I wasn't sure of the street address, but we turned on Twelfth and I had the driver slow to a crawl as we passed the storefronts there. If I had guessed right, Frank Stevenson would be there even late on Sunday: His piece was due to open within a week—the kind of deadline that keeps artists working late.

The reflection of worklights glared around the edges of the installation and through the glass panel of the door. He had to be there.

"Wait," I told the driver. "I'll be back with the fare." He had no idea how much blind faith in a fellow artist was behind the promise.

By God it was cold! In California shirtsleeves and without a coat, I knocked, and froze, and prayed a little to the god of the deaf, waiting for Stevenson to catch the vibrations of my presence there. If only he would open, I could talk to him. What were the chances he'd see me and hurl imprecations through the door?

"Stevenson," I yelled at him as he lumbered up and squinted into the darkness. "It's me, Jake Molnar!"

He scowled.

"For Christ's sake, let me in! I'm freezing half to death out here!" I mouthed the key words out and mimed my meaning.

There was a moment when I thought he wasn't going to, but he opened up and I slipped in through the crack he allowed me. Thank God for artists!

"Listen," I said, careful that he could see each

movement of my lips, "I'm desperate. My clothes and money are gone, I've nowhere to go. I need help. I can explain why I came to you, but first I need a twenty."

He looked at me as though I had lost my mind.

"To pay off the cab," I said. "I'm good for the money. I'll pay you back."

With an expression that showed he questioned his own sanity as much as mine, he reached into his pocket and pulled out a tattered bundle of notes. He sorted out a twenty and handed it to me without a word.

"Thanks," I told him. "I'll be right back."

I paid off the cab driver and got back to find Frank sitting by his electric heater with a cigarette. A bottle of Beam stood on the bare boards in front of him, and a pair of aluminum tumblers. With a gesture he invited me to join him and ran a hand through his hair as he watched me. He pushed a paint-splattered thermal jacket over to me and slowly nodded as I put it on.

"I think I was wrong," he said, with his curious words and gestures. "I'm sorry."

"That makes two of us," I told him. "I should never have tried to bullshit you. I'm sorry, too."

We drank, and the whiskey brought a glow not only to the belly but to the surface of the skin that I had thought was never going to thaw. We drank some more as we talked. Rather, I talked, letting him watch the words take shape on my lips and link with each other into a continuous narrative. It was strange—and strangely comfortable—to feel the story take this physical form. It became curiously more believable as it passed from lip to eye, rather than throat to ear.

By the time I finished, I felt that Stevenson's eyes had devoured whatever truth was in me. He had made no comment and asked no questions along the way.

I touched his knee, to bring his eyes back to me. "What I need," I told him, "is a place to spend the night. I can't go back to my place. Everyone's looking for me and I can't tell the good guys from the bad. I don't want to meet up with any of them yet."

He sat there, nodding and thoughtful, caught in the drift of the smoke from his cigarette.

"I need somewhere that no one would think to look for me. Tomorrow I'll contact my ex-wife and follow up on some of the leads we've put together. Do you have a spare bed? Can you put me up? I'll pay you back for any expense, of course."

He rejected the last thought angrily, shaking his head.

"You're welcome to stay at my place," he told me, "for as long as you like. If you don't mind being a little primitive." He grinned at me. "My clothes won't fit you, though."

He threw his head back and laughed a huge, braying laugh and slapped an arm around my shoulder. I had found a friend.

THIRTY-NINE

◇

"I was nearly finished anyway," said Stevenson. "Let's go."

I kept the paint-splattered jacket that had brought me back to life in the studio—a loan I had more reason to be grateful for when we emerged into the streets again: It was late, and colder still.

Reason argued that there was no way I could have been tracked to Stevenson's storefront, but I checked the street before we started out. Nothing. It was filled with as much silence and darkness as you're ever likely to find in a Manhattan street.

It was impossible to walk and talk with Frank Stevenson. It was barely possible to walk with him.

At the corner of West Broadway and Houston, a patrol car parked at the curbside pumped white exhaust plumes into the night air. I wondered again about Richards and the police. What chance did I have if they were with Traceman? With that trust blown, I had only friends to fall back on. Old friends and new. Cynthia. Elmer and Stevenson.

Frank's head was somewhere up ahead of us, forging a way through the night air. It never occurred to him to do anything but walk. How easily I had slipped into the cultural change from the sidewalk to the roadway.

We ended up in Tribeca, at the far southwestern tip of Manhattan. The moon appeared between deserted buildings, its light reflected frostily on the uneven, potholed surface of still cobbled streets. Rows of steel roller doors, all lowered at this time of night like eyelids, fed my impression that we'd surfaced in some De Chirico painting.

Frank's studio was in a block-long building whose ground floor was a wholesale produce outlet. There was no elevator. Our footsteps pounded up flights of wooden steps to the fourth floor.

Primitive, Frank had said. Well, it was warm—and I couldn't think of anything that mattered more. It was small by comparison with SoHo lofts. A single, fair-sized room with a platform at the far end from the window, it didn't even boast the luxury of a high ceiling.

Up on the platform, a kitchen range, refrigerator, sink, and tub with plastic-curtained shower were installed without concern for privacy. A single cot with a nest of blankets was crowded in, and a waist-high curtain veiled what I guessed to be the toilet. There were sketches pinned up everywhere on the walls, and down at the far end by the window, a drafting table was buried in books and papers. Beside it stood a handsome relic from the Twenties, an enormous over-stuffed sofa. That was it. It was clean and cared for— home to a man who could sacrifice the creature comforts.

Frank dug another bottle of Jim Beam from a kitchen cabinet and waved it at me. This time I turned him down, preferring the sleeping bag and pillow he retrieved from under the sofa.

Whatever else, I couldn't but feel safe, this far from every path I had beaten in the past ten years, and the sofa welcomed me with ample comfort. I could have slept a night and a day, but for the roar of produce trucks backing in to loading bays, the clatter of doors and dollies, and the yells of early workers before dawn.

Even so, I must have slept again fitfully for some time and I found that Frank was already gone when I woke. It was close to ten.

He'd left a note on the table under a jam jar. "Help yourself," it said. "I won't be around here much myself. If you need to get in touch, try at the storefront.

I'll be there most all the time. Meantime, the place is yours. I'll be back late. Good luck!"

With the note, he'd left a small stack of shopworn dollar bills and a pair of keys.

While I drank the remains of his coffee, still hot on the gas burner, I realized that what I needed most was what Frank might well not have: a telephone. What use would a deaf man have for such a thing? But I nosed around anyway and unearthed a strange black box that featured a small panel of lights along with a dial and a receiver. It looked like no phone I had ever seen, but it made a dial tone when I lifted the receiver. I dialed Cynthia's office number and sat down with my coffee, listening to the ring.

"Artresearch."

"Cynthia?"

"Jake! Is that you? Jake?"

She'd been worried and was relieved to hear from me. I grinned.

"Hi, Cynthia. Yeah. It's me."

"Jake, where the hell have you been? I was expecting you back last night and you didn't call. I just spent half the night trying to reach you at the studio. Are you home?"

"No, I'm not home. I'm back in New York, but not home. They're after me, baby."

"After you?"

"They tried to kill me. At the airport, just after I arrived."

The fact of it hit me as I put it into words. I felt nauseated. The idea of being dead was never so real. More important, the need to stay alive had never seemed so vital.

"Jake? They tried to kill you?"

"It must be in the papers. Have you seen this morning's *Daily News*? Gunman at Kennedy, that kind of thing?"

"I haven't seen any kind of paper yet. But listen, Jake, where the hell are you now? For Christ's sake, let me help!"

I was ready to practice some self-restraint and fore-thought for a change. "I can't tell you, Cynthia."

"What do you mean, you can't tell me? This is me, Cynthia! Don't be ridiculous, Jake."

"Listen," I said, "we already know what happens to anyone who helps me. They get clobbered. They already know I've been in touch with you and probably that you've been feeding me information. Now they've lost me. What do they do? They do the same thing I'd do if I were them: I'd go to the person who might know and knock it out of them. It's better you don't know, for my sake as well as yours."

There was a silence at the other end of the line while Cynthia thought through this scenario.

"You have to trust someone, Jake," she said. "You're quite sure you're not exaggerating this whole thing?"

It was my turn to explode.

"Jesus Christ, Cynthia, what kind of a child do you take me for? I've seen three people slaughtered in the past week. I've been attacked with knives and guns and damn near pushed a man to his death off a free-way bridge, and you ask me if I'm not exaggerating! Grow up! If you want to help, for Christ's sake help. Don't waste my time with bullshit!"

Another silence. "Right," she said. "I guess you're right. Just tell me what I can do."

"I assume you called Richards?" I asked.

"Of course. You asked me to, didn't you?"

"If it hadn't been for yesterday at the airport," I said, "I'd have had you contact him. You might need protection. Now I'm not sure where I stand with the guy. Better hold off on that. But I do need Nicholas's address, he's one of the keys. Have you tracked him down?

"Well," she said nervously, "I've been having some trouble . . ."

I knew she was stalling. She didn't want me going there by myself.

"Cynthia," I said, "don't bullshit me. Just give me the address."

I almost heard the tumblers fall as she made up her

mind. Then she gave me an address in the upper eighties, West Side.

"I still haven't heard what else you've managed to find out," I said. "About those paintings, and the Dmitri artists. I'd have thought you'd have managed to turn up something by now. What's with the Fortune?"

"Listen, I have everything legitimate under the sun. When it comes to shady deals, I just don't get the information. I've been trying, Jake. I'll keep trying for you. Is there anything else?"

I thought a moment. I had found two addresses for Traceman in the telephone book—from their locations, I guessed a residence and a business.

"Yes," I said. "You can check around to see whether Traceman has a warehouse of some kind for his collection. There's no way he'd be keeping the Worthing Nelsons at home or at the office. So where are they? Once I find them, I've got everything I need. Okay? Meantime, stall everyone."

She wasn't too happy with the arrangement. "How am I going to reach you, Jake?" she asked.

"You're not," I said, "I'm going to reach you."

FORTY

◇

Try withdrawing a couple of thousand bucks in cash from a New York bank with no ID, no driver's license, no major credit card. Frank Stevenson's thermal jacket didn't help.

Even at my own bank in the Village I had to go all the way to the top before I got authorization, and then only because the manager knew my work. A New York banker. You couldn't hope to find another one like that outside the city.

"Do I have to draw you a picture?" I asked him with a grin.

He had a print of mine from the Sixties in his collection. By sheer good luck, it was one I happened to remember and could tell him about. He thought he knew my face from the magazines.

"Would you be interested," I asked, "in an original? A drawing, I mean, not a print?"

I borrowed a yellow pad from his desk and sat down opposite him at the desk, exploring his face. In five minutes, I had come up with a sketch that seemed headed in the right direction, signed it, and passed it to him. He gasped.

"I didn't know you did this kind of work," he said.

"Nor do most other people," I assured him. "You're the first. Take a look at the signature."

All in all, he was ready to take the risk.

My next stop was Macy's. Frank's jacket wasn't a big hit there either. I climbed into new long johns and jeans, a heavy, big-check Pendleton, ski cap, and jacket—and a pair of sunglasses. New man, new image. I had them wrap Frank's jacket up with a bunch of other work clothes and truck it off to his job site.

I felt more like a visiting lumberjack than a New York artist. Heading north from Macy's, I stopped off at the nearest barber shop. I had worn the fierce red stubble on my chin for twenty years. It was time for it to go. It was worth the sacrifice, even if a naked chin would only stall pursuit for a little while. I sat up in the chair when the job was done, and glared at my rediscovered chin in the mirror, pointing it this way and that. Even with the mustache still in place, my face felt naked.

I took a cab up to the eighties and walked across the park to reach the address I had copied down from Cynthia. The cold air bit at my chin, but the walk was marvelously bracing. I felt alive again by the time I reached the double glass doors to the apartment building.

The only surprise in getting past the doorman was that it proved so easy: I slipped the guy in uniform a ten and told him I wanted to surprise my friend Nick Lazarus on his birthday. He gave me a curious, big wink. Maybe he knew that Nicholas was gay. Maybe everyone in the building was gay. That was the least of my worries.

I took the elevator up to the eighteenth floor, where there seemed to be only two apartments. I found Nicholas's place down to the right and rang the bell. No answer. Nicholas could have been at work, but work was something I had never associated with the man. I rang again. There was still no answer, but I could make out sounds when I put my ear to the door. I tried the handle. It was locked.

It wasn't hard to guess from a glance down the corridor at the configuration of the two apartments. There were four doors, two of them unmarked, suggesting service entrances to each. I tried the handle of the one that had to lead into apartment B.

It was unlocked. I tensed. Something had to be very wrong if a door was left unlocked in this city. I pushed gently and waited.

God, the place stank. Cats.

Even before the door was fully opened, the stench was overpowering. I stepped inside and found my leather soles scrunching on grit. I fumbled for a light switch.

Kitty Litter. Green stuff. Everywhere there were shallow boxes of it that couldn't have been emptied for a week. A whole bag had been knocked down, perhaps by kitty paws, and emptied over the red-brown kitchen tiles.

In another corner, they'd done the same with cat food—ripped the bags apart, leaving mounds of pellets spilling over the floor. And there were furry creatures moving everywhere, stalking or sleeping, high and low. A few of them ran toward me when the light went on. Others looked up and blinked. Most didn't even bother.

There had to be a score of them in there.

Aside from the spilled cat food, I noticed that cabinets were open where no cat could have reached. Packages seemed to have been thrown out and exploded on the floor.

I managed to pick my way through the mess and found the sitting room in darkness. In light reflected from the kitchen, I found a lamp and reached to switch it on. I barely had my fingers on the switch when a creature hurtled into my leg with a yowl fit to wake the dead and attached itself to flesh with razor claws. Matching his yowl with mine, I kicked him scudding across the room.

I switched on the light and looked around. There were cats here everywhere, too. What had once been expensive furniture was covered with hair and mutilated by their claws. Good Persian rugs were ripped apart. Adjusting with difficulty to the smell, I paused to inspect the room. As in the kitchen, I had the impression that it was more than cats that had destroyed the place.

It was strangely barren. You'd have expected books, pictures on the wall, the usual decorative things. Here there were only a couple of chairs and a couch. The furniture had been upended, slashed apart. Its stuffing spilled out onto the floor and the cushions were scattered in torn fragments. A hall closet had been emptied, its contents strewn in tattered piles around the door. Nothing was left untouched.

And then there were tapes—videocassettes, dozens of them, pulled from their neat black boxes and scattered on the floor by the television set. I picked up a couple. Cheap porn, from the titles. But every last one had been opened. Why?

The bedroom was the same. Ruins. Clothes were pulled out of drawers and closets, and the queen-sized bed was ripped apart. Feathers from pillows carpeted everything like snow.

It was in the bathroom that I found Nicholas. In the bath. Stark naked. Dead.

Stark indeed. I'm used to seeing human bodies nude. It goes with the job I've given myself to do. But I had never seen anything that approached this sight. The flesh was a shocking blue-white against the porcelain that contained it. The scrawny genitals were so far removed from anything like human sex, I barely recognized them for what they were.

I had no way of guessing how long he'd been dead, but I knew the meaning of the length of rubber tubing stretched and knotted around his upper arm and the syringe hanging from the flesh.

In a sudden rush of nausea, I emptied my belly in the toilet. I flushed and grabbed a towel from the rack to wipe my mouth.

Still gagging with the stench of Nicholas, his cats, and my own vomit, I staggered back into the sitting room, more than ready to move on. Yet there was something there that made me stay. The destruction was focused, purposeful, and logic suggested that if they had searched the apartment for anything, it was likely a videotape.

Had they found it? I looked around. The completeness of the job made me think they hadn't. They would have stopped when they found it. Yet there wasn't a corner anywhere undisturbed. Okay, Molnar, use your eye.

Did you ever play those games you find in puzzle books for kids: What's wrong with this picture? Or find the hidden monkey in the tree? I was the champ.

It turned out to be as simple and childish as the game. A fresh dab of color against an old coat of paint on a heating duct. Two screws, I discovered, recently removed and then replaced. I bent down, scraped away the paint, and took the screws out again with the blade of my pocket knife. The black cassette was taped to the inside of the duct.

I read the label: "Brian Brain."

Slipping the tape from its box, I snapped the switch of the VCR beside the television. Even Nicholas in the bathroom couldn't hold me back from this one.

The cassette sank easily into its bed with a click and began to roll. The titles were scrawled in the big, childish writing I had found on the picture of Laura in my studio. "DIRTY OLD MAN," they said. "A VIDEOTAPE BY BRIAN BRAIN." The background for the titles was a crude erection, dripping blood. "TELEPLAY STARRING" —new frame—"THE INCOMPARABLE"— new frame— "WORTHING NELSON"

There's no way you can prepare for such moments in your life. You never expect them, they can't happen to you. And there's no way to describe them when they do. Something happened, painfully, inside my chest—a constriction, an acceleration of the heartbeat. Something in immediate correspondence with the panic in my head.

As the mind builds the sound of the alarm clock into its nightmare, waking from it, my panic found an unexpected echo from outside. The sound of sirens.

Get out.

My reaction was immediate, unhesitating. I popped the cassette from the recorder and ran with it. Slamming the kitchen door behind me, I found the fire stairs and ran, half-stumbled down the eighteen flights and paused at the ground floor. I pushed the door open slightly and found the lobby noisy with police. I caught a glimpse of the doorman's face. It was pale, sweating slightly.

I closed the door. I followed the stairs to an underground garage. I prowled around panting, until I found an unlocked car and sat there in the gloom to catch my breath.

I fought off the image of what had once been Nicholas. Accident, suicide, or murder, it took no expert in police work to question the timing of the thing. One: No question that Nicholas is up to his eyeballs in stealing Worthing's pictures. Two: Starting with Carlos's efforts and continuing with mine, the curtain starts to fall on a highly profitable operation. Three: Nicholas is obviously a weak link in the chain. It must have taken him years to reach the state I had found him in. Four: Someone starts asking questions about Nicholas—myself in Los Angeles, Cynthia, possibly Richards in New York. It won't be long before one of us tracks him down. Five: Nicholas turns up dead. To coin a phrase.

A new idea: My discovery of the body was no more an accident than any other of the events in the sequence. I had become a part of the plan and everything I did had been ordained elsewhere before I did it. I was no longer acting, I was being moved from place to place.

It was time to get out. The sirens had stopped but not the rest of it. They had come for Nicholas, that much was clear. But why now? He had been dead some time. Had someone been waiting for me to show up before they tipped off the police? Was I being watched again?

It was an uncomfortable thought, but at least it got me moving. On the doorman's word they would be starting to look for me, and I wasn't about to stay trapped in the garage. The elevator and the fire stairs were both out of the question. The steel gates to the parking ramp were closed. The owner of the car I had sat in had been thoughtful enough to leave it unlocked. Perhaps . . .

I searched the glove compartment. Nothing. I felt along the top of the visor on the driver's side. A card key. I slipped it out, turned up my collar, and pulled the ski cap down a little farther over my hair, and made myself walk, not run, to the ramp.

I pushed the card in the slot and waited while the gate retracted with quiet precision into the ceiling.

At the top of the ramp I paused, twenty yards east of the front entrance to the building. There were three police cars and an ambulance. A small crowd had begun to gather, held back by a couple of uniformed police. They formed a kind of reception line on each side of the doors, as though some celebrity might emerge at any moment.

I joined the crowd, feeling curiously protected, somehow invisible as one of them. There was a tension in the air, but we were very patient, standing there waiting for something to happen. Very little did. Richards arrived in an unmarked car, with Callahan at his side, his arm in a sling. I stood and watched them with this strange feeling of privilege, as though in the audience of a movie whose star is a personal friend.

A kind of euphoria.

There was a stir in the small crowd when a van from the city sanitation department pulled up beside the ambulance, followed shortly by another from the animal shelter. "Dog bites man," speculated a neighbor.

I had visions of Richards and Callahan chasing cats around the apartment.

The crowd hummed with satisfaction when they finally wheeled Nicholas out—no more than a lump under a gray blanket. I began to feel absolved, at least of this one. He was their business now.

FORTY-ONE

◇

My business was with Dan Traceman. There was no point in pussyfooting round the issue any longer.

I stopped to pick up a *Daily News* and grabbed a southbound cab.

There was a sense of urgency now; this was the final push. It couldn't be long before Richards found out that I had been at Nicholas's apartment: The uniformed doorman had a good look at me, and the missing beard alone was not enough to fool anyone for long.

In any event, I had already added Richards and the New York Police Department to the list of people to be avoided. Whatever the reason, they wanted to get their hands on me. And Traceman would be headed out by now.

The newspaper confirmed it—"material witness" was the phrase. I searched through the final edition of the *News* as I rode back south. It wasn't much of an item among the disasters of the day—a single paragraph item under the headline AIRPORT SHOTS: ARTIST SOUGHT. Callahan had been hurt, not seriously, but enough to earn a mention.

Traceman. I still didn't have the address of his downtown warehouse, but at least I knew where his midtown office was. That was a start.

It was mid-afternoon, a little after three. I paid off the cab driver outside the high-rise on Sixth Avenue—one of those stacks of glass and steel that pass for architecture.

I wouldn't have taken no from anyone. The first to try it was the receptionist at Traceman Enterprises.

Below the image of a soaring eagle, the legend was stenciled on the double glass doors that led to the office suite. The receptionist's desk was opposite the elevator banks, a brushed aluminum job with a brushed aluminum occupant at the center of a huge white space. A monumental Ellsworth Kelly, juxtaposing two resplendent rectangles, one black, one white, hung on the wall behind her. The thing was impeccably minimal, just the job for the corporate wall.

She smiled. "Can I help you?" she asked.

"I need to see Mr. Traceman."

"You have an appointment?" The look she gave my Macy's winter outfit made it clear that she knew I didn't. Happily, I was able to remove the decision from her hands. One of the glass doors opened and a three-piece-suited young man blinked at me as I jumped to hold it open for him and slipped through after him. The woman at the reception desk had barely time to register disapproval.

Offices have a spatial logic of their own that usually leads you to the top if you follow it. I did so, briskly, aware of the decorously subdued alarm that spread in my wake and awaited me, thanks to the intercom, by the time I reached the inner sanctum. The executive secretary, a woman of dedicated competence in her mid-fifties, was already on her feet.

"Mr. Traceman," I said, and strode on past her desk.

"Mr. Traceman isn't in," she insisted. She edged her neatly tailored hips and thighs around the angle of her desk and was hard on my heels as I crossed the threshold into Traceman's office.

She was right. He wasn't.

It was as though a wall had been sliced away, where the glass afforded a panorama of the Manhattan skyline. Outside, similar stacks of glass and steel jockeyed for sky space everywhere. It was breathtaking, as unreal as a photorealist painting.

The office was furnished with a desk, which looked as though it had been positioned for some purpose other than use, and an arrangement of easy chairs around a coffee table.

The other three walls were stacked, salon-style, with a history of the past twenty years of American art. Johns, Rauschenberg, Warhol and Lichtenstein, de Kooning—all the main men. Even, I noticed to my chagrin, a Jacob Molnar. If I remembered right, it was the very painting I had refused to sell him. Plastered like wallpaper across the walls, the paintings might have been so many treasury bills.

Along the wall to my left, a pair of workmen had already started taking them down and stacking them against the wall to be wrapped. They wore Artcart caps, the specialists in crating.

"Where's Traceman?" I asked my escort rudely.

She gave me a look to let me know she wouldn't tell me if she knew, but answered far more pleasantly than she thought I deserved.

"Mr. Traceman," she said, "will not be in today."

"Where can I find him?"

"Surely you can't expect me to let you have that information," she told me calmly. "You haven't even had the courtesy to tell us who you are."

It was entirely possible, I realized, that Traceman Enterprises was legitimate and that no one here had reason to question Traceman's ethics. Whatever they might have thought of him as a boss, I was the invader.

"Listen," I said, with an attempt at patience. "I need to see him desperately. I know he'll want to see me. This may sound ridiculous, but I'm the artist who painted that picture."

I pointed out which one, but it was her turn to shrug.

"It doesn't really matter who you are," she said. "I don't know where Mr. Traceman is today, and I wouldn't tell you if I did."

I gave it one more try.

"Can you tell me where these pictures are being taken?" I asked.

Her look told me it was none of my business, but I suppose she thought the answer to this one wouldn't get her into any trouble and would make the firm look good.

"They're to be included," she told me primly, "in a museum exhibition."

"All of them?" I asked.

She nodded. "All of them," she said. "It's the Traceman Collection."

"And where is the exhibition?" I asked.

She began to look uncomfortable again. "I don't believe I'm at liberty to discuss that," she said, "without Mr. Traceman's approval."

Understandably, I thought. Traceman seemed to be moving as fast as I had feared, and faster than I would have hoped.

"Perhaps Mr. Traceman's at his downtown warehouse," I suggested. "Could you give me the address?"

This time I read a different meaning in her eyes. It seemed to me there was a genuine confusion, but she wasn't about to confess ignorance of the Traceman empire.

"Warehouse?" she said. "Downtown? I'm sure you must be mistaken. Traceman Enterprises has no such facility, to my knowledge." She conveyed the conviction that anything she didn't know about Traceman Enterprises was either a fiction or wholly not worth knowing. Looking at her, I was inclined to believe her self-appraisal.

"And you have no telephone where you can reach him when he's not in the office?"

Clearly she had, but just as clearly she was obliged to persist in the lie. "Mr. Traceman can't be reached today," she said.

"Suppose you called and asked him if he'd see me?"

"I can try to set up an appointment for you, if you leave your name and number. Otherwise, there's really nothing I can do."

She led me back to her desk as she answered my questions and, now that she was back behind it, punched a couple of numbers on the intercom.

"Security?" she said. But I was on my way before help arrived.

FORTY-TWO

◇

Cynthia's part-time help was on the job that afternoon. Ginni came to the door to check me out when she heard the buzzer. She stared at me through the glass pane in the door for a moment without recognizing me, until I realized what the problem was. I had already forgotten about the beard.

I grinned at her and traced a finger round my chin.

"Beard!" I mouthed at her through the glass. "It's gone!"

She smiled and let me in. Ginni wore her hair in a 1920s flapper style, with a band around it. She was usually bubbling with much more enthusiasm than art world chic dictates, and I liked her for it. Today, I found her solemn.

"My God, Jake," she said. "You look so different! I never saw you without a beard before." She was too well bred to mention the clothes.

"Not many have," I told her. "You should be so old. Where's Cynthia?"

"I was just hoping you'd be able to tell me," she said. My blood froze. "It's the strangest thing," she went on, "I got here a while ago, my usual time, and found Cynthia still not back from lunch. It's two hours now. The Hoppers are gone, too. I couldn't believe she'd have taken them off like that, without a note or anything. I've been wondering whether I should call the cops."

I sat down on the arm of one of the chairs and stared at her. Cynthia gone. And the Hoppers. The thing seemed impossible.

The trouble was, it wasn't impossible at all. It was

frighteningly logical. Ginni was right: With Cynthia's obsession with perfection—her own and others'—she'd never be gone intentionally for more than ten minutes without leaving instructions.

There was only one explanation that made sense. They knew I was back in town and didn't know where to find me. They knew I had been in touch with Cynthia. It didn't take much to figure out where I would go if I wanted to track down Traceman. The Hoppers were just a bonus.

I thought of Laura and shuddered. "You haven't called anyone?" I asked.

"I tried her at home, of course, and I got no answer. Who else would I call? The police? To tell them my boss had been missing for a couple of hours? You can imagine how thrilled they'd be."

"The Hoppers," I said. "They could have been stolen."

"But I don't know that for sure. She could just as well have taken them, they're so tiny."

There was still the computer. It was the only thing I could think of now. "Did you check the Fortune?" I asked.

"Well, that's how I knew she must have been in this morning. The power was left on—not that there's anything unusual about that. We wouldn't normally log out at lunch time. But anyway, there wasn't anything special on the screen—some collection she'd been tracking down, is all."

"Let's check it out again."

The Fortune sat whispering impassively on its desk in Cynthia's office. Its green phosphor eye glowed like a benighted Cyclops, offering the data of some person's life. The cursor winked at us knowingly and I felt uncomfortable, as always, in the presence of the device's peculiar power.

Ginni's fingers darted about the keyboard, registering a fresh set of commands, and an unseen eyelid wiped out the current information, replacing it with a whole new screen.

"This is the log," Ginni explained. "Cynthia likes to

keep tabs on the daily use of the computer and punches everything into the log before accessing files. The last entry of the morning was listed at eleven-thirty."

The name on the file was unfamiliar to both of us, but Ginni called it up anyway and I studied it over her shoulder. It was the owner of one of the Edward Hoppers. The screen showed us a collection of very limited interest, mostly American watercolors from between the wars.

I saw no possible connection. "Does Cynthia ever do things she doesn't enter on the log?" I asked.

"Oh, yes, it happens sometimes," Ginni told me. "When she's just playing around. Or working on something that doesn't have much to do with business."

"Did she ever mention Traceman to you? Dan Traceman, the collector?"

"Traceman. Well, I know the name of course, but I don't know whether Cynthia ever worked for him. We're bound to have a file on him."

She punched in the name and drew a blank. She made a face and punched it in again, with the same result. "I don't understand," she said. "I could have sworn we had a file on him."

I watched her as she went back through the system, searching for the file. I had a feeling she wasn't going to find it. "Can you tell if a file has been erased?" I asked.

She thought about that one for a moment. "When the file's been erased, the directory information goes with it," she said. "But I guess, through a kind of deduction, you might be able to tell. Everything in the system is cross-filed, you see. Under the artist and work, you'd find what collection it belonged to. If there were enough references to any one collection, you'd know it would have to be cross-referenced under the collector's name."

"Try Molnar, Jacob," I told her. "Look up a painting called *Red Menace, Sixty-Nine.*"

The scene at Marlborough flashed back in my memory: Traceman, livid with anger, left to pick up his money from the gallery floor while I turned on my heel and walked away. It was a humiliation that in hindsight was more than he deserved. Perhaps he had simply been too ignorant at the time to know what he was doing. But if it was ignorance back then, it was something different now.

I watched as Ginni's short fingers punched my name out on the keyboard and scrolled through screens of titles before she turned up the one I was looking for.

"Wow," she said. "I never knew you were so prolific."

Ginni was young enough not to have been around in the art business when I was still active. Still, it was amazing that I had done so much—and just as amazing that it could all be reduced to so little.

Red Menace, Sixty-Nine, 1969, acrylic on canvas, 36 inches by 60 inches. Collection, Dan Traceman. Provenance—the painting was bought originally from Marlborough by Leo Wolff. Of course. It was sold a short time later to the Traceman Collection for an unspecified amount.

"What does that tell you, Ginni?" I asked.

"It tells me the guy didn't keep your painting very long," she said.

"Maybe he didn't like it," I said.

She laughed. "Beyond that," she said, "like I thought, we must have had a Traceman file. But Cynthia would never erase a whole darn file. They meant too much to her."

"Someone else could have done it, though?"

She looked at me thoughtfully, her gray eyes clouding with doubt.

"That would have been tough," she said. "Unless it was actually on the screen—or unless she gave them the password. All these files are accessed through passwords, and there are some I don't know myself. But if it was right there on the screen, it could have been done reasonably easily. Jake, is Cynthia in some kind of trouble?"

Suppose she had been working on the Traceman file for me—she might even have found the address of the warehouse. Then Traceman decides to pick her up and sends someone over here. She opens up for them and they find her working on Dan Traceman's file, so they say, okay, let's get rid of this. They erase the file, or persuade her to erase it. Then punch in something else and zoom, they're gone.

"I don't know, Ginni. I don't know what to tell you."

FORTY-THREE

◇

The warehouse had to exist, but where the hell was it?

I couldn't believe that Cynthia would have just gone along, without having made some kind of attempt to let me know what had happened.

"Have you checked around the office?" I asked Ginni. "Where would she normally leave a message if she was planning to be out when you arrived?"

"She'd scribble something down on a scrap of paper and leave it on the keyboard," said Ginni. "And, good Lord, how dumb! There's a message pad on the Fortune! I hadn't even thought to look."

She punched it up. "We've got a hit here," she said. "I've no idea how much use it is."

I peered over her shoulder. The message was cryptic, just a single word: "Corman." It looked to be some kind of memo to herself. Had he called? "Can you tell when this was written?" I asked Ginni.

"Not if she didn't note the time," she said. "But I can tell you it wasn't there when I left last night at six. Cynthia had already gone by then."

So it must have been this morning. I could call Dick, but it seemed more urgent to move on. The first thing was to find Cynthia. If they could get their hands on me, what were the chances they would let her off the hook? Especially now with Brian Brain dead. Suppose Traceman only wanted her as bait to bring me in? If that was the case, it was time to break cover. The sooner the better.

I decided to take a risk on Richards. If he was with me, it couldn't hurt. If he was with Traceman, so be it. Let them find me and I would worry about it then—at least Cynthia might have a chance.

There was one other possibility I could check out.

"Listen," I said to Ginni. "You've got to do something for me. For Cynthia, really. Get hold of a Lieutenant Richards at this number." I wrote it down on a scratch pad. "No one else, okay? Get hold of him and tell him that Cynthia's disappeared. Just that. He'll know what it means."

I tore the sheet of paper from a memo pad and added a couple of names. Stevenson, with his storefront address and number. And Samantha Dmitri, with a question mark for the street number or West Broadway. Telephone? Home number?

"See if you can fill in the details and give them to Richards with both these names. Tell him I'm trying to find a warehouse belonging to Dan Traceman. Maybe he'll find it quicker than I can. Answer anything he asks, if you can—but don't try to answer anything you can't. No bullshit, okay?"

I was halfway out the door when I thought of the videocassette in my pocket. I remembered that Cynthia kept a tape deck in the office as an information service for her clients. Jesus! Where was my head?

I came back in.

"Can you switch on the VCR, Ginni?" I asked. "I've got a tape here that I need to run."

I pulled the cassette from the inside pocket of my coat and watched it settle down into the deck. After the title that I had seen at Nicholas's apartment, the credits rolled across the monitor. Camera: Brian Brain. Lighting: Brian Brain. Very funny. Narration: Brian Brain. Script: Brian Brain. Editing: Brian Brain. Directed by: Brian Brain.

The surprise was kept until last—I guessed he had left it to the end for the effect. It came in large letters, filling the screen: PRODUCED BY DANIEL TRACEMAN—TRACEMAN ENTERPRISES. Little wonder Traceman had Nicholas's place searched.

I knew I would hate myself for doing it, but I watched anyway as the dreadful images materialized on the screen. I told myself it was all an illusion, the effects of light. I listened to the appalling, insistent sound of Brian's voice and his obscene, delighted, blow-by-blow description of each sad episode.

This wasn't the great artist I remembered. It was a man obsessed by flesh and the ecstasies of the flesh. Rather, its ecstatic agonies—not the agonies of inflicted pain, but of degradation. A pathetic, crawling, pissed on, beshitted creature, moaning in exquisite pleasure at the maltreatment of a succession of sultry boy-men, contemptuous, sullenly naked and commanding.

Enough said. The images will stay with me for the rest of my life. The pain of having witnessed the dismal parade of a friend's iniquities is something I have to live with and live down—for Worthing's shame was my shame, too, and perhaps the shame of everyone who entertains a sexual fantasy now and then. Which of us doesn't? For Worthing, the only difference was that someone happened by who made them real.

The tape may have lasted twenty minutes and I watched it to the end. Ginni didn't. I heard her gasping after the second minute. She said, "Oh, God, Jake, I'm not watching that," and went back to her desk. I don't know if she managed to block out the sound as well.

It lasted twenty minutes, anyway, and I was about to switch off the recorder. But the images had scarcely faded when a second title flipped up on the screen and turned my heart to ice.

"PATTY CAKE, PATTY CAKE, DRAYTON'S MAN."

The thing was a single take, black and white. It started with a long shot, interior: an artist's loft. Its white walls made a space for invention, a space to be filled.

Something at first was unidentifiably wrong, no more than a movement of white against the white rear wall. Your eyes continued to work uneasily until you made out a human figure, pale and thin and naked, as the shot closed in. And then you realized that the figure was hanging. Hanging and turning slowly toward you as you came in close with the camera. It was Patty.

The obscenity wasn't simply the tortured angle of that thin, snapped neck. Nor the dreadful, lifeless emaciation of Patty's boyish torso with its tight black button nipples. The obscenity was below. There, at the pathetic, scrawny bush of hair, in grotesque parody of Patty's work, a half-opened switchblade was planted, handle up, inside her.

It was on a tight shot of this image that the camera's movement finally came to rest and faded without comment.

The tape moved on to gray and the silence continued. I found Ginni behind me, her face a ghastly pallor and her eyes reflecting disbelief at what she had seen. I stood up and put my arms around her.

"It's a setup," she said. "Bloody artists. It has to be a setup."

Given what artists have been known to do these days, it wouldn't have been farfetched as somebody's art work. But it wasn't a setup. What we'd seen was Patty Drayton's suicide—except that it wasn't a suicide. Carlos was right again.

"Listen," I said. "I can't tell you any more about it now, I've got to get moving. But I promise I'll explain it later. Are you okay? Can you handle things?"

She took a deep breath and nodded.

"First off, get the tape in a safe place. Locked. Okay? Then put in that call to Richards. I'm going to look for Cynthia."

"Should I stay here by the phone?" she asked.

I thought for a moment. Would Traceman try to get me at this number? What other number would he have? He knew I wouldn't show up at the studio. Besides, I needed a home base where I could check in—somewhere that Richards could leave word for me. An umbilical. "Could you do that?" I asked. "How late could you stay?"

"How about ten?" she said. "If you call before then and no one answers, call back. I'll be out a few minutes to grab myself a sandwich. Otherwise, you can count on me."

"You're a dream," I said. "Bless you. But for Christ's sake, lock the front door after me and keep it locked while you're in here. Let the building security know you're working late and call them before you open it. Don't trust anyone."

I kept an eye open for a tail as I left the building, but I seemed to be alone. My face felt naked as I burrowed down in the subway, seeking the safety of numbers. Perhaps they weren't bothering to follow me because they knew I would come to them. They had Cynthia.

There was still no one with me as I hurried past the New School and walked the extra block to Frank's work site. I beat on the window until he heard, or sensed the vibration or the change of light—whatever it was that told him I was there.

He blinked through the window at me, grimacing at the change.

"Jesus Christ, Molnar. What did you do to yourself? You look terrible."

There wasn't time for anything but the essentials. "You've got to get me in to see Samantha right away," I told him. "I need you to get me past the door. She'd never let me in. Okay?"

He stared at me. He stood there holding three different brushes with different colors in his hand. The guy wanted to paint.

"You're crazy, Molnar. Wait until morning. I've got to work, I've got to get this damn thing finished."

"Frank," I said, "Frank. You don't understand. They've got Cynthia, my ex-wife. God knows what they'll do to her. I told you what they did to Laura." I laid a hand on each of his shoulders and refused to let his eyes escape me as I spoke. You ask an artist to cross his dealer, you're asking more than you should ask of anyone. Especially a dealer who does well.

"Frank," I said. "Samantha may be the only person who could tell me where to go. She's maybe the only person who knows where Traceman keeps his stuff.

For Christ's sake, that must be where they are. It's the only place they could be. You've got to help me, Frank."

He knew he had no choice. He couldn't keep his eyes on mine and tell me no. Frank sighed and began to clean the paint out of his brushes, his shoulders heavy with frustrated energy.

It was still early evening, not yet seven. If we could get there in decent time, we'd have a better chance to catch her at home. I found myself panting, not only with the effort of keeping up with Frank, but also with an agony of anticipation. Samantha was it. Failing her, I knew I had no way to catch up with Traceman.

The approach to her loft apartment was as unprepossessing as to any New York artist's loft: cold stairs or a dilapidated elevator, bare wood floors and drafty corridors. By contrast, I remembered the interior shots from Andy's *Interview*. Luxury built on the backs of artists. A rococo heaven for the gallery queen.

I grabbed Frank by the arm to get his attention before we reached the door.

"Listen," I said, "you've got to get us in there. After that, it's up to you. Stay or leave, whatever you feel. I'll stand back out of sight here. Tell her it's urgent. It can't wait till tomorrow. Okay?"

He nodded and rang the doorbell.

"Who is it?"

The voice came at the squawk box and I relayed it silently to Frank. Thank God she was in.

"Frank Stevenson," said Frank. Because he was nervous, his voicing didn't work too well and I wondered if she would understand it through the intercom. There was a silence.

"Frank. What in God's name are you doing here?" He didn't hear her and started to talk again before she'd finished.

"I can't wait," he said. "I have to see you now."

I heard the sound of bolts and chains and the door opened a crack. I still couldn't see her, but I heard her voice.

"Frank," she began, "this is very inconvenient . . ."

He pushed the door further open and stepped in.

"Samantha," he said, "I'm sorry. I'm truly sorry. But you've got to talk to Jake Molnar."

He held the door open and waved me in. And then simply left. He turned on his heel without a further word and clumped off down the corridor toward the elevator.

FORTY-FOUR

◇

We stood and stared at each other for a few moments in silence, in the improbable environment of her vestibule. Richly flowered wallpaper decorated the walls behind the wedding-cake woodwork of an interior gazebo. There was the sound of water and birds.

Samantha didn't smile and wasn't pleased to see me. She glared at me, tipping her head and shaking out the famous black hair. Then she shrugged.

"You'd better come in," she said. She stood back to let me through and I brushed past her into the loft. And then stopped dead.

I looked around with the sudden, uncomfortable realization that I'd come to do battle with someone other than the woman who lived here. The place was so kinky, I almost had to laugh. It was a hilarious mismatch of moods and styles, extravagantly juxtaposed with total aplomb. Perhaps the most amazing thing about it was that it worked. An impeccable sense of color and an eye that reflected unquestionable taste. For the first time since I'd heard about it, the gallery seemed to make sense. Samantha's act, too, with its extravagance. I felt an absurd inclination to like the woman.

"Well . . .?" she said.

For the moment, I couldn't think of anything to say. She sat down at the end of a Victorian fainting couch and twisted a cigarette into a holder.

"You hound me and my artists, you invade my gallery space and raid my files. You sic the cops on me. You do your best to screw up my entire business. Then you come crashing into my private life without an invitation. What is it with you, Molnar? I should have you locked away."

Suppose I'd been wrong?

"Carlos . . ." I started.

"Carlos was a terrific artist," she interrupted. "But a damn fool person. Jesus, the guy had everything. Or could have had. He got this damn fool notion in his head about Patty . . . oh, yes"—she waved me back into silence—"I knew about that. He was obsessed with Patty, always had been. He never accepted that they'd simply grown apart. It happens to people. She grew apart from him. She went her own way. God knows, we all wish she'd chosen a different way. But that was her, that was Patty, God help her. And Carlos had to juggle the whole thing into some kind of giant conspiracy. Some artists behave like kids."

She glared at me though her cigarette smoke to make it clear that she included me in the list. Was it possible she really didn't know?

"Listen," I said, "just an hour ago, I was sitting at a videotape monitor, watching the most appalling obscenity I've seen in all my life. You want to know what it was? It was Patty. Patty in the act of being murdered. Patty hanging from the ceiling with a switchblade planted in her crotch. Carlos was right, goddammit. He was right!"

Samantha's face changed in seconds from the flush of anger to a startling pallor. A flicker played across the surface of her eyes. Unlike Eduardo Guerrero, I've never prided myself on knowing when people are lying.

"You know Brian Brain?" I said. "He made the tape. He was working for you."

Visibly, she shuddered.

"Brian Brain was the most vicious little bastard I ever met in my entire life," she said.

"You heard he was killed?"

She nodded. "Hot off the grapevine. Best news of the week."

"You lied to me before. You told me you didn't know him."

"You expect me to tell my most regrettable secrets to a total stranger?"

"But he worked for you."

"He didn't kill Patty Drayton for me, if that's what you're suggesting." She was angry again now. "If you want to know how he came to be working for me, it's quite simple: Dan Traceman pushed him onto me. He said he felt sorry for the guy, and he'd like to help him out. Some patrons do that for an artist. The arrangement was that Dan would pay his wages and I'd get the back-room labor. I could use the help in those days. Besides, Dan was a good customer already."

"So you hired him?"

"Kind of, yes. But I always had the feeling he was snooping around. And he liked to touch, he was always pawing at me. Ugh! Anyway, I had to get Dan to call him off."

There was little doubting her conviction.

"What about his work?" I asked her. "Did you ever handle him?"

"Are you kidding me?" she asked, outraged. "He only did performance stuff and that was long before I knew him. He gave that up. I don't think he ever did anything again. He said he was making tapes."

"Tell me about it," I said. She shuddered again and stubbed her cigarette.

I shook my head to get the cobwebs out. What else had I based all my assumptions of her guilt on? Carlos's evidence of hype? Selling art works for a profit? Brown-nosing with the rich and famous?

"If you knew that Carlos was suspicious about Patty's death," I asked, "did he talk to you about Worthing Nelson?"

"You asked that before," she said. "Something like that. And the answer's no. He didn't. What's more, I never had anything to do with Worthing Nelson in my life. Never met the man. Never sold a painting. Never owned one. Nothing."

"You sold a drawing once."

She raised an eyebrow, thought back, and then

shrugged. "That must have been ten years ago. I hadn't even remembered."

"And you never saw any of the paintings from the silent years?"

She shook another cigarette from the pack in front of her and watched me curiously as she fixed it in the holder. She took her time lighting it.

"As a matter of fact," she said, "I did. I happened to be at the Conners' in Beverly Hills. I'd never seen one like it before, so I took a Polaroid, out of curiosity. But I don't see what that could have to do with Patty Drayton."

"There's a whole lot more Nelsons from the silent Seventies that have showed up. Carlos found the slides. That's what started the whole thing rolling. You know who has them? Your friend Dan Traceman."

Samantha crossed her legs and raised her chin to blow out a plume of smoke.

"So far as I know," she said, "Dan Traceman's only friend in this world is Dan Traceman. Oh, sure I've worked with him, who hasn't? He must have bought a million paintings from the gallery. So what's the big deal?"

"He had no financial stake in the gallery?"

She looked at me, genuinely startled.

"Is that what you thought? Are you kidding? Traceman? I wouldn't trust him farther than I could throw him."

My card house began to fall apart completely.

"Wasn't it Traceman who worked out the deal with Burke Chung in Los Angeles?" I asked.

"What deal?" she asked with a shrug. "The guy shows some of my artists on the coast, is all. Sure, Dan arranged it. For all I know, he might get some kind of a cut from Burke. But nothing from my end, I just collaborated. It can't hurt my artists to show out there, if they have the work. The best of them don't—I sell it all in New York and Europe."

"Chung has been selling those Worthing Nelsons from the Seventies," I told her. "You know Leo Wolff?"

"Of course."

"Did he and Dan Traceman work together?"

She shrugged and looked at me as though I were a total fool.

"Grow up, Molnar. I should teach you the facts of life? Of course they worked together when there was a buck in it for both of them. Jack up the price at an auction. I've seen that. Who hasn't? So where's the big conspiracy? Dan Traceman must have done the same with fifty other people."

It was true. It could have been anyone.

"Can you help me find the Worthing Nelsons?"

"I wouldn't know where to look," she said. "Besides, I'm not sure what you have at stake in this?"

"Worthing Nelson was a friend," I said.

"I'm sorry," she said.

She really was, I thought, looking at her. A different Samantha Dmitri than the one I had concocted—a mixture of my prejudice and fears. The real Samantha was more complex, more thoroughly dimensional. More human.

"Listen," I said, "if I'm right about one thing, it's that people have been getting killed. You have to feel the same way about Patty."

Samantha nodded.

"Carlos thought you'd hyped her out of reality."

"Sure," she said. "I hyped her. And I guess in a way I sold her out to Traceman. He made a heavy investment in the work. But that's my job, isn't it? Then suddenly she's this art star, right? Suddenly she's not so ready to work with you anymore. She got bitchy, high on the image. Patty Drayton, queen of punk. Okay. So we all got pissed at her. But kill her? Jesus, Molnar, kill her? Would he do that?"

"Would Brian?" I asked.

She didn't answer that one. We both knew that he would.

"What about Nelson?" she asked. "Was Carlos right about that, too?"

I had been trying to think it through and there were still some things I hadn't been able to figure.

"They destroyed the guy," I said. I told her about

the tape. "I'd like to bet that Nicholas was a Traceman plant right from the start. Remember, back in those days, around the end of the Sixties, Traceman was an upstart back-stager. Maybe he needed money. He sees Worthing's love life breaking up and latches on to what could be an opportunity. He picks up a kid like Nicholas who can turn a nice trick and sends him out to stud. He gets Worthing hooked on his pecker and runs him for all he's worth."

It sounded as though it might have worked. I mean, Worthing was no fool, but he knew a nice piece of ass when he saw it. So it might have been worth a couple of pictures to him. Traceman turns them over fast and makes a hundred thousand on the deal.

"The tape would be just a few years and a hundred fantasies down the road. Between them, they sold him blissful dreams for paintings."

"Blackmail?" she asked.

"No, it wouldn't have been blackmail. Worthing wouldn't have cared enough, he'd never have gone for that. More like extortion. He just got hooked on his own id. He looked like a junkie in those pictures. It could happen to anyone."

"His whole production? I mean, everything?"

"Where did the silent Seventies go? Where are the paintings from the Sixties that Worthing held back for his own collection? The thing he wanted most was to see it go to a foundation of some kind. Then he died without a will and everyone supposed the earlier work had gone. I'd like to bet it had. Traceman had laid his sticky hands on it. Where else did he get his money? Traceman Enterprises! The Traceman Collection! The whole damn thing was bought with Worthing's blood."

I got up from my chair and went to sit beside Samantha on the fainting couch.

"Listen," I said. "It's not too important what either of us believes right now. What matters now is that they've got Cynthia—my ex-wife, Cynthia Molnar, you must know her?"

"Sure, I know her. Artresearch, right?"

"I had her helping track down works with the computer. I've got to find her. Will you help?"

She nodded.

I leaned forward and placed my hands on hers. "Tell me," I said, "of all people, you're the one to know. Where can I find Traceman's warehouse?"

She knew. She had to know.

FORTY-FIVE

◇

She didn't.

"I wish I did," she said. "I've heard it rumored about this fabulous place, but I've never been there. I don't know who has. I've always assumed it was some kind of art world myth. I wish to God I could help, I really do."

I couldn't believe it. I'd had it in mind so long that Samantha was the direct pipeline to Traceman, it hadn't occurred to me that I would reach the end of the line right here. I had run full tilt through the darkness into a wall.

And now there was no other possible way to reach him. Unless . . .

Unless Richards had run down the address.

"Do you mind if I use your phone?" I asked Samantha.

I dialed Cynthia's office number and Ginni picked up right away. Thank God for Ginni.

"Listen," I said, "have you talked to Richards yet? It's absolutely vital that I speak to him."

"No," she said. "You said not anyone but Richards, so I left an urgent message for him to call. They're trying to reach him, but he hasn't called back. But listen, your friend called a moment ago. I just put the phone down. If you'd called two minutes sooner . . ."

"My friend?" For a moment I couldn't think of any.

"Corman," she said. "The name you found in the message file. Dick Corman. He said to tell you he's in town. He flew in from the coast to find you. He called from Kennedy, says he's tried every number where you might have been."

Dick? In town?

"Did he say why? I don't understand the connection here. What's the guy doing in New York?"

"Here's what he said," Ginni told me. "I told him you might check in with me, so he said if you did, he couldn't say much but to tell you that Lieutenant Richards asked him to come. He couldn't give me the details on the phone, but you should drop everything. He said to tell you to wait. Very emphatic. Wait where you are. Oh, and contact Richards. Not to do anything until you'd talked to Richards."

"That's it?"

"Well, I gave him the two addresses you asked me to give Richards. I hope that was okay."

Stevenson's work address and telephone. Samantha's.

"Did you find the numbers?"

"Yes, of course. I kept him on the line while I tried them, just in case. There was no answer at Stevenson's. Same with the gallery, no answer. And Samantha Dmitri's home number is unlisted."

"Okay. He just left Kennedy?"

"He was just about to leave when he called. Two minutes, not more. He said he'd try Stevenson's first."

It would take him an hour to get there. I thought for a minute. It was after eight. Better to try the police from here, directly. Then, if there was no way to get to Richards, I could perhaps get through to someone familiar with the case. At least I had to get them started. Richards could be out for dinner and a movie. It could be too late.

"Listen, Ginni," I said, "you're doing wonders. Thanks."

"Jake? Hold on, there's more."

"Yes?"

"I've just spent hours cross-referencing some of the files to see what I could track down. I think I may have that address you're looking for. The warehouse."

My head started to pound. "My God, let me have it, Ginni!"

I copied it down on the telephone pad, my fingers trembling with the effort to control the pencil. Downtown. Another piece of luck. There's something about the nature of crisis that brings its own response, a mysterious energy of need sent out like microwaves and returning miraculously as an answer. It happens. Ask any artist.

"Ginni," I told her, "you're a genius. God knows how I could thank you. But thanks, anyway."

"I'm going to wait here for Lieutenant Richards's call. And I told your friend Dick I'd be here if he needed me."

"You said you could stay till ten?"

"I'll stay later, if I'm needed. Where are you now?"

I read off the number from Samantha's phone and hung up. Samantha had her feet up on the fainting couch when I got back. She was smoking another cigarette.

"I guess you'll be going, then," she said. She couldn't help but overhear the telephone from the hall. "What do I say? Good hunting?"

Dick had said wait, but it wasn't the moment for that. I wondered if Ginni had told him what was happening with Cynthia. I assumed she had.

"If anyone calls," I asked, "will you tell them where I've gone?" I gave her the address from the memo pad.

"That's it?" she said. "Do I have to get used to Jake Molnar storming in and out of my life like a tornado?"

She took my hand at the door and grinned at me.

"No need to say anything," she said. "I love a good storm. I'll catch up with you, one of these days."

In other circumstances it would have seemed a short walk from Samantha's to the warehouse. That night it was endless.

I suppose it occurred to me that I was alone and unarmed, but I didn't give it much thought. I was simply carried by the momentum, and by a desperate need for action. I don't think I felt afraid. God knows I had every reason to. Yet, as I had done earlier, I felt a kind of euphoric invulnerability, as though everything were happening in a dream and could not, in some way, actually touch me.

I couldn't have been more wrong.

Approaching the address, it was a moment before I realized what was happening. A moving van was backed up to a loading bay ahead of me, with light spilling out into its open doors from the building. A packing case was dollied noisily across the bridge as I approached. Art. I could smell it. I had been around enough museums and galleries and had enough carting services around my studio at shipping time to know what was happening. Traceman was moving out.

Still a short distance from the van, I moved back into the shadows and stood for a few moments, catching my breath and watching. More packing crates were dollied out. Through the open doors, I could hear the sound of hammers pounding nails.

I waited for the right moment to slip in, swinging myself up around the edge of the loading bay and into the light, following close behind a carrier on his return trip to the storage area. The whine of a power saw drowned out even the rolling dollies, and the place was filled with the smell of fresh-cut knotty pine. Overhead track lights glared down on a half-dozen workers.

There was art everywhere. Most of it crated, ready to be moved. But a few pieces still stood, wrapped up in plastic sheets and propped against the walls, waiting for the craters to pack them into boxes. I saw a Warhol and a Rauschenberg, a big Johns target. Enough to guess at the contents of the big crates they were loading.

But these were nothing to the Worthing Nelsons. Unnoticed among the workers, hands in pockets, I strolled through the main storage area to the back.

I found what must have been a hundred of them there, stacked in neat rows or crated. I slid one from its plastic covering and set it down against the wall. There was no question but that it was Worthing's. Like the two I had seen in California, it was a Worthing Nelson changed by time, charged with a deeper and more angry passion. But it was his. Somber colors— ochres, blacks.

Pulling out others, I ranged them by the side of this

one, absorbed in the incredible, dark vision to which Worthing had penetrated in his latter years. There was a desperation I wanted to attribute not only to his personal life, but to a growing realization of the futility inherent in this great work, the discovery of the final limitations of a mode of painting. It was as though he had had to test every avenue to prove the process.

I must have had a dozen of them out before I was aware of Traceman standing there. I had no sense of how long he had been there. Only that he was there, smiling pleasantly enough and nodding as he watched me, perfectly at ease with the enormity of his possession.

"Hello, Jake," he said. "My God, you look wan and desperate without the beard. Would it be presumptuous to say I've been expecting you?"

FORTY-SIX

◇

He held a gun on me without fuss or apparent embarrassment, as though it were something he did every day.

"So you've found your friend," he said. "Go ahead, I invite you. Take a good look." He waved the small black thing from me to the paintings in a gesture of invitation.

"Traceman," I said, "you've got Cynthia."

He smiled briefly and I realized how Cynthia could have thought of him as handsome. He looked as fresh as if he had just arrived for a day's work at the office.

"Oh, yes," he said. "I've got her. But don't let it worry you. She'll be just fine, so long as I have your help. But tell me, I'm curious, really. What do you think of these paintings? Remarkable, isn't it, how a man can change so much and yet remain the same?"

"Remarkable," I agreed shortly. "How did you get them, Traceman? Is this what you killed for?"

Traceman allowed himself the gesture of a man too concerned with the larger issues to worry over details. He wore his self-confidence almost as easily as the immaculate three-piece suit, yet there were tiny lines of tension in his face. He turned the gun away from me for a moment to look at his watch.

"You always were a cocky bastard, Jake," he said. "Come in the back." The gun came level with my chest again. It was hardly an invitation this time. He ushered me back down the corridor to an office that appeared to have been recently cleared out. The sliding doors of a credenza behind the desk were left open, and the drawers of a filing cabinet.

Wherever Traceman planned to go, the disappearance was going to be complete, I thought. There was nothing left here. Even the surfaces had been cleared—the desk and credenza, a small coffee table, all stripped clean. There were hooks in the walls that showed where pictures had been.

I sat where I was told, in an upright, aluminum-frame chair. Traceman retrieved a length of picture wire from his pocket and wired me hand and foot to it with painful thoroughness.

"What happened to Worthing, Traceman? Did you kill him too?"

He didn't bother to reply—he didn't need to. He left the room for a few moments and returned with a red five-gallon can. It was the second time I'd been condemned to death by fire.

"I've got the tape," I said. It was worth a try. Anything now was worth a try. "From Nicholas's place. Your man never found it there. Are you still looking for it?"

It wasn't much to bargain for my life with, but it was all I had. At least he paused and looked thoughtful and the cap stayed on the gasoline can a moment longer. It didn't help to remember what happened to the last man who had used the tape for insurance.

"I don't think it really matters that much, Jake. Not anymore. A week ago, maybe. But you've forced my hand in a thoroughly unpleasant way. I wish you hadn't done it—I even tried to warn you not to. But you did. This used to be a very comfortable arrangement. Now I have to skip town. There's no way back for either of us that I can see."

"The tape's going public soon unless I stop it. I've seen to that."

Maybe neither of us believed the lie, but he paused a little longer. There were seconds gained.

"By then I'll be long gone, my friend, believe me. It'll take more than a pornographic memoir to dig me out. You can keep it, Jake. Much good may it do you."

Assuming there was nothing I could do to stop him,

could he hope to get away? There were ways, I knew, of changing one's identity. They did it for underworld informers. Plastic surgery. A subtle change in the facial structure. I had drawn enough faces to know what a tiny change can do. And there are ways to invent a new life story, fully researched and documented. Why not?

"What happened to Worthing, Traceman?"

I had the man talking, perhaps I could keep him at it. The wires cut into my wrists and I noticed now that they had begun to bleed.

Traceman looked at his watch again. He was itching to be moving. At the present rate, I guessed, it could take at least another hour to get the paintings loaded.

"Worthing?" I prompted.

"He died a natural death," he said. "If you call his binges natural. Those we supplied him with, but I'm sure you've found out about that already, if you've seen the tape. The guy was a turd. Disgusting." Traceman's face expressed the contempt for weakness of a man who assumed he had none of his own. "A sick, sick man, I promise you. But I didn't kill him. He killed himself. Heart attack, like the papers said."

He laughed. "Overexertion, more like it. All I did was have him moved to the street in the Bowery. There was a certain poetic justice in the move, I thought. Back to the gutter where the guy belonged." He laughed briefly. "Carlos, too. You'll have to forgive Brian's humor. But then, you never did forgive much, did you, Jake?"

He looked at the gun in his hand and then at me. Shrugging, he moved his jacket aside and returned the thing to a tidy shoulder holster.

"Nicholas . . . ?" I began to ask.

"A victim," he said. "A loser. Always was."

"He manipulated Worthing," I said. "Didn't he?"

Traceman studied me with cool brown eyes. You really believe that? they asked me. And I didn't anymore. I knew who had manipulated Worthing, start to finish. No matter who had been his bait or tool.

"Nelson," he told me, "gave all his work to Nicholas. And rightly so, for what he did to him. Payment in kind. By the same token, it all passed on to me. Services rendered. All fair and legal, I can promise you. I took care of him, you see, after Worthing died. Took care of Nicholas, poor stinking turd."

The memory of the pathetic remains of Nicholas in the bathtub came back to me with a wave of nausea. "How long had he been like that?" I asked.

Traceman looked at me levelly. I remembered the feeling of having been set up to discover that scene—and to be discovered there. How? There had to be a piece somewhere I had missed, something I had overlooked. The guy had been playing with me all along the line. But how?

"Nicky always liked cats," he said absently.

The pet name hit me with a shock of familiarity. Nicki. It looked like the end of that story, too.

"Come on, Traceman. You know that's not what I meant. The drugs, the squalor."

He puckered his face in disgust. "How long? Too long," he said. "I had the guy set up for life. For life. He had everything he could ever have wanted, and he blew it. Can you imagine," he asked me, "sticking a needle in your arm?" He looked at me reflectively. "No," he said, "I don't suppose you could. Anyway, we did the man a favor," he concluded.

The picture wire had bitten deep into the flesh around my wrists. I tried to force myself to relax, if only to ease the pain. But I also knew that at this point anger would buy me less than patience would. I emptied it out of me with an effort of concentration, felt it expel through fingertips and feet. Keep talking. It seemed about the only thing I had going for me. He was waiting, annoyed, I thought, to be delayed. I watched for anything that could upset his balance.

"Worthing wanted to set up a foundation for the work," I said.

Traceman just laughed again. "So much for artists' dreams," he said. "And artists' egos. The man had no idea how much the stuff was worth."

"And all that new work, in those last few years. How did you persuade him not to show them?"

He looked at me pityingly. "What's the matter, Jake? You didn't see the tape? You haven't been listening? The guy had discovered sex. He was hooked, a junkie. He'd have done anything to get his fix. Boys, Jake, boys! He painted his tail off just to have Nicholas find him more and better ass. And speaking of which . . ."

Whoever it was he had been waiting for had arrived. The door opened behind me and I could watch the tension slacken from his face. He looked at his watch again.

"You got him, Dan?" she asked.

I knew the perfume right away.

FORTY-SEVEN

◇

Cynthia.

It was like a sudden, devastating blow to the head, a physical fact. A moment of total disbelief followed instantly by total comprehension. Traceman had known everything from the start.

"Jake, is that you?" she said. "Christ, I wouldn't have known you without the beard."

That was it? She wouldn't have known me?

"Jesus, Cynthia," said Traceman, "where in hell have you been?"

"Packing," she said coldly. "What did you think?"

"I was expecting you here an hour ago."

"They wouldn't have finished loading yet. Will you calm down, Dan? Nerves don't help."

He had seemed remarkably cool to me, but he wasn't a patch on Cynthia. She wasn't finished yet. She came up close to look at me. Then she hauled off and slapped me hard across the face. Strangely, with little expression on her own. As though it were something she had to do and did, perfunctorily, to get it done.

Tied up in the chair, my head reeling and my wrists and ankles cut with picture wire, I couldn't think of one damn thing to say. The questions came later—what I should have asked her. At the time, I was literally struck dumb. Mouth open, bleeding a little at the lip, I simply stared.

She stood and looked at me for a moment, her eyes filled with . . . What? Anger? I'd screwed her project for her. Without knowing it, I'd stumbled on a million-dollar enterprise that had taken years of planning.

But there was more in her eyes. There was the

stubborn Iowa farm girl, her moral rectitude twisted into its own reverse—as rigid, perhaps, in its principle, as the code with which she had grown up. There was the woman, the years of living in the shadow of Jake Molnar, artist and egotist extraordinary, who'd known nothing better than to use her, as he had used everything and everyone around him in those days. A critical mass of intelligence and human capability frustrated. By rights, it should have exploded then—better for her if it had.

For myself? I was surprised to feel no anger. Only the deepest misery I had ever felt. Even after I'd come to accept that she couldn't stay with me, I always hung on to the love I'd imagined us to share.

"You'll never know, will you, Jake?" she said. "You never saw anything but yourself."

Then she turned and left.

Traceman stood there and grinned at me as though he couldn't have done better himself. He couldn't. Nothing he could have done would have hurt as much as that single slap.

"That's it," said Traceman lightly. "Bad guy exits with good guy's girl. Credits. Curtains. House lights."

It seemed a pitiful ceremony, to watch him unscrew the cap from the gasoline can and douse the liquid generously round the room and over the remaining furniture.

He emptied the last gallon over me. The foul-smelling stuff soaked my hair and my shirt. It saturated my jeans and seeped through to my flesh.

"Sorry, Jake," he said. "We can't take any risks. Think of it this way: You brought it on yourself. Take care, okay?"

He paused at the door and turned around one last time. "Oh, by the way," he said. "I thought you'd like to know who'll inherit all your work. The new stuff." He jangled a set of keys on a ring with an African charm that I recognized as Laura's. My studio keys. "We thought it should go to Cynthia. She's admired it for so long. Me, I could live without it."

He grinned and left. I heard a key turn in the lock.

If he'd thrown a match, the whole place would have exploded—a risk he likely didn't want to take. In the silence that followed the click of the latch, I could imagine what he would do. The racks must have been cleared off by now, the warehouse empty. Another five-gallon can splashed through the open storage space could be safely lighted and left to burn awhile before it reached the office.

Then, *whoom!*

The stench of gas fumes overpowered me. I retched, choking on the nausea that surged up from my stomach. My eyes began to sting and water, obscuring my vision and leaving me disoriented, on the verge of panic. To make things worse, the picture wires dug deeper if I moved, and tore into flesh that was already ripped and bleeding.

In a way, it was just as well. To be a spark away from annihilation seemed momentarily less important than the need for relief from pain—or to catch a single breath of unadulterated air.

God knows how I did it, I began to move. I found I could rock, using the weight of my upper body, using the tips of my toes that touched the floor, chair and body together, walking us inch by painful inch toward where I thought the door had to be. If I rocked too far, I knew, I would risk the delicate balance and bring myself crashing to the floor. Once there, I would never get up again.

So I rocked gently, painfully.

At some point, late in that dreadful odyssey, I became aware of a change in the chemical composition of whatever it was I was breathing in place of air. It thickened, changed in density and smell.

Smoke.

With watery, distorted vision I could make out clouds of it, billowing from where I had guessed the door would be. If there were flames beyond it, I knew what would happen if I got it open.

Incineration.

Burned if you do, burned if you don't. Instant ash. But I had to try it anyway.

I was still rocking toward it when the door began to disintegrate without my help.

What registered in the brain was at least as distorted as my vision. An unbelievable din, what I would imagine to be the sound of high explosive ripping through a city block, accompanied by a strange, wild, extra-human yell.

The swimming white surface that had been the door shattered in on me and the smoke came in. A solid bank of it, from behind the door, swelling to fill the interior of the room.

"Jesus Christ!"

Another braying war cry, striking a memory chord somewhere, way back.

"Grab him! For Christ's sake! Grab him! Run!"

Voices I knew and didn't know. Faces. It all faded in and out. I knew I was losing consciousness and fought to keep it. I was swept up, chair and all, miraculously, by some panting, giant creature, and wafted through canyons of smoke to freedom and fresh air. Not wafted: trundled and bumped. Dropped and half-dragged.

But I might as well have been wafted. I had lost the battle for consciousness.

FORTY-EIGHT

◇

Within what may have been seconds, I was stunned back to my senses. Whatever had happened originated somewhere behind the eyes.

I squinted down and took from a small white stick another sudden shock that hit me like a cattle prod. Smelling salts. I found myself giggling insanely. I was sitting upright in an aluminum chair in the middle of the street, outside a building engulfed in flames.

"Is he okay?"

My eyes felt like volcanic craters rimmed with molten lava, but I found that with effort I could focus them again. I just wasn't ready to believe what I saw, still less to understand it.

What was I doing here?

The first improbable vision was Dick Corman. He was kneeling beside the chair, unwinding picture wire from the bleeding mess around my wrists. Then I pulled Frank Stevenson into focus, standing behind Dick, somewhere in mid-distance, breathing hard and gazing back into the inferno. I turned my head to the other side and was astounded to find Nicki bending over me. For a while I sat still and stared at her, trying to put things together.

My brain refused to do what I asked, but it managed to kick out a single image very clearly. "Cynthia," I said. I didn't know exactly why.

Dick paused in his work and looked up at me. "I know," he said. "Richards phoned us in L.A., but you'd already left. He'd put her together with Traceman and wanted to warn you."

What was he talking about? I struggled to make

sense of words that must, somehow, have had some meaning. He turned back to the picture wire and I flinched, beginning to feel the pain that my brain had been too numb to register before.

"I don't understand," I said.

"We've all been trying to reach you, Jake. Richards had sent a man to the airport, but you know what happened there. Then you dropped out of sight and there seemed to be no way to find you. Richards thought you would trust me more than you trusted him. So I came."

He had finished with one hand and laid it on my knee, where it sat, impotent, wanting to reach out to Nicki. I looked back to her.

"Me," she said, "I just came along for the ride." She gave me a shrug of elaborate indifference and then smiled. Somewhere she had found a handkerchief and was swabbing at the sweat and salt around my eyes.

"You think I'd have let Dick come without me?" she added.

Did it all make sense?

The cold air reached my lungs like a sledgehammer. I guess I must have opened my mouth several times and closed it without saying what I had planned to. Nicki laughed and laid a hand against my lips.

"It's okay," she said.

I wanted to believe it. There was nothing more I wanted than to close my eyes and go to sleep. But it wasn't okay. What kept coming back was that I hadn't finished. There was more I had to do. What was it?

"Don't move," said Dick. "We've got to get you to the hospital." He held up a length of bloody picture wire and dangled it in front of me. "This stuff has cut you up pretty bad. Police and fire should be here any moment now. Jesus, what a mess!"

It may have been Dick's gesture, or the sound of sirens, or the effect of the cold air. Remembered images began to fall back into sequence like the tumblers in a lock. Cynthia. Traceman. My brain accelerated with my heartbeat as it raced toward the final image I had been searching for.

What I saw was Dan Traceman dangling the studio keys in front of me. The African charm on the ring that Laura had been killed for.

Now they were going after my work, too. Traceman had given himself the satisfaction of the final insult. He had delighted in the anticipation of getting rid of me and reducing everything my life had meant to chattel. With Cynthia.

Never. The battle between ultimate physical exhaustion and the anguished fury of an ego as stubborn as my own was barely a contest.

I was free of my bonds—and I was awake, and powerful. "Dick," I said, "no questions. Nothing. Just get me to a taxi now."

The sirens were distant enough for me to be gone before they arrived. But there wasn't time to argue.

"Now," I told him.

It was as though the chair had become of a piece with me, and all my own parts were its aluminum frame. To drag myself away from it required not only a dreadful effort of the will, but a physical strength I had never had to draw on in my life. I pulled myself up.

There was a taxi waiting across the street—the one, it turned out later, they'd arrived in. I started toward it. The engine was running, perhaps to keep the driver warm.

Dick was soon with me, carrying half my weight. Frank was behind us half a moment later and Nicki followed, scolding.

"Shut up," I said.

"Why don't you let us deal with it?" said Dick. "We can take care of it."

"It's my work," I said. "My drawings. Last chance."

Something broke inside me. I was finally enraged. Crazed by lingering fear, or pain, or the effects of the gasoline fumes, I was seized by a drunken arrogance: I'd handled the whole thing so far. I didn't need their help.

I shoved Dick aside as I reached the cab, climbed in, and slammed the door on the lot of them. I pushed the lock button down.

The driver would have demurred. With the sirens approaching fast, smoke and flames billowing from the loading dock, and my own bloody wrists, I could hardly blame him. I reached into the pocket of my jeans and was relieved to find what remained of the money I had withdrawn that morning.

I took two hundreds from the wad of bills.

"Five-minute drive," I said, and waved them at him. "And another hundred when you get there." He stuck his fingers into the tiny cash window and took the bills.

Dick was still rattling furiously at the door, but we pulled away just as the first of the emergency vehicles hit the intersection, skidding around in the direction of the fire. I couldn't have cared less. I sat, slumped back, and watched the reflection of the lights on the ceiling of the cab. Closing my eyes, I took a sobering breath and concentrated on gathering what strength I could.

I don't know where you find the energy when you need it. By rights, my own supply had long since been exhausted. But I know that I needed it, demanded it, and found it. In the ten-minute cab ride, I shed exhaustion like an unneeded skin.

It wasn't simply a day or a week I needed to purge. Those came first, and slipped behind me with surprising ease. Then came the years, the isolation of the intellect and the emotions, the skepticism and mistrust that I had called independence, the prejudice and presumptions I had called judgment. The blinkers I had called vision. These were dead things that had been desiccating with the skin. They needed only to be let go. Or so it felt.

If the new man climbing out of the cab was less than perfect, it was only to be expected. Yet I was amazed at the restoration of my body and what seemed like the composure of my mind.

The driver thanked me for his extra hundred and

took off. It must have been late. I had no idea how late. I stood alone on the street and gazed up to where lights were burning in the studio. Double-parked outside the front door, its orange emergency lights blinking in the darkness and its side door open, stood a late-model van with the Artcart logo. A small Mercedes was parked directly in front of it. As I watched, the house door opened and spilled light down the steps. Two Artcart movers emerged with my drawings in their arms.

They were very young—little more than kids. I nailed them at the van door. They took one look at me and realized this was trouble they didn't want.

"Those are my pictures," I told them simply. "These people are stealing them. This is my business, please stay out of it. Move."

There's a certain intensity that carries a message more effectively than words. I remembered how Carlos had first approached me, how it was his conviction that carried me along. These two could easily have overpowered me, but they didn't stop to question what I told them. They climbed into the van without a word.

I stacked the drawings carefully and started up the steps.

Once in the house, I could see that the door to my studio on the first-floor landing had been left open, too, though the landing was in darkness. I climbed the stairs and left the drawings at the top.

They would have been expecting the movers to return, so I made no special effort to conceal my own approach.

I paused at the door. I had been gone only a few days, yet the studio had that tentative familiarity of a place you return to after long absence—as if it were not days but years that separated me from the life I had played out here.

On the telephone table by the door, the little red light on the answering machine still glowed. I hadn't switched it off.

Traceman was in the studio with Cynthia. They

didn't even turn around when I reached the door and leaned against the sill. Traceman was holding a study of Laura to the light.

"It's Jake's black whore," he said.

He was still laughing when they both turned round and saw me. Then the laugh froze and his face turned dark. Cynthia went white.

"Jesus!" he said.

"Jake . . ." said Cynthia.

Nothing could have held me back from him at that moment, not even the gun he wrestled from his pocket. I don't think I even hurried. He was too late, anyway.

Oh, the gun went off. It didn't hit me and I jumped on him before he could fire a second shot.

It must have been a stupid and ungainly sight—a wild, flailing battle, incompetent, angry, and eventually indecisive. I would have liked to knock him clean off his feet and pound his face and body with my fists. But that wasn't the case. Once I had grappled him down, I just clung on and tried to bash his head against the floor, with Cynthia yelling at both of us, trying to drag me off him.

It was like this they found us. At least I was on top.

EPILOGUE

◇

New York, April

Well, Nicki, love . . .

It's been a while, but that's what we agreed on and I think it was best for both of us. For me, there's been so much to get tied up at this end, I've barely had the chance to miss you. (That's not true—I've missed you. Maybe that's something we can begin to make up for now, if you're ready.)

The last act's over now, so far as I'm concerned. Richards came by last evening and we shared a beer. I tried to get him to guess at what might happen in court, but he wouldn't stick his neck out. Traceman has an army of lawyers, and Richards is cynic—maybe realist—enough to believe that justice is something that you buy, these days.

At least the foundation's pretty much settled now. We've put a board together, all good people, who'll see to it that a good part of Worthing's work gets back where he always wanted it—in the public domain. I think I told you about Elmer Rothstein, the writer who helped me out along the way? I managed to get him an exclusive on the foundation for the *Village Voice*. That, and the update on Jake Molnar he'd been clamoring for.

I tried to see Cynthia, to get that part of things squared away, but she wouldn't have it. I've tried every way I know to figure her out. Among other things, we both went sour on each other as we did on the art scene. We just dealt with it in different ways. My way was to drop out and pretend it wasn't there. For her, that was the ultimate cop-out. She turned cynical instead, exploiting what she pretended to deplore.

Here's a thought that's haunted me: The best guess I can get from Richards is that she'd been with Traceman for much longer than I could imagine—maybe even since the Marlborough scene. Did she know about Patty? Worthing? According to Richards, she says no. She blames the killings on Traceman. He tells it differently. There's no love lost between them now.

Sex? I get the impression that was part of the business arrangement—not much passion there. According to evidence Richards has put together, they'd planned to go separate ways. Cynthia had done an incredible job creating lives for them on the Fortune. Traceman would have disappeared completely, surfacing with a whole new identity in Seattle.

Cynthia was planning on international expansion. She'd created a base of operations in Paris. Even after they'd figured Traceman couldn't survive with his own identity, she seemed safe. They thought that if I hadn't caught on to her, no one would. She was smart enough not to trust him a hundred percent, however: She had a new life planned for herself that even Traceman didn't know about. In case.

I've got no more excuses, have I, love? Will we be together soon? I've been wondering if you still want me out there, and thinking more than ever that I want to come. I miss your sweet face and your phony accent.

Call me, okay?

Best love,
Jake

P.S. Guess who called to offer me a show? I told her I'd do it.

About the Author

PETER CLOTHIER writes regularly for *Art in America* and other journals. A published poet who wrote the "In Verse" column for the *Los Angeles Times*, he has been Dean of the Otis Art Institute and also Loyola-Marymount, both in Los Angeles. He is a native of Newcastle, England.